MYSTERIES
OF
GOLFTON HILLS

MYSTERIES
OF
GOLFTON HILLS

CRIME,
PSYCHOLOGICAL SUSPENSE,
AND THRILLER
SHORT STORIES

R. Barri Flowers

Author Photo Credit: R. Barri Flowers

First edition

ISBN: 978-1-68512-568-4

Cover art by Level Best Design

This book was professionally typeset on Reedsy.
Find out more at reedsy.com

To the memory of my wonderful parents, Marjah A. and Johnnie H., who gave me the wisdom and tools needed to succeed beyond my wildest dreams; and to the great love of my life and best friend in the whole world, Loraine, to whom I am forever indebted for her unwavering support and tireless commitment to assisting me in completing one book after another for many, many years of concerted efforts and achievement. And lastly, to the loyal fans of my crime fiction and lovers of riveting short stories.

Contents

Praise for Mysteries of Golfton Hills

"Flowers may be a new voice in modern mystery writing, but he is already one of its best voices."—*Statesman Journal*

"R. Barri Flowers is among the best of them."—John Lutz, Edgar-winning, bestselling mystery author

"With his amazing background and varied stories, Flowers's tales of crime in paradise will pull the reader right in."—Karen Harper, *New York Times* bestselling author

"Vivid details of police procedure one would expect from an author who is also a top criminologist."—Douglas Preston, bestselling mystery writer

"R. Barri Flowers writes with the passion and knowledge of someone who truly knows his craft."—Allison Leotta, former federal prosecutor and crime novelist

"Gripping writing, wonderfully rounded characters you really care about, and vivid locations."—Peter James, bestselling mystery author

"Flowers once again has written a page-turner legal thriller that begins with a bang and rapidly moves along to its final page."—*Midwest Book Review*

Teachers Fatal Lessons

They were in bed, a ceiling fan spinning overhead, making love like there was no tomorrow. At least it seemed that way to Edgar Armstrong as they went at it hot and heavy. Marjorie was stunning with long and curly raven hair, a svelte body with long, lean legs wrapped around him, and seemed just as insatiable as he was, if not more. Both were teachers at Golfton Hills High School in the sleepy little beach town of Golfton Hills in Corall County on the Florida Panhandle. Both were married, just not to each other.

Having been down this road before, Edgar had no problem with that. His wife, Harriet, was away on business, leaving their spacious Cape Cod-style home on Appalew Lane all to himself. With just the right and desirable company. As for Harriet, she seemed content to have as little sex as possible, her thoughts often elsewhere. He wasn't. The fact that he'd connected with a like mind in Marjorie, who apparently couldn't be satisfied by her husband, Joaquim, made the experience all the more enjoyable and exciting to Edgar.

They had successfully finished what they started on the sleigh bed and had come up from beneath the linen sheets for air when he heard a noise that sounded like someone was coming up the stairs. Edgar's heart skipped a beat as his first thought was that Harriet had gotten back earlier than expected and never bothered to call or text with a heads-up. How would he even begin to explain what spoke for itself? Had he just blown his marriage? Would Marjorie find herself in the same boat?

Before he could try to figure out how to play this and somehow extricate himself from being caught in bed with another woman, someone stepped inside the primary bedroom. Edgar cocked a thick brow; his gray eyes widened with shock to see that it wasn't his wife after all. He recognized the person standing there. It was one of his students. A tall and husky senior named Rod Palmer. His blonde and brown hair was worn in an undercut style. He was wearing black gloves.

"What the hell are you doing here?" Edgar demanded as, unlike him, Marjorie frantically covered herself up again, though a bit too late for what had already been exposed in full. "How did you get in?" Had he forgotten to lock the door in his haste to get Marjorie naked and into bed?

"I came for some payback," Rod responded, his lips pursed angrily. "I think we both know what I'm talking about, Mr. Armstrong."

Edgar did at that, unfortunately, but tried to play dumb to buy time. "I'm afraid I have no idea what you mean," he said with a straight face.

"Yeah, right." Rod rolled his blue eyes. "You should've thought about that before you ruined my life, you bastard!"

Before he could come to terms with exactly what the vengeful-minded student had in mind, Edgar watched in horror as Rod lifted a handgun from beneath the blue hoodie he was wearing. Edgar recognized the firearm as a Smith & Wesson M&P M2.0 9mm pistol that was just like the one he owned. Right down to the suppressor on the gun's barrel.

"Put that down!" Edgar ordered him, as if his hard tone carried enough weight to get the senior to comply.

"Not before I do what I came to," Rod spat. He aimed the gun at Edgar's head and, without flinching, pulled the trigger, hitting the mark. And did it again, as if for good measure.

* * *

Marjorie Hernandez was aghast as she watched her handsome lover's head explode—ruining the textured thick dark locks of his hair around a handsome face and splattering blood over the sheet covering her nude body—after he was shot twice at close range by Rod Palmer, who was a student in her English Literature class. What would possess him to do such a

2

thing? What had Edgar ever done to him? How exactly had he ruined Rod's life to make him take Edgar's?

Is he going to kill me, too, as a witness to the cold-blooded execution? Marjorie asked herself with dread. How would her husband Joaquim react when he discovered from the authorities that she was found stark naked in bed with her colleague, Edgar Armstrong, both shot to death? But not before they had engaged in passionate sexual and clearly consensual relations. Would Joaquim hate her? Believe she deserved to die after killing the fidelity of their marriage, betraying him in the process?

When she managed to get past the stunned silence, knowing she had to say something to the shooter—if he was to be the last person she ever spoke to while still alive—Marjorie peered at the student and had to beg for her life. "Please don't kill me, Rod. I have a husband...a life—"

"I know." To her shock, he calmly tucked the gun back into the waistband of his jeans. "I have a mother and father. And they were happy together. Until Mr. Armstrong seduced my mom six months ago and caused my dad to file for divorce rather than have to ever look at her again. I don't want that to happen to anyone else. Not even you, Mrs. Hernandez. You were drawn into his selfish, sick web, just like my mom. Now I've taken you out of it so you can get back to your real life."

So he's not going to shoot me to death, too? Marjorie dared to hope. Why would he leave a witness to the carnage inflicted upon Edgar? "I won't tell anyone," she muttered weakly, knowing he would probably dismiss this out of hand.

"You know what? I don't think you will," Rod said arrogantly, grinning lustfully at her. "That's why you're still alive, unlike him." He glared at Edgar's head. Or what was left of it. "I used Mr. Armstrong's own gun to take him out. Fitting, don't you think?"

Aside from still trying to process that her lover lay dead beside her, murdered before her very eyes, Marjorie was admittedly forced to come to terms with the revelation that Edgar had cheated on his wife with someone other than her. Especially when he indicated otherwise, making her feel special and believing it was worth it to betray Marjorie's own husband.

3

"Maybe he did deserve it," she tossed out, mainly to appease the vengeful student. Even if at least part of her believed that to be the case, feeling hurt by Edgar, as though having been jilted by her lover.

"Yeah, I think so." Rod rubbed his nose. "But you don't, Mrs. Hernandez. You made a big mistake when you decided to get involved with Mr. Armstrong. Now you get the chance to put it behind you, if you're smart. It'll be our little secret. You keep mine and I'll keep yours. I'll take the gun—in case I need to use it again—and steal a few other items from the house to make it look like a home invasion that got out of hand. I'll slip out through the back door, and you can do the same—or however you choose to make your own getaway. We both get to carry on with our lives as if we were never a part of this." He caught his breath and regarded her intently. "What do you say?"

Given that he still had the murder weapon and—with his veiled threat—could turn it on her at any time, Marjorie didn't exactly feel that she was in a position (while naked beneath the sheets) to argue the point. Beyond that, did she really want to be at the center of a police investigation that exposed her affair with the victim for all the world to see and would likely also mean the end of her teaching position at Golfton Hills High?

Even worse was what this would do to her own marriage. Joaquim would never forgive her for cheating on him, right under his nose. Just as she would never have forgiven him had she discovered he was sleeping with another woman. Never mind that it ended tragically. That was almost beside the point.

I can't be caught like this, Marjorie decided. She looked the killer in the eye and said straightforwardly, "It's a deal, Rod. If you let me leave here, this will be our little secret. I want to keep my marriage and career intact. I'll do whatever it takes to make that happen."

"I was hoping you'd say that." He grinned crookedly. "Cool."

"Okay." She waited beneath the sheets, beside her lover's corpse, for Rod to leave.

He headed for the door, turned back to face her and said intimidatingly, "Oh, and if you change your mind and decide to spill your guts, I'll say we planned this together so your husband wouldn't find out you were banging another teacher. I'll deny it had anything to do with my parents, and I'm guessing they would back me up. Either way you slice it, you're screwed should you go to the cops. Keep that in mind. See you in school, Mrs. Hernandez—"

Marjorie cringed as she watched him walk away coolly. She heard the sound of items being tossed and overturned, before he left.

Only then did she climb out of the bed. Instinctively, she did her best to smooth out the bloodied sheet and mattress she'd laid on to hide this as best as possible. She couldn't even look at Edgar, hating to see him that way, knowing he would never again open his eyes. Or make love to her the way he had so thoroughly.

Quickly picking up her clothes off the hardwood floor, Marjorie put them on, ignoring Edgar's blood on her. Though tempted to go into the en suite bathroom to wash it off, she knew that this would only give the police evidence that could lead right to her front door. She would hop into the shower and wash her clothes when she got home.

Only then would she be able to better assess the damage and how best to cover her tracks.

* * *

Rod Palmer pulled the hood over his head before slipping out the back door and running into the woods from whence he'd come to kill Edgar Armstrong. He had been thinking about this for a while. Or ever since his dad left him and Rod's mom high and dry, using her infidelity as an excuse to abandon them. Rod was really pissed about it. Why did a teacher whom he had respected up until that point have to seduce his mother—making her believe she was in love with him—and ruin their lives?

When he discovered that Mr. Armstrong had turned his attention to Mrs. Hernandez—and had it reciprocated—Rod knew he had to act. She was one of the hottest teachers at the school, but was supposed to be happily married. Till Edgar Armstrong—who obviously wasn't happy with his own wife—put

5

the moves on Marjorie Hernandez, seemingly determined to screw up as many lives in Golfton Hills as possible.

Well, Rod put an end to that and didn't regret it in the slightest. In killing the teacher, at least he had given Mrs. Hernandez the chance to repair whatever was broken in her marriage. For her sake, Rod hoped she took it and never looked back. Otherwise, he'd come gunning for her, and she would join her late lover in an early grave.

For his part, Rod fully intended for things to be business as usual in his life. He still had his girlfriend, Tabitha, who would never cheat on him. And lots of friends who would stand by him through thick and thin. Then there was college. Set to begin in the fall, he had already been accepted at Florida State University and planned to get his degree in civil engineering and go from there.

But first, he needed to pretend he'd never shot to death his teacher and hope it blew over while counting on Marjorie Hernandez to do her part in keeping the authorities off balance as the two of them went back to their normal lives.

Rod went inside the two-story craftsman-style home on Frandon Road, which he now shared with only his mother. With her still being at her job, working as a hygienist for a local dentist, it would give Rod time to get himself together and, if need be, establish an alibi for his whereabouts during the break-in at the home of Edgar Armstrong.

Even if he didn't believe it would happen, Rod still clung to the hope that just maybe, with the adulterous teacher out of the picture, his parents could get back together as though never apart.

* * *

Marjorie couldn't stop shaking as she drove her Subaru Legacy home. She had never seen anyone being murdered right before her very eyes. Till now. It was totally unexpected and something she would have to live with for the rest of her life. But at least she had a life left. That was more than she could say for Edgar, who had his life snuffed out by an obviously mentally

6

unhinged student whom he had wronged. Or at least it was perceived that way by Rod when Edgar chose to get involved with his mother.

Though the thought of Edgar seeing her as merely another notch on his belt of charming married women into his bed irked Marjorie, she had to look past that betrayal for self-preservation. She couldn't allow a big mistake in judgment to cost her everything. Not if she could prevent that from happening.

She arrived at her ranch home on Platlyn Place. As expected, Joaquim was still at work as a mechanic. She had time to clean up and prepare dinner without him being the wiser of how horrible her day had been. After starting off on a good note before ending very badly.

She went inside and headed across the bamboo flooring and past contemporary furnishings to the laundry room, where Marjorie wasted little time in stripping her clothes off and putting them in the washer to clean.

Then she headed to the bathroom, turned on the shower, and stepped inside. She applied shampoo to her hair and lathered her body, scrubbing away the evidence of having been at the scene of infidelity and murder. As if she could ever truly rid herself of this. She couldn't help but wonder if Rod Palmer was doing the same. Would he really be able to so easily put behind him the cold-blooded murder of one of his teachers, like it was little more than a walk in the park?

Or would guilt eat away at him like a hideous disease, causing Rod to confess what he'd done? And maybe bring her down with him, as if to further punish her for having ever gotten involved with Edgar in the first place.

Marjorie tried not to think about that as she put on some fresh clothes and made macaroni and cheese, along with pork chops for dinner, knowing that both were favorites of her husband. She had to believe that good food was still the key to a man's heart. Especially when she needed him now more than she'd ever realized before—with their future hanging in the balance.

* * *

When Joaquim arrived home, Marjorie greeted him warmly, giving him a passionate kiss. "Hey," she uttered, like it was just another day. She only wished that were true.

"Hey." Joaquim was a year older than her, at thirty-five, and a year younger than Edgar. Her husband had a medium build, was a little taller than her, and had thinning dark hair in a slicked-back style and brown eyes. He gave her a strange look. "Is it my birthday or something...?"

She showed her teeth. "How about something?"

"I'm good with that." He chuckled. "So, what's up?"

"I just felt like being with my husband," she told him in a desirous tone. "Dinner's ready, but it can wait."

"Why don't I jump into the shower and..."

"Later," Marjorie insisted, taking his calloused hand. "I want you—now." In her mind, it was the best way to vanquish, if only temporarily, the guilt she felt in being with Edgar. And worse, watching him get executed by Rod.

"Okay." Joaquim didn't argue the point. "You've got me."

They went to bed, and Marjorie made her husband feel good while wishing she had resisted temptation that sent her right into the arms of another man. And the trouble that followed.

Now she hoped to put that behind her and focus more on what—or who— was right in front of her, the man she had fallen in love with before things between them began to grow stale, and she turned her attention elsewhere.

* * *

The next day, Rod passed on breakfast with his mother, using the excuse that he was running late for school, knowing it worked every time. His education was as important to her as it was to him. In truth, he was too tense to eat right now, while wondering when it would be discovered what happened to Mr. Armstrong. Had he covered his tracks sufficiently to keep the police from showing up at their house and pointing the finger at him? Just as importantly, Rod wondered if he could count on Marjorie Hernandez to hold up her end of the bargain and not rat him out. He banked on the teacher, wanting to hold onto her marriage more than she wanted to see him in jail for taking out her lover.

He regarded his mom, who was standing by the kitchen sink, sipping coffee. Loretta Palmer was petite and blue-eyed, with short crimson hair worn in a pixie. "So, any chance you and Dad might get back together?" he asked.

She shrugged. "That's up to him."

Rod furrowed his brow. "But you're definitely through with Mr. Armstrong?" he asked, knowing the teacher had moved on to Marjorie Hernandez and probably others in between and was no longer around to cheat anymore on his wife.

"Absolutely!" Loretta said in a firm tone. "He was a big mistake, and I regret it deeply for what it did to my marriage and you. But I can't go back. If your dad can ever forgive me and doesn't find someone else—then maybe there is a chance we'll get back together. No promises, though."

The mere chance was good enough for Rod at this point. At least he had done his part to eliminate one potential roadblock to his parents reuniting. The rest would have to take care of itself.

"Gotta go," he told her and kissed her cheek before grabbing a bagel on his way out the door. Rod was already starting to feel better about things, even while dreading the wait for the news to come out about Edgar Armstrong.

* * *

Marjorie tried to keep things as normal as possible as she taught her English Literature class. But in truth, she was on pins and needles in knowing that her former lover and colleague, Edgar, would never return to the school. Or sneak away to an empty room with her to make out, leaving them both hot and bothered. Rod Palmer had seen to that in deciding to play judge and jury as he ended Edgar's life without so much as blinking an eye in a brazen act of revenge.

Now she had to look at him, sitting forebodingly in the front row, staring her down, as if to say that both their hands were dirty—only his, a little more so. She didn't disagree. But what he had done was totally unforgivable. Sooner or later, he would need to be held accountable. If not by her, then someone else.

Marjorie watched as Rod turned his attention to the pretty girl beside him, Tabitha Ainsley. She was green-eyed and had thick brunette hair that Marjorie could only dream of. The two seniors were dating and were apparently planning to attend the same university together. Before what happened to Edgar, Marjorie had once thought that Rod was a good catch for Tabitha. Maybe even marriage material. Now she knew better. He didn't deserve to be with someone who likely had no idea what Rod was capable of.

I hope she'll be able to see right through him before it's too late, Marjorie told herself. As it was for poor Edgar, his apparent cheating addiction notwithstanding. She thought about his wife, Harriet. According to Edgar, they hadn't been happy with each other in a long time. Had that only been a convenient excuse to get Marjorie to cheat on her own husband? How could she have been so gullible and stupid to fall for Edgar's lines? Had he spotted her a mile away as someone vulnerable and easy to seduce? How many others had there been besides her and Loretta Palmer, Rod's mother?

Marjorie could only guess. Or maybe she shouldn't. That would make the trap she had allowed herself to fall into that much more painful. No, she needed to push aside the pity party and own up to her own naivety, while at the same time doing what she could to make amends to Joaquim. Even as she tried to remove herself from the quicksand that Rod Palmer had pushed her into.

Once class ended, Rod gave her the evil eye as he passed by, seemingly having second thoughts about approaching her to talk. Not with Tabitha watching his every move like a hawk, as if sensing that something was off with her boyfriend. If she only knew just what.

Just as Marjorie was ready to take her afternoon break while keeping a cool head, Principal Paul Eckersley entered the classroom. He was in his forties, short, and had a salt and pepper pompadour haircut and blue eyes behind horn-shaped glasses. He had a dour look on his face.

"You have a minute?" he asked tersely.

"Yes." She met his gaze. "What's up, Paul?"

He hesitated, as though something weighed heavily on his mind, before responding, "I have some very sad news to report..."

"What is it?" Marjorie braced herself for what she could see coming.

"Edgar Armstrong is dead."

Her mouth opened with feigned ignorance. "What?"

"He was murdered in his own home—shot to death," Paul reported, looking like he was in a state of shock. "His wife, Harriet, found him dead when she came home from a business trip this morning."

"I'm so sorry to hear that," Marjorie said, with a catch to her voice. "Do the police know what happened...or why?"

"From what I've heard, they seem to think it was a home invasion that turned violent," the principal reported.

She sucked in a deep breath. "I can't believe it... Edgar dead..." Marjorie pivoted somewhat. "I mean, we weren't really that close," she stressed, "aside from being colleagues. But I wouldn't wish something like this—being murdered—on my worst enemy." She wasn't sure if this sentiment held up when she considered Edgar's killer, Rod Palmer, no matter his reasoning.

"I know. Who would?" Paul asked, pushing the glasses up his nose. "Anyway, I'm just making the rounds to everyone. Seemed less painful that way somehow. I'm guessing that the police will probably want to interview the entire staff and student body at some point in the course of their investigation, given that Edgar taught here, and it could've been a pathway for a killer. Though, hopefully, the killer was not connected to Golfton Hills High School."

"I understand," Marjorie said levelly. "I'll make myself available if the police would like to speak to me, though I don't think I'd have much to offer in their investigation."

"Good." Paul sighed. "Well, I'd better share this with others."

She nodded and waited for him to walk away, before realizing that her wobbly knees were threatening to give. She wondered if the principal could possibly have known about her affair with Edgar. Had he been bragging about it behind her back? And, in the process, implicating her in his murder, before or after the fact?

As Marjorie mulled this over, fearful of her sordid affair being exposed and then being shown the door by Paul Eckersley, who would surely view this as, at the very least, behavior unbecoming for two married teachers at the school. Even worse was if she were in any way associated with Edgar's murder. Having been blackmailed and bullied into silence by the killer was not going to fly with Paul, the police—and certainly not Joaquim.

I have to fix this, Marjorie told herself. She couldn't allow Rod to forever hold her hostage to his homicidal behavior, knowing full well that he could turn on her at any time, should he find himself backed into a corner like a rat. The way she saw things, it was either him or her. That made it clear as day to Marjorie for what she must do.

She left the classroom and didn't take long to spot Rod, who was chatting it up with some friends, seemingly without a concern in the world. Much less, that the police were looking for him, without realizing it.

Her first thought was to warn the student who murdered Edgar. Should she send him a text, knowing she could get his cell phone number easily enough under the guise of needing it for an assignment. But she quickly dismissed that idea, realizing that text messages could be traced to the sender—no matter how clever her wording—giving the authorities a reason to believe they were somehow in on it together. As Rod had promised he would claim, were he to go down and she were to testify against him.

Instead, she managed to make eye contact with him for a long moment and walked way. As expected, he followed her. She waited till they were in a private spot and fixed him with cold eyes before saying in a low voice, "The police know about Edgar."

"Yeah, I heard," Rod muttered. "No big deal. They have nothing on either of us."

"You don't know that," she told him. "I don't want to talk here. Meet me at my house at six. I'll leave the side door open."

"Whatever you say, Mrs. Hernandez," he said arrogantly. "I'll be there."

"Good." Marjorie wrinkled her nose at him, then walked away without looking back.

* * *

Marjorie waited patiently for Rod to come through the side door, as instructed. He showed up right on the money. As usual, he was smug, and mistakenly believed that he was calling the shots. Under other circumstances—such as had he caught her and Edgar in bed and hung this over her head without killing her lover—this might have been the case. But given the stakes of the current situation, she had taken that privilege from him.

"So, what's so urgent that you needed to see me?" he asked suspiciously, walking toward her in the living room.

She gave him a disingenuous smile. "Oh, I don't know. Guess I was just hoping we could brainstorm on how best to handle more questions that the police could still throw at us."

He shrugged. "Don't tell them anything. Not unless you want your sordid little secret exposed for everyone in town to know about—including your husband."

Marjorie frowned. "That's just it, Rod, I don't want anyone knowing what went on between me and Edgar. And, right now, you're the only one who can spill the beans. I can't let that happen."

He cracked a smile. "Then keep your mouth shut, and we're good."

"I only wish it were that simple," she told him.

"It's only as hard as you choose to make it," he countered.

"Afraid that's not good enough." She gave him a sharp look. "You made this hard when you chose to murder Edgar. You need to pay for that."

"I don't think so." Rod's eyes narrowed. "He had it coming. Looks like you do too."

"Actually, it's the other way around," Marjorie told him. "You're going down for what you did—no matter what happens to me. I can't allow you to get away with this."

"Watch me!" he snapped, and she watched in anticipation as he started to reach inside the pocket of his hoodie.

Anticipating this, Marjorie removed from her own pocket, the SIG Sauer P365-380 robin's-egg blue 9mm pistol she had her fingers around. Without giving it a second thought, she fired it at him, before he could remove Edgar's gun from his pocket.

"You bitch!" Rod sputtered with shock as he clutched his chest. "You shot me."

Unmoved, Marjorie stepped closer. "You bastard," she countered. "You started this and left me no choice but to finish it. Goodbye, Rod." She shot him again, this time in the head, and watched as he fell to the floor on his back. His eyes were wide open, but devoid of life. "Sorry, Rod," she snorted. "But you brought this upon yourself."

By the time Joaquim arrived home, the police were already on the scene, as well as the medical examiner. Marjorie was in complete shock by all appearances as she ran into her husband's outstretched arms outside the house.

"Are you okay?" he asked with concern.

"Yes, but barely," she cried. "Rod would've killed me had I not killed him first. He broke into the house, looking for something to steal, I guess, when I confronted him with the gun you got me. Everything just happened so fast."

"You did the right thing," Joaquim insisted. "I know the police will back me up on this."

Marjorie was counting on the same thing as Rod's corpse was wheeled out. Detective Suzanne Gohara followed and approached the couple. The slender, thirty-something detective ran a hand through her blonde hair, in a choppy bob cut and, eyeing Marjorie, said smoothly, "We think the gun found next to deceased was the firearm stolen from Edgar Armstrong's house and used to kill him during the home invasion. Apparently, Rod Palmer had staked your house out for his next burglary, before it all went wrong—for him."

Marjorie wiped tears from her eyes. "I never wanted this to happen," she stated convincingly. "Rod was one of my students—"

"It wasn't your fault," the detective insisted. "Mr. Palmer blew up his own life when he decided to go into the business of home invasions. It was bound to catch up with him sooner or later. Looks like sooner." She paused. "If I have any more questions, I'll be in touch. But as of now, it looks like a case of self-defense," she said matter-of-factly.

Marjorie let that sink in satisfyingly while clinging to her husband, who said, "We'll get through this."

She nodded to that effect. "That's all I needed to hear," she told him sweetly, knowing that her secrets were safe, having died with Edgar and Rod, allowing her to work on rebuilding a marriage that had suddenly become more important than ever and was definitely worth fighting for.

A Dire Dilemma

Ever since losing his wife, Kendre, two years ago after a long and expensive battle with colon cancer, Jordan Westbrook had been more focused on his work as the chief financial officer for a tax preparation business in Portland, Oregon. When he did go out on occasion, he'd been content to play the field, not looking for a serious relationship and more heartbreak. Maybe someday, someone would come along to give him a real reason to pursue love again. But he wasn't holding his breath.

This was the last thing on his mind as Jordan stepped inside Creighton's Place on West Burnside Street in downtown Portland. For whatever reason, he felt a sense of dread when one of the principals of Ollin Tax Services, Tom Gleason, asked to meet with him at the dive bar. Actually, there was a good reason for concern. Jordan was aware that the company had cut a few corners to maximize profits while crossing the line into illegality. Though his own hands were stained—needing the extra money to help pay for his wife's medical bills and the mortgage—he'd done his best to stay on the right side of the law to the extent he could and still keep his job without another to fall back on.

Gleason waved him over to his table. In his mid-fifties, the chief executive officer was thickset and had a gray horseshoe-shaped hairline and brown eyes. He looked tense as he said, "Thanks for meeting me here."

Jordan, who was twenty years younger and much fitter, wore his dark hair in a short quiff style and sported a three-day stubble beard. He nodded, sat, and gazed at the CEO through deep blue eyes. "What's going on?"

"The company's in trouble," Gleason said, downing the whiskey left in his glass in one gulp.

"Meaning what exactly?" Jordan asked straightforwardly, even if unsure; he really wanted to know the depths of the trouble.

"There's no easy way to say this other than to just come right out with it." Gleason paused nonetheless, then said, "The IRS is about to bust our whole operation wide open. According to a contact of mine, they've been investigating us for a while now, and a federal fraud indictment for tax fraud and more is said to be imminent."

Jordan felt his heart skip a beat. "Are you sure about this?"

"I'm sure." He studied his empty glass. "You, me, and the rest of the management team—we're all facing some heavy-duty time behind bars, fines, and who knows what else. I wanted to give you a heads-up."

Jordan muttered a couple of expletives. Not that he hadn't seen this coming. Deep down, he'd known it was only a matter of time before the roof caved in. He was only glad that Kendre was not around to say she told him so, having been privy to his ill-advised attempts to make ends meet and looking the other way when it served his purposes.

He watched as Gleason ordered two more whiskeys, one for each of them. Jordan drank a generous amount of his alcohol and asked unnervingly, "Is there any way out of this?"

"Yeah, there's one way," Gleason said bluntly. "Get the hell out of Dodge."

"You mean make a run for it?" Jordan peered at him.

"That's what it's come down to, I'm afraid. Unless you're into prison cuisine. I heard that the feds are not in the mood for any pleas: eager to make new examples of white-collar offenders."

Jordan found it hard to imagine being on the run, having to look over his shoulder at every turn. But being stripped of his freedom and dignity was not an option that made him feel warm and fuzzy.

"How long do you think you could last as a fugitive?" he had to ask the CEO.

Gleason shrugged. "Guess I'll have to find out. The alternative for a guy my age is more than I care to deal with, frankly."

"I hear you." Jordan knew Gleason was divorced and liked to travel to

South America. On his own part, leaving the country was something he couldn't imagine doing. But something short of that, maybe. He finished off the drink. "Thanks for letting me know what's going on."

"I owed you that much, for getting you involved in this," Gleason told him. "The rest is up to you."

Jordan took that for what it was worth, realizing he was in a real dilemma, for better or worse. And only he could extricate himself from this, if possible.

* * *

Golfton Hills, Florida. Population: Less than 45,000. Seaside resort. Palm trees. Great weather year-round. No state income tax. Low crime rate. Young professionals and retirees living in the community. Laidback lifestyle. Activities galore.

It seemed to Jordan like the perfect place to lose himself in. And maybe find what he was looking for in another life. Could he really make this happen? Or was it only a pipedream borne out of fear and desperation?

I can't go to prison, lose my house, my job, what money I have left...and my freedom in the prime of my life, Jordan told himself, as he sat before the laptop in the colonial-style home on Cardinal Drive in Lake Oswego, a suburb of Portland, where he'd lived with Kendre till the day she died.

Admittedly, Jordan didn't know if he could pull this off, but he suddenly felt as though he had to try and let the chips fall where they may. He checked out more information on Golfton Hills, how to disappear without a trace, faking one's death, and anything else he could think of for setting up a new identity and world to call his own.

Then he called a childhood friend, Derrick McClatchy, who Jordan had helped out through the years when he had some rough times. Derrick, a recovering addict, was streetwise and familiar with the ins and outs of identity theft and how to make living people disappear.

When he picked up, Jordan said without prelude, "I need a favor, Derrick—"

* * *

It wasn't at all lost on Jordan what a dramatic turn his life was about to take. But there was no turning back. This was his last chance to leave the life he'd known behind and start fresh. Before the authorities showed up at his door with an arrest warrant and slapped handcuffs on him. If he could go back in time and do things over, he would. But there were no re-dos in life. He had no choice other than to own up to what he'd done. Or didn't do. Only with the mindset that he wasn't up for paying for this to the full extent of the law. Payment would come through giving up everything he'd spent much of his life working for and delving into an unknown future.

Jordan drove his black Land Rover Range Rover Evoque onto the Interstate 205 Bridge and pressed down on the accelerator. His heart was pounding as he considered this action—danger and all. But he had come to believe it was the only way he could pull this off.

Bracing himself, he kicked up the speed another notch and lost control of the vehicle enough to send it airborne, before plunging into the Columbia River—with him still behind the wheel and watching the real prospect of death flash before his very eyes.

* * *

Six months later, he was now Mason Underwood and living in Golfton Hills, Florida, where he had rented a room in a beachfront cottage on Butlertonne Street and drove around in a used red Honda Accord Sport. By most accounts, he was believed to be dead, having succumbed to the depths of the Columbia River, though no body had been found. Still, to feel more confident that he wouldn't be exposed as alive and well, he had dyed his hair from black to brown, changed to a more textured undercut style, and gone smooth-shaven on his face. Whether that, and working part-time as a bookkeeper and assistant manager at a small bookstore inconspicuously, was enough to stay under the radar and out of reach of the IRS or other federal or local law enforcement remained to be seen.

Jordan wasn't about to let his guard down, knowing he might have to skip town at a moment's notice. Or be taken away by force, if the IRS somehow figured out that he was still amongst the living and were able to track him down and arrest him.

But until such time, were it to ever come to that, he had been able to settle into life nicely in this coastal community. That included dating his landlord and employer, Vivian Carlyle. Two years his junior, Vivian was an attractive redhead and divorcée who was easy to get along with and just the type of person he had hoped to meet in starting over in romance. As Mason Underwood, she had asked little of his backstory, and he offered little more than what he had created while staying true to his real character.

The two of them were stocking shelves with new books one afternoon when he snuck a kiss and said coolly, "So, what do you say I make you dinner tonight? Or we can go out to grab a bite to eat? Your choice."

Vivian, who had a sexy hourglass figure and aquamarine eyes behind brow-line glasses, flashed him a toothy grin and said, "Well, when you put it that way, since I'm more of an eat-at-home type of gal, as you know by now, you can cook the meal yourself. Or better yet, why don't we do it together?"

"Sounds like fun." He smiled at her, happy to go with the flow. "You're on."

"Cool." She ran a hand through her short and layered hair. "Where have you been all my life, Mason?"

Jordan pondered the question while wondering what life would have been like had they met years earlier, before responding equably, "Just waiting for the right time to find you and hope we could make up for lost time."

"Good answer." Vivian offered another smile, gave him a quick kiss, and they returned to putting out books, as he contemplated his secret past and their potential future.

* * *

Vivian Carlyle wondered how she could have gotten so lucky as to meet someone like Mason Underwood. After ending a relationship with her abusive ex-husband, she had nearly given up on finding someone who was a gentle soul and seemed to get her. Then, six months ago, Mason walked into her life looking to rent the room she had available at her beach house, hoping to bring in some extra money to help pay the mortgage. She hadn't expected to hire him as well for the vacancy at Carlyle Books, the independent bookstore she owned and operated on Ferry Street.

But he had proven to be a good fit in both departments. Getting involved romantically was an added bonus. When considering this tripartite relationship, it scared Vivian a little, as it was almost too perfect: like Mason dropped from somewhere in outer space to mold into her world magically. She couldn't help but wonder if there was more to him than met the eye. Or was she looking for something that wasn't there to ruin what they had developed?

She hoped she never had to find out.

* * *

Criminal Investigation Special Agent Lydia Finneran sat at her desk at the Internal Revenue Service Headquarters in Washington, DC. She was going over the case against the now defunct Portland, Oregon, based Ollin Tax Services. During the COVID-19 pandemic, several members of the tax preparation business had conspired to defraud the IRS, as well as the Paycheck Protection Program meant to assist businesses in paying employees and covering expenses during the pandemic. They had successfully convicted and sent to prison the tax preparer's chief executive officer, Tom Gleason, having extradited him from Brazil to face charges, and other principals of the firm, including Shirley Kadoyama, the vice president of operations.

One person who had managed to escape justice was Jordan Westbrook, the company's chief financial officer. Nine months ago, he had apparently killed himself before he could be taken into custody by driving his SUV off a bridge and into the Columbia River. His body had never been found, but he was presumed dead.

Lydia wasn't so sure about that. At twenty-nine, she had always had a suspicious nature for as long as she could remember. That included being suspicious as a girl that her father was cheating on her mother, which unfortunately proved to be all too true. Then there were Lydia's instincts that something was off with her ex-boyfriend, Richard Ferreira, Jr. when she attended Stanford University. Turned out she was spot-on, as he was dealing in drugs and unapologetic about it when caught.

Now, her gut feelings were telling Lydia that Jordan Westbrook was still alive and had gone underground to live his life. But proving this was a high hill to climb.

Or at least it was when it came to convincing her boss, CI Deputy Chief Perry Ulbricht, that it was a legitimate path worth pursuing.

Perry, who was fifty-something and had gray hair in a comb-over style, rolled his blue eyes at her and asked skeptically, "So, what—you think that Westbrook was able to somehow swim his way out of the river and dodge the Coast Guard, FBI agents, Portland Police Bureau detectives, and the rest of us—then just vanish into thin air? Or should I say, under water...?"

"Stranger things have happened," Lydia responded, looking up at him with her big hazel eyes. "What better way to avoid capture than by pretending to be dead?"

"I suppose. But there's been no activity on any of his accounts that we're aware of," the deputy chief pointed out. "And no indication of him reaching out to family members, acquaintances, or past co-workers."

"He wouldn't," she said surely and scratched her scalp inside a brunette bob. "On the other side of things, Westbrook's bank accounts were emptied around the time of his disappearance, and his credit cards maxed. Sound odd to you?"

"Maybe he thought about making a run for it, then thought better." Perry pinched his nose. "Keep working on this, if you think something can come out of it other than a dead end."

"Okay." Lydia read between the lines, in which her boss wanted her to focus on more winnable investigations should she find herself stymied for too much longer.

She would keep pressing forward.

* * *

Jordan walked hand in hand alongside Vivian on the beach, sidestepping the footprints of others, while enjoying the scenery. It seemed like such a natural thing to him that they had clicked so easily. He dared to dream that this fantasy could turn into a reality if he played his cards right. The stars lined up. Or whatever. He even made himself believe that his late wife, Kendre, would have approved of Vivian as someone worthy in taking her place in his life.

Yes, he had made some mistakes—who hadn't made a wrong turn or two in life—but he was doing his damnedest to turn the corner and recalibrate his life into one he could be proud of.

Vivian was helping him with that in more ways than she could imagine. Now it was up to him to do right by her by being the best version of himself as possible.

His only concern was that the feds would somehow figure out his secret and pounce on him like a pack of hungry animals. Or should he not let paranoia rain on his parade when, thus far, there had been no indication that those who wanted to see him join his former co-workers behind bars had even a clue that he had survived the murky waters of the Columbia River? Or had pieced together the fact that he had excelled in high school as a member of the swim team?

"What are you thinking about?" Vivian asked curiously, as if she could read his mind.

Jordan turned off the negative musings, regarded her with a half but genuine grin, and responded in a way that he felt was indicative of the strong feelings he had for her, "You and what you've come to mean to me these past months, Vivian."

"That's so sweet." Her lashes batted coquettishly. "It works both ways."

He gave her a kiss and said happily, "I was hoping you'd say that." Now he knew the trick was making it last, while hoping his past didn't come roaring back to haunt him.

* * *

Bingo! Lydia thought jubilantly. An IRS investigation linked to a case of identity theft and tax fraud led her to check out Derrick McClatchy, a known perpetrator of tax identity theft and crimes related to falsifying one's identity through fake IDs and more.

Lydia found it more than a little curious that McClatchy appeared to have been involved with creating information for a man named Mason Underwood at around the same time that Jordan Westbrook supposedly took his own life eight months ago. When she dug deeper, Lydia learned that a Mason Underwood had died fifty years earlier, whereas the current version had no history to speak of—as though his life had only just begun to be established.

She was able to track down this modern-day Mason Underwood who was living in a Florida beach town called Golfton Hills. He worked there at a bookstore, where his duties apparently included bookkeeping. This would have been par for the course on a lesser scale for Westbrook, were he to be living there incognito, while making use of some of his know-how.

Lydia felt that it was more than worthwhile to pay Golfton Hills a little visit and see if she had struck gold in her pursuit of a supposedly dead, and buried in a watery grave, fugitive.

* * *

Inside her rented Toyota Corolla, Lydia waited for Jordan Westbrook, who was using the alias Mason Underwood, to emerge from the house on Butlertonne Street after catching him entering it with an attractive red-haired woman. Reading their body language, it was obvious to Lydia that they were an item. She wondered just how much—or how little—Westbrook's female companion knew about his past life.

Or how it was about to impact his future life, which would see him behind bars for a good stretch of time, putting an end to the cozy existence the fugitive had made for himself in Golfton Hills.

Lydia was beginning to feel antsy. She wanted this over and done with so she could return to her life, even if it wasn't everything she desired in an ideal world.

She stepped out of her car in anticipation of making the arrest of Jordan Westbrook, who had clearly faked his own death—fooling everyone, herself included—and see to it that he paid for his role in the PPP fraud and income tax evasion he and his cohorts at Ollin Tax Services willfully engaged in.

Now, it was time to end this, once and for all.

As Lydia was about to cross the street, she reached inside her blazer for her Glock 23 .40 caliber firearm. At the same time, she caught movement with her periphery. Whipping her head in that direction, she saw a thickly built man with a bleached mohawk and dark eyes move toward her so quickly that she didn't have a chance to react before he slugged her squarely in the jaw.

Lydia went down and saw stars. By the time she cleared her head and tried to reach for her gun, she realized that the holster was empty.

"Looking for this?" the man asked, brandishing the firearm.

"Is this a robbery?" Lydia put a hand to her sore jaw while trying to buy time.

"Something like that. I'm taking your car—and you with it," the man declared in a triumphant tone of voice. "Get up!" he ordered.

Lydia struggled to get to her feet and told him, "I'm a federal agent—on a mission. Give me the gun back, and we'll pretend this never happened."

He regarded her intently while considering her words and then said, "I hate feds, but I'm going to love being with you. Now get the hell in the car, and we're going to go for a little ride."

"I don't think so," she retorted, realizing that to yield to his demands would probably be signing her own death warrant. Not to mention whatever else he had in mind for her. "If you want to shoot me, you'll have to do it here in broad daylight—and then have every law enforcement officer in the state after you."

"Okay, have it your way," he spat arrogantly. "I'll finish you off here and take the car afterwards."

As he aimed the gun barrel at her face, with just enough distance between them to keep her from trying to wrestle the weapon away from him, Lydia couldn't help but shut her eyes in silent prayer, believing she was about to die.

But then she heard some footsteps and a deep voice bellow, "Hey, you—!"

Lydia opened her eyes to see Jordan Westbrook confront the carjacker and would-be killer from behind, forcing him to look in that direction. When the man tried to shoot Westbrook, the two fought for control of the gun. Westbrook forced the man's arm up in the air, and then head-butted him twice, causing the firearm to fall out of his hand.

As the two men traded blows, Lydia scurried to get hold of her Glock 23 pistol. Once she did so, she watched as Westbrook used his fist to apply two hard shots to the man's face, putting him down and out.

Only then did Westbrook look at her and ask, "Are you all right?"

"Yes," she told him, catching her breath and staring at him. "You saved my life."

He shrugged. "I just did what anyone would have done when seeing someone in distress."

"I wish that were true. Not everyone would have risked bodily harm to help a stranger."

He grinned sideways. "Guess it's just part of my nature."

"It's a good nature to have."

"I take it this was an attempted carjacking?"

"That and more victimization he had in mind."

Lydia looked to see his female friend run over to them and say, "I called 911, Mason."

"Good," Westbrook told her, a catch to his voice as she hugged him.

Lydia could tell he was ill at ease where it concerned having to speak with the police. Yet he still risked this to save her. "By the way," she said evenly, lifting the identification from her pocket. "I'm IRS Special Agent Lydia Finneran." She eyed Westbrook keenly, watching as he squirmed even more. "And who do I thank again properly for saving my life?" Lydia glanced at his female friend and back at him again. "She called you Mason...?"

"Mason Underwood," he spoke hesitantly.

Lydia regarded the woman, who said, "I'm Vivian Carlyle."

Turning back to Westbrook and meeting his gaze squarely, Lydia stuck out her hand and said affably, "Nice to meet you, Mason Underwood. You too, Vivian."

"You too," he told her, his features relaxing somewhat.

Lydia smiled at him for an instant, then said, "If you'll excuse me—" She pulled the handcuffs from her pocket and cuffed the carjacker before he woke up. She stepped back over to the couple and said, "I think I can handle it from here while waiting for the police to arrive and arrest the creep. You can feel free to go about your business. Have a nice day."

"All right, and same to you," Westbrook said, sporting a soft grin of gratitude.

Lydia watched as they walked away, arm in arm, lovingly. She knew that she couldn't take into custody the man who had put his life on the line to save hers. Duty-bound or not, Jordan Westbrook, aka Mason Underwood, had earned his ticket to freedom. As far as she was concerned, the man had died in the chilly waters of the Columbia River, and that was where he would stay, effectively closing the IRS investigation on Jordan Westbrook for good.

* * *

Talk about dodging a bullet in more ways than one, Jordan thought as he sat in the passenger seat of Vivian's white Lexus ES 350 while she drove them to a restaurant for lunch. IRS Special Agent Lydia Finneran seemed to look right through his Mason Underwood persona, as though she knew otherwise. Had she identified him and actually been on the scene to make an arrest? How would he have explained the situation to Vivian while being handcuffed and hauled away like a common criminal?

But if Lydia had been onto him, why did she let him off the hook? Had his act of gallantry had the unintended effect of literally saving his life?

"I'm still shaking after that," Vivian remarked thoughtfully.

"Me too, a bit," Jordan admitted, though for totally different reasons, he suspected.

"I can't believe someone attempted a carjacking right outside my cottage."

"These things can happen anywhere."

"I guess." She paused. "It was really heroic of you to step into the fray, but if something bad had happened to you…"

"It didn't," he broke in, seeing where this was leading and not wanting her to go there. "I just felt it was the right thing to do, as it looked like she was in serious trouble in resisting the carjacker."

"You're right, and I commend you for being such a selfless person." Vivian glanced at him with a smile.

"Not totally selfless." Jordan grinned at her. "I'm pretty selfish when it comes to not wanting to lose you."

"You won't," she promised and gazed at the road.

"Good." He knew a good thing when he had it and was glad that she seemed to see the same in him.

"Wonder what an IRS agent was doing here?" Vivian remarked.

"Probably looking for tax cheats," Jordan tossed out in what was meant to be half a joke and half for real.

She chuckled. "Good thing I have you to keep my taxes up to date."

"You're in great shape there," he made perfectly clear. "I promise, the special agent won't be knocking on your door."

"That's nice to know." Vivian pulled into the Golfton Hills Food Palace restaurant parking lot on Judd Avenue. "Whatever Agent Finneran's mission was, I suspect it paled in comparison to having to fight for her life."

"I was thinking the same thing," Jordan stated candidly and had a feeling that Lydia Finneran may have been on the same bandwagon when she suggested that they vacate the premises before the police arrived and started asking questions. He pasted a boyish grin on his face and said to Vivian amorously, "Let's go eat."

The Abduction

Using binoculars, he watched the house from the wooded area behind it in Golfton Hills, providing the perfect cover of spruce pine and Areca palm trees to see and not be seen. That was the only way his plan would work, as getting caught wasn't an option. Not that he was doing anything wrong. Not yet, anyway. It wasn't a crime to look or even think about what he wanted to do. And that was a good thing, for his thoughts, dark and utterly delicious, were menacing, to say the least. This excited him on that basis alone.

Focusing again on the rustic two-story house, he looked from window to window, getting a feel for each room. He caught a shadow of someone passing by in an upstairs bedroom. Another room had a light on. Then it was turned off. Downstairs, the blinds were raised on a side window. Suddenly, they were lowered as if to block his visual intrusion.

This angered him, but only for a moment. How could they know he'd been spying on them? He'd been very careful to keep this his dirty little secret. Until it was too late to do anything about it. He drew in a deep breath. The family who lived there seemed to more or less go about their business without a care in the world. Or so it seemed.

He was especially interested in the girl. She was in the backyard playing with a puppy. He guessed she was ten or eleven. Perfect. He liked the long blonde ponytail that bounced this way and that as she tossed the ball up in the air and giggled as the dog went after it.

The sun was beginning to set as shadows crept up around him like ghouls. It was nearly time to get down to business. He waited patiently, though salivating with anticipation for what was to come.

* * *

Jodie lay quietly in bed. Her goldendoodle puppy, Tasha, slept on the floor right next to her. She could hear her parents making loud sounds downstairs. She wondered if they were talking about her or each other. Maybe it was neither. Suddenly, there was only silence until Tasha barked.

"What is it?" Jodie whispered, propping up on an elbow. There was mild anxiety in her voice. She looked down through the darkness and saw that Tasha had gotten to her little feet and was staring toward the doorway. Jodie turned her big green eyes in that direction and saw nothing. "Don't be afraid," she told the dog. "There's no one there."

Tasha seemed to get the message as she finally laid back down. Jodie did the same. She wondered what had gotten into the puppy. Maybe some of the creaks in the old house had scared her. Sometimes, they scared Jodie, too. She hoped they would one day move into a brand-new house with a huge swimming pool.

Jodie had half fallen asleep when she suddenly felt something wet over her nose and mouth. She opened her eyes and saw what looked like a boogeyman standing above her. As fear gripped Jodie like never before, she tried to scream for her parents, but no sound would come out of her mouth. She could hear Tasha whimpering as if in distress. The boogeyman held Jodie down so she couldn't move. Soon she got very sleepy, and then there was nothing but darkness…

* * *

Ethan Beckett was making love to a hot blonde woman named Sharon, whom he met at a bar before they ended up in a cheap motel room on Levell Street, when his cell phone rang, disrupting the momentum. He tried to lift up, but she had her hands firmly around him.

"Just let it ring," she urged through his mouth.

Though tempted, he wasn't afforded that luxury and broke away from her kiss. "Sorry, but I really need to get that."

Ethan picked up his pants from the floor and dug out the phone. As a detective sergeant for the Homicide Division of the Golfton Hills Police Department, he was waiting to get word that the rich perp he'd arrested two days ago for murdering his wife in a fit of jealous rage would continue to be held without bail.

"Beckett," he spoke routinely, his tall and muscular body turned away from Sharon.

"It's Justin Montrose."

"Yeah," Ethan said to the assistant county attorney of Corall County.

"The judge denied Sheldon Victorino bail," Justin said satisfyingly. "In spite of his high-priced lawyer's impassioned plea about him being a so-called pillar of the community and all that."

"That's good to hear." Ethan's blue eyes glanced at his shapely bedmate. "I'll look forward to testifying at his trial."

"I'll keep you posted on that."

"Okay." Ethan disconnected. He had just run a hand through his thick and coarse gray hair with a side part thoughtfully when the phone he was still holding rang again.

The caller was Detective Rodney Fleisher of the PD's Missing Persons Unit. "Hey, Beckett. We just got a call about a missing girl. She was apparently abducted from her house while the parents were in their bedroom. When they heard the girl's dog barking, they went upstairs to her bedroom, and she was gone." He paused. "Thought you'd want to know..."

Ethan tensed upon hearing the disturbing news. "How old is the girl?"

"Ten."

"Are they sure she's actually out of the house and not just playing hide and seek or something?" Ethan had to ask, remembering how his daughter liked to play tricks on them.

"A neighbor reported a man carrying the girl—her name is Jodie Yancy—to a dark SUV and forcing her inside."

Ethan certainly didn't like the sound of that. "How long ago did this happen?"

"About half an hour ago," Fleisher reported. "We just issued an Amber Alert and have officers looking for her and the SUV even as we speak but, as you know, the first twenty-four hours are crucial—"

"Yeah." Ethan sighed. "Thanks for keeping me in the loop." With that, he disconnected and started putting his clothes on.

"Aren't you coming back to bed?" Sharon lifted her head, frowning.

"Something's come up," he told her unapologetically. "Have to go."

"Do you want me to wait for you to return?"

"Probably not a good idea." It wouldn't be fair to her. "I likely won't be able to return anytime soon. Sorry." He believed it was probably for the best that they ended things here, knowing that his busy life wasn't one that could even count on a repeat performance.

After grabbing his Glock 42 .40 caliber S&W duty pistol and 380 holster from the table, Ethan left the motel room. He climbed in his white Dodge Charger Pursuit, an official vehicle that was permitted for personal use as well, and drove off. His mind was weighing heavily on the missing girl, Jodie Yancy, which, in turn, brought Ethan back in time to a heartbreaking tragedy that turned his own life upside down in ways he couldn't have imagined. Or at least wouldn't have dared to.

* * *

"Help me, Daddy." The desperate words rang loudly in his ears as though he had just heard them yesterday. In fact, it was eleven years ago that Ethan received the pulse-skipping call from his nine-year-old daughter, Angela, who had been abducted from their ranch house by a knife-wielding male assailant.

"What's happening?" he asked her before realizing the gravity of the situation.

"The man and Mommy are fighting," she cried. "He's hurting her."

"Get out of there and go for help," Ethan ordered, knowing it was the best thing he could do at the moment to protect her and try to save his wife from the intruder.

"He won't let me," Angela uttered, her voice cracking under the weight of the crisis.

"I'm on my way," Ethan told her, his blood pressure rising while feeling helpless till he could get home to stop the attack.

By the time he arrived, it was too late. His wife, Justine, had tried valiantly to fight off the attacker, to no avail, as she was killed in the process.

The perp had taken Angela. Days later, her small body was found in a shallow grave. It nearly broke Ethan. At the same time, this gave him a whole new reason to carry on as a police detective.

Seeing to it that justice was served.

He got his wish when the unsub was identified as local handyman Terrence Reynaud, who was captured while attempting to flee Golfton Hills. Reynaud, a career criminal and sex offender, was convicted and sentenced to spend the rest of his life in prison.

* * *

Now, the nightmare was starting all over again for another family. Ethan cringed during the drive. For an instant, he wondered if Terrence Reynaud had somehow managed to escape from Apalachee Correctional Institution, East Unit. But Ethan quickly dismissed this possibility, knowing he would have been notified had this been the case.

No, whoever kidnapped the latest little girl was another child predator with, undoubtedly, the same devious intentions. Or a terrible omen of things to come for the abductee. Maybe this psychopath had gone after other girls elsewhere before setting his sights on Jodie Yancy.

The mere thought was grating to Ethan's nerves as he drove down Main Street. For him, this was personal. He owed it to the memory of Angela—and his late wife Justine—to do everything in his power to prevent what happened to them from ruining another family and additionally be able to reunite Jodie Yancy with her parents.

He got on the speakerphone and tried to get as much information on the child abduction as he could, which wasn't nearly enough as far as Ethan was concerned. But at least it gave him something to work with if he was to find Jodie before it was too late.

Having been a cop for going on twenty years, he'd developed an acute sense of sizing up criminals in trying to figure out their next move. In this instance, every second counted, and every minute that went by without the child captive being rescued was one more that the perp could find ways to harm her.

I have to do for Jodie what I was unable to do for Angela, Ethan told himself, more determined than ever to give her a happy ending, relatively speaking, to her ordeal.

* * *

He looked in the rear-view mirror at his little prize. She was still snoozing, thanks to the chloroform he'd given her. Just as well. He'd hate to see her whining for her mommy and daddy, especially when it wouldn't do her any good. No one would come to save the girl, no matter how hard she cried and begged for that to happen. He had waited long enough to fulfill his dark fantasies and now only needed a bit more time to put them into practice before getting rid of the body and seeing who else out there might be ripe for the picking.

Rubbing his aquiline nose, he glanced again at the girl lying in a fetal position on the back seat. Soon, they would arrive at the secret hideaway he'd lined up just for this occasion—and others to follow.

He drove down Greenhaven Lane, making sure to stay well within the speed limit. The last thing he needed was the cops, surely looking for them, to stop him for speeding and ruin everything. He'd planned this too carefully to make a mistake now. Everything had worked out to perfection thus far. It had almost been too easy to grab the girl and toss her into his SUV like a sack of potatoes. Still, he didn't want to press his luck.

For all the world, he was just another above average looking, down to earth person who most would say couldn't hurt a fly let alone another human being. No one would ever suspect him to be far more dangerous and deadly to not only the delicious little one, but anyone who dared to get in his way.

* * *

"We've got something…" Detective Fleisher reported over the phone.

"Go on," Ethan said to him eagerly while heading down Greenhaven Lane.

"Surveillance video was able to pick up, near the scene of the abduction, an SUV that matched the description of the vehicle the girl was put into. It's a black Ford Expedition. We ran the plates and found that the vehicle is registered to a Dominic Axelrod, whose address is 1843 Gapport Street. We think that Axelrod, who is thirty-four years old and has a record for crimes against children and various drug offenses, may be headed there."

"That's not far from where I am," Ethan told the detective.

"We've got a unit en route there and have issued a BOLO for the suspect and his SUV," Fleisher informed him.

"Good." As Ethan was pondering this and the need to rescue the victim at all costs, he happened to approach a black Ford Expedition. "Run that license plate number by me again."

Fleisher did so and asked, "What do you have?"

"The vehicle we're looking for," Ethan told him, seeing that the number on the license plate was a match.

"What is your location exactly?" Fleisher pressed. "For backup?"

Ethan gave it, but he wasn't about to wait around till the suspect either managed to give him the slip. Or had more time to hurt the girl. Though there was no visual of her, he suspected that she was still inside the vehicle, lying unconscious but probably still alive on the back seat. Till her abductor was able to get her to his intended destination to complete the victimization.

That's not going to happen, Ethan told himself. This had to end here and now. He banked on the fact that the element of surprise in his unmarked vehicle and swift action would work in his favor in giving him the upper hand he needed to get the jump on the suspect.

Without giving it a second thought, he dipped into the other lane and sped past the SUV, before sharply cutting it off and causing the driver to swerve and slam on the brakes at the same time to avoid hitting him.

Quickly climbing out of his car, Ethan removed his firearm and moved up to the driver-side window of the Ford Expedition, identifying himself as an officer of the law before directing the suspect to step out of the vehicle.

"Or what?" he spat defiantly.

"Or I'll shoot you for resisting arrest!" Ethan retorted, taking aim to make it clear he was not bluffing. Or fooling around here.

The suspect seemed to be weighing his options while Ethan never took his eyes off him, in case the man went for a weapon or tried to back the car up and drive off.

"Get out of the car!" Ethan repeated, a sharp edge to his voice.

Finally, the suspect did so with his hands up and asked coolly, "Mind telling me what this is all about? Was I speeding or what?"

It's the or what, Ethan thought perturbed, glancing toward the rear seats and seeing no one. He turned back to the suspect, who was blue-eyed and as tall as him but not as well built and had brown hair styled in a messy undercut and a circle beard. He was wearing a black logo jersey T-shirt, stretch denim pocket jeans, and black sneakers.

Eyeing him sharply, Ethan continued to keep the gun on him and responded cautiously, "Is this your vehicle?"

"Yeah," he answered snappily. "Why?"

"Are you Dominic Axelrod?"

"Yeah." The suspect tensed, then tried to play innocent. "You have no right to detain me. I didn't do anything," he claimed.

Ethan asked him straightforwardly, "Where's the girl?"

"Girl? What girl?" Axelrod wrinkled his nose, as though totally at a loss.

"A ten-year-old girl named Jodie Yancy was abducted a short while ago from her house." Ethan peered at him. "Know anything about that?"

"No. It wasn't me," he insisted.

"Your vehicle, which matches the SUV the girl was put into, was captured on a security camera video leaving the immediate area of the child kidnapping," Ethan told him. "Care to explain that?"

"Nothing to explain. I was visiting a friend—a lady I've been seeing—and that was it." Axelrod took a breath. "I never abducted a girl or anyone else."

"In that case, I'm sure you won't mind me searching your SUV," Ethan told him.

"Feel free to," the suspect said calmly. "I have nothing to hide."

Ethan wasn't about to take him at his word. Especially when instincts told him the man was lying through his teeth. "Turn around," he ordered him.

"Why? I've given you permission to search the car."

"I'm going to handcuff you during the search, just routinely," Ethan said, though he knew it was much more than that. Letting his guard down and giving him the benefit of the doubt could prove to be a fatal mistake. "Now turn around."

"Okay, okay," Axelrod said irritably and began to do so.

At that point, Ethan lowered his firearm just slightly while removing the flex cuffs from his belt. Before he could react, the suspect swiveled and landed a solid blow on his jaw. As Ethan tried to recover, Axelrod went for his Glock 42 pistol.

A fight for control of the firearm ensued between the two of them. No longer seeing stars, Ethan slammed his head against the bridge of the suspect's nose and again harder, hearing the bones break in it.

As Axelrod howled from the pain and continued to try and wrestle the gun from him, Ethan drove a knee into his crotch and shot him once in the leg. These maneuvers were enough to give him the upper hand in regaining control of the situation. He forced the suspect to his knees and handcuffed him, then stated, while still feeling the discomfort of being sucker punched, "You're under arrest, asshole, for assaulting a police detective."

Just then, Ethan watched as the back door of the SUV opened, and a young girl crawled out. "Are you Jodie Yancy?" he asked.

"Yeah, I'm Jodie." Tall for her age and slender, she glared at the suspect defiantly and pointed a thin finger at him. "That man came into my room and took me."

"Did he hurt you?" Ethan asked though she did not appear injured on the surface.

"No, not really," she said. "He put something on my face that made me go to sleep before I woke up, lying on the back seat in his car."

So, he drugged her, Ethan told himself. She would need to be checked out by a doctor before being released to her parents. He furrowed his brow at her abductor and said, "You can add child kidnapping to the charges you're facing, along with any others we come up with—"

Axelrod muttered an expletive or two while moaning from the pain he was feeling. When more police arrived, the suspect was taken into custody.

Ethan was surprised when, before she could get into the ambulance for medical evaluation, Jodie ran up to him and wrapped her small arms around his waist in a hug. "Thank you for saving me from him," she uttered tearfully.

He responded emotionally while thinking about his late daughter, "I was happy to do so. I'm just glad you get to go back to your parents, safe and sound. I'm sure they'll be elated to see you at the hospital and take you home."

"Yeah." She giggled. "And I can't wait to see my puppy, Tasha, again."

He grinned, having been told that the puppy went unharmed during the abduction. "I'll bet Tasha won't want to let you out of her sight."

Ethan watched as the ambulance drove off to the hospital. He knew that Jodie Yancy was indeed one lucky girl. If only he had been able to save Angela. Along with his wife, Justine. His whole life would have been different for the better. But he was unable to do anything for them except for trying to be a better person in all the ways that counted most in their memory.

* * *

The next day, Ethan was on hand as formal charges of drugging and kidnapping a juvenile and assaulting a police officer were issued in court against Dominic Axelrod, along with unlawful possession of fentanyl. All of which would ensure a conviction and lengthy stay behind bars.

Afterwards, Ethan visited the Golfton Hills Cemetery on Hollow Lane, where his wife and daughter were buried. He laid flowers at their gravesites and took a moment to remember them as each was when they were a whole family.

"Miss you guys more than I could ever say in mere words," he spoke out loud. "I got an opportunity to give an abducted girl back to her parents— and took it. I know you'd both be proud that I'm still out there, hitting the pavement and trying to do for others what I failed to do for you. But something tells me that we're still in this together, no matter what twists and turns my life takes moving forward."

Ethan put a hand to his lips and touched each granite headstone affectionately before heading off with them still very much in his thoughts. Along with a little girl named Jodie Yancy.

The House Sitter

Sally Berenger had big plans for the evening. She had met a man. He seemed nice enough. Or at least a better bet than some of her most recent and mostly unforgettable dates. So what if he was older and had a ready-made family? Was that so bad? Though she was childless while pushing thirty, she was open to having children of her own. Or inheriting children with the right partner. Particularly one who was well-established as a businessman, matching her own success in the investment community.

Sally slipped into the off-the-shoulder red dress that flattered her figure and was a good match for her long and blunt-cut raven hair before stepping into stiletto pumps. She coated her mouth with rose-colored lip gloss and was ready to go.

The doorbell rang. Her date was half an hour early. She appreciated a man who didn't keep her waiting for a change. Another good sign?

Sally strode across the plush dark gray carpeting of her Golfton Hills condo and opened the door. Her blue eyes flashed with disappointment when realizing that the visitor wasn't her date after all.

He was nearly the same height as him, probably just as fit, and younger. His dark hair was in an angular fringe cut, and dark eyes stared back at her. He was wearing a brown uniform and, she just noticed, was carrying what looked like a tool box, as though a maintenance man.

"Ms. Berenger?" he asked evenly, with a crooked grin on his lips, as if already knowing the answer.

"Yes...?" she acknowledged quizzically.

"I'm Hal from the Sinclair Plumbing Company. Your neighbor's kitchen sink is backed up—with whatever they put in there—and it will soon make its way through your pipes and into your sink. I'll need to run a snake through it and avert the crisis before it happens. At least on your end."

Sally bristled with annoyance. She had run into a pipe problem once before caused by her neighbors. But, right now, the timing stunk. "How long will this take?"

"If all goes well, only a few minutes," he promised.

She had little choice but to take him at his word, hopeful that this would be over before her date arrived, as Sally didn't want to keep him waiting any longer than necessary. "Okay, go do what you have to do—but please hurry, as I have somewhere to go." And someone to go there with.

"I understand." Hal grinned again. "I'll be out of your hair in no time flat."

She stepped aside and watched him head for the gourmet kitchen to do his work.

* * *

He stepped toward the kitchen, glancing back over his shoulder at the attractive dark-haired woman. She was now holding a cell phone, checking her messages, or whatever. More importantly, she had given him free rein to do what she was expecting him to, without giving it any consideration that he just might have ulterior motives for being there. Worked like a charm seemingly every time.

He might have laughed loudly, had he not wanted this to alert her that she had let trouble inside her condo. She would find out soon enough—and before the man she had apparently expected at the door could arrive and try to be a hero.

He sat the toolbox on the marble countertop, opened it, and removed the silk scarf. Flexing it, he wasted little time in coming up behind the distracted Sally Berenger and wrapping the scarf around her neck. By the time she came to terms with the fact that he wasn't there to unclog pipes—but something much more sinister—it was too late for her to do anything but accept the reality of the situation she found herself in.

She was going to die, and there was nothing she could do about it. Just like the ones who came before her.

And those to follow.

* * *

I listened with interest to the radio while driving down Jaffe Road in a blue Audi Q5 Sportback as it was reported that a third woman in less than a month had been strangled to death in Golfton Hills. It was believed that they were the victims of a serial killer, who had apparently been able to enter their residences under false pretenses—catching the victims off guard. The press had dubbed the killer the Golfton Hills Strangler, who was still at large.

The thought of being strangled under any circumstances gave me the chills, as it would anyone dying in such a frightening way. But it wasn't enough to scare me away from my current plan of being a thirty-year-old, single house sitter. The homeowner, Lilian Henriksen, a bestselling author, and friend, was overseas on an extended book tour.

The hope was that the unidentified serial killer would be stopped, one way or another. Of course, that was always the desired outcome whenever such an unsettling scenario existed. But I was confident that the authorities had this one—and that justice would prevail at the end of the day.

Until such time, I needed to stay the course and let things play out as they were meant to. Or adjust accordingly if it seemed I was in harm's way.

I drove up to the Florida-style pastel colonial beach house on Dolen Way. It was one story and quite charming, with lots of windows and wooden shutters.

I grabbed my leather hobo bag and one piece of luggage and headed past cabbage palm trees to go inside. Just as I remembered, with an open concept, it was spacious and well-appointed, with high ceilings, hickory hardwood flooring, and attractive traditional furnishings.

I checked out the rest of the place, my blue-green eyes taking careful note of every angle, twist, and turn—including the den, which looked to be halfway through being remodeled, perhaps to house more of Lilian's writings—before going into the modern kitchen. Opening the stainless steel refrigerator, I saw that it was well stocked with food and drinks.

I took out a bottle of white wine and poured myself a glass, then sipped while giving the place another survey, pondering the tasks before me as a house sitter.

* * *

He watched her through his telephoto zoom lens as she stood out on the porch. Tall, slender, and attractive, just as he liked them. The past the shoulders, yellow hair with bottleneck bangs was a definite bonus. So what was her story anyway? He was aware that the house had been vacant of late, with the celebrity author who owned it—and not at all his type—having gone to Europe for a book tour.

Was she simply making use of the place with beach access for a day or two? Or perhaps house-sitting while the owner was autographing books far from home?

Either way he sliced it, the blonde excited him as he enjoyed checking her out. Was that a smart move? Should he be cautious about targeting her? Or throw caution to the wind and take advantage of an opportunity that had deliciously presented itself?

He opted for the latter, salivating at the prospect of wrapping his scarf around her pretty neck. Then gloating thereafter while waiting for the next female to come into his crosshairs.

He watched as the good-looking blonde woman went back inside, undoubtedly oblivious about what he had in store for her.

* * *

I called Lilian Henriksen while sitting in a comfortable mid-century modern chair to let her know I had arrived safe and sound.

"Hey," I said to her in the video chat.

Lilian, who was like a mother to me—having been there when my real mom passed away a decade ago—flashed a smile as her aging face crinkled, surrounded by silver hair styled in a pixie bob. "I see you made it."

"Yep, I'm here." I grinned. "Thanks so much for letting me stay here for a bit."

"I'm happy to have you there, Ash," she said, which was short for Ashley. "The place needed someone to look after it while I'm away."

"I'll do my best."

"I know you will." She furrowed her brow. "Sorry about the mess in the den. I was in the process of having it remodeled before needing to delay it while on the book tour."

"Not a problem," I assured her, imagining how it might look once the work was completed. "So, how's the book tour coming along?" She wrote historical novels known for their verisimilitude and attention to detail.

"Wonderfully," Lilian said with a lilt to her voice. "Seems like everywhere I go, my fans are more than willing to show up and make me feel extra special."

"You deserve every bit of that adulation," I assured her.

She blushed. "You deserve such even more for the important work you do, Ashley."

"Thanks." I colored, knowing it meant a lot to have her approval.

"You be careful," she advised, narrowing her blue eyes sincerely.

"I will." I favored her with a look that illustrated the seriousness with which I took her words to heart.

Once the conversation ended, I made a couple of other calls before contemplating my next move.

* * *

The next morning, Ashley was up bright and early. After putting on a tank top, running shorts, and low-top sneakers, she tied her hair in a ponytail and set out for a run on the beach.

On an overcast day, she jogged past art galleries and a farmer's market, then across the walkway, till making her way to the white sand beach, where

Ashley took in the glistening clear water with soft ripples before slowing down when approaching a man and his dog.

"Morning," the man said, grinning crookedly. He was tall, tanned, and muscular, with short black hair and dark brown eyes.

"Good morning," she told him evenly, then gazed at the dog, a black Dutch shepherd. "Who's this?" The dog seemed friendly enough.

"This is Grady," the man answered.

"Hi, Grady," Ashley said and crouched down just enough to pet him under the chin and chest. The dog seemed pleased with the attention and licked her hand.

"He's warmed up to you quickly," the man said, as if unexpected.

She stood upright. "I guess I have that effect on animals," she said, having left her own French bulldog at home.

"I can see that." The man smiled. "So, are you a visitor in Golfton Hills? Or a resident?"

Ashley took a moment to consider how to answer. Too much information was never a good idea. Too little might seem paranoid. Not that the latter was a bad thing right now, locally speaking.

"I'm house-sitting for a friend," she replied simply. "So, I guess that puts me down as a visitor."

"I see." He met her eyes unblinkingly.

"What about you?" she threw out. "Local, tourist, or something else?"

"Something else. Just here for business," he said tersely.

She didn't bother to ask him to elaborate—or what his dog was doing with him on a business trip—seeing no need to get more out of the man than she was willing to give in return. "Well, I better get back to my run."

He nodded. "Have fun."

"You too." She amended this, as it was clear that he wasn't there for fun, "Hope you succeed in whatever your business endeavors are in Golfton Hills."

"Me too."

Ashley eyed the dog and said, "Bye, Grady."

The dog barked, as if it understood, causing her to smile at him and his owner before she resumed her jog down the beach without looking back.

* * *

He watched as the blonde-haired woman ran across the sand in a good and steady trot that made it obvious that she was more than just an occasional runner. Part of him wanted to run after her, keeping her in his sights. But then that would be too obvious, wouldn't it?

Tipping his hand by showing his eagerness to add her to his victims of strangulation wouldn't be very smart. No, he needed to fight his urge to appease his inner self and play it cool. He knew where she was staying. He also knew just how to get to her. And what to do once she was trapped with nowhere else to go.

Soon, very soon, he would get this over with, once and for all. Only then could he take credit for ending her life and making his own seem that much more worthwhile.

He moved across the beach in the opposite direction from his prey, but never allowed her to stray very far from his mind—and his sinister plans for her.

* * *

That afternoon, I had lunch at a small café on Brooker Street before going back to the beach house.

I was just about to pluck one of Lilian's novels off the shelf to read a few chapters of, when there was a knock on the door. I tensed while peeking out the window. A man stood there. He looked to be in his mid-thirties, was tall and solid in build, with dark hair in a fringe cut, and wearing sunglasses. He had on a gray uniform. There was a black van parked on the street in front of the beach house.

As he knocked again, I contemplated whether or not to open the door before doing just that.

"Yes?" I peered at him coolly.

"Hi. I'm looking for Lilian Henriksen."

"Lilian's not here."

He wrinkled his nose. "Do you know when she'll be back?"

"Not for a while. She's out of the country on a book tour," I felt at liberty to tell him. "And who are you...?"

As if he had forgotten to introduce himself till now, he responded sheepishly, "My name's Dean Parrish. I'm a contractor with Thayer Construction & Remodeling. I was hired by Ms. Henriksen to complete the work on her den."

I wondered if this had slipped Lilian's mind when we spoke yesterday. "She never mentioned this to me," I told him honestly while noting the company logo on his shirt. "I'm sure when she gets back..."

"I had to work my schedule around to fit this in," he said, an edge to his voice. "Do you suppose I could take a quick look at the den to gauge what still needs to be done? Then I can come back and complete the work whenever Ms. Henriksen returns and gives us a call to set it up."

It seemed reasonable enough. *Maybe too reasonable to the point of being suspicious*, I told myself.

"All right," I relented. "You can check out the den and see where things stand for when Lilian gets back."

"Thanks." He grinned at me in what I took as disingenuous. Then he came inside the house, where he removed his shades and put them in his shirt pocket.

"This way," I told him, as though he had no idea.

"Cool."

I practically felt him breathing down the back of my neck as I led him into the den while wondering if he would actually hit me from behind.

He didn't. Instead, he actually appeared to size up the rather large unfinished den with interesting angles and a combination of retro and contemporary furniture before pivoting on me so swiftly that I took a step back involuntarily.

"Did you see what you needed to?" I had to ask guardedly.

"Yeah, thanks." He stuck his hand in the side pocket of his pants. "What I

47

needed to see was you, I'm afraid…"

"Excuse me?" My heart skipped a beat as his eyes were suddenly menacing as they fixed upon my face.

He removed a silk scarf from the pocket and said coldly, "Turns out I'm not really here to remodel the den after all."

I backed up a bit more. "What do you want?" my voice cracked pretending I hadn't a clue.

"Your life."

I remained as calm as I could. "You're that serial killer I read about?"

He chuckled. "You got me. Too bad it won't help your cause any."

"So, you strangled all three of those poor women?" I wanted to get him to confess.

"Yeah, guilty as charged," he bragged. "Or I would be if the cops were ever to arrest me. Not happening."

"Why are you doing this?" I had to ask, as though there was any justifiable rationale.

"Because I can," he said straightforwardly. "That's what makes all serial killers tick, for the record." He laughed. "We just can't help ourselves."

"Not if you don't even bother to try!" I glared at him, feeling nothing but contempt.

"Too hard. Especially when you and the others have made this so easy." He bared his teeth like a rabid animal as I found myself backed up against the wall. "I'm going to strangle you to death—and there's nowhere to run. And no one to come and save you—"

"I won't fight you," I told him, lowering my guard just enough to increase his level of confidence. "Just please make it as quick as possible so I don't have to suffer too much."

He seemed to resent the thought of me not begging for my life and, at the same time, looked a bit out of sorts before saying, "If you say so…"

The moment he flexed the scarf, I made my move. I grabbed a hardcover book that happened to be lying on a wooden end table and, before he could block it, threw it as decisively as I could so that the book slammed right into his face, landing squarely between his eyes and the bridge of a long nose.

While he screamed in pain and tried to shake it off, I was removing the Canix TP9SF Elite 9mm Luger pistol from the nylon concealed weapon holster I had just inside the waistband of my linen pants and further hidden by the oversized button-down shirt I was wearing.

Pointing it right at his bloodied face, while beyond arm's length, I announced in an authoritative fashion, "FBI Special Agent Ashley Anderson. You're under arrest for attempted murder...for starters..."

"You got me there," he muttered, breathing heavily. "Never saw that coming."

"Maybe you should have, asshole!"

He flexed the silk scarf, as though willing to take his chances for a date with death. With one eye half shut, he hissed cockily, "You're not good enough to get me before I get you."

"I wouldn't even try that if I were you—" a familiar voice uttered warningly. "We won't let you commit police suicide."

I looked over my shoulder and saw my fellow special agent and current boyfriend, Hamilton McCroy, whom I'd last run into on the beach, standing in the den. Next to him was his trusty working dog, Grady. Hamilton released him from his leash, and the dog charged the suspect.

Grady jumped atop him, and both went crashing to the floor, where the barking dog kept the Golfton Hills Strangler at bay, till Hamilton handcuffed him. "Sorry I was late to the party," he told me. "Got held up, even though we heard everything that was going on in here. Including the perp's confession to the serial strangulation murders."

"I won't hold it against you," I told him lightheartedly. "I think I had things pretty much under control while waiting for the cavalry to arrive."

Hamilton laughed as he got the suspect up on his feet. "Yeah, I can see that."

As if on cue, other FBI agents and personnel from the Golfton Hills PD came storming in and took the culprit into custody.

Three hours later, I shared a glass of wine with Hamilton at the beach house and said thankfully, "Nice to get past that ordeal."

"Absolutely." He nodded, regarding me in earnest. "Going undercover was a good idea in giving the then-unsub just enough rope to hang himself. You played your part to perfection."

"Ditto," I told him, smiling. "As did Grady."

"He's always up for a challenge," Hamilton joked. "Glad that your friend, Lilian, agreed to allow you to borrow this place to set up the serial killer."

"Truthfully, she was much more concerned with something bad happening to me than her wonderful beach house," I made clear. "But I assured her that I would be fine, knowing that you and others had my back, while we rooted out the Golfton Hills Strangler."

We had learned through his DNA that the perp's real name was George Sheppard, who, as it turned out, actually was a general contractor—when not murdering women by ligature strangulation.

"It was a team effort," Hamilton emphasized, "with you leading the way, Ashley, to get Sheppard to confess and to make sure he's never, ever able to stalk and hurt anyone again."

I flashed him a warm smile. "That's a comforting thought."

"So is this," Hamilton said and tilted his head for a sweet kiss. "While I'm here and before our next assignment, we might as well make the most of this idyllic setting by the beach."

"I couldn't agree more," I told him and clinked our wineglasses before continuing to take full advantage of the captivating circumstances afforded us.

An Unforeseen Awakening

E lla Hampton woke up early as usual, giving her at least half an hour before everyone else got up to make breakfast, lunch, and maybe steal a few minutes for herself. Careful not to wake her husband, Brett, she eased quietly out of his protective long arms. She noted that the only time he seemed to touch her these days was when he was asleep, as if any other time he couldn't be bothered. Or was opposed to it, like he was repulsed by her.

She pretended that this didn't bother her, though how could it not? Was it so wrong to wish that her husband desired her as much as she did him?

Slipping into a terrycloth robe over the chemise lingerie nightgown covering her slender body, Ella left the bedroom that had once been her pride and joy of the Spanish-style home they had purchased ten years ago in Golfton Hills. That was before it became primarily a place to sleep and get up rather than make love and cuddle afterwards. She had pretty much reconciled herself to the fact that this was probably what she had to look forward to in their marriage. Apparently, Brett was content to keep things just as they were, as if there were no other choice.

She padded barefoot to the en suite bathroom, where she washed her face, her tired blue eyes regarding her reflection through the mirror. Her short brunette hair, layered with baby bangs, was disheveled from sleeping on it. She wondered if her husband still found her attractive now that she was pushing forty, as was he. Was that the problem?

Moving down the hall across rosewood flooring, past the rooms of their children, Melissa and Ryan, Ella headed down the spiral staircase and through the contemporary furnished great room and into the gourmet kitchen.

In routine fashion, she made scrambled eggs, toast, and oatmeal and brewed a pot of coffee. Then a ham sandwich, apple, and slice of apple pie were brown-bagged for Brett and Ryan's lunches. Ella didn't bother making lunch for Melissa, knowing her sixteen-year-old daughter—a year younger than Ryan—had chosen to skip lunch these days as part of her attempt to remain rail thin in keeping pace with her friends.

Ella could only hope this wasn't the first step toward anorexia. How does a mother reach out to a typical know-it-all teenage girl these days without her rebelling? Something that Ella knew all too well from her own teen years and overly strict parents whom she struggled to get along with. Might it be a genetic predisposition where it concerned her relationship with Melissa? Or lack thereof?

She set the table and fell into a swivel armchair in the breakfast nook to sip coffee. Having quit college in midstream to become a wife and mother, Ella wondered if she might have taken a wrong turn in life. Perhaps instead of being the stay-at-home wife of a police detective, she should be out in the workforce, making her own money and otherwise leaving her mark on society. She shrugged at the reverie.

I suppose I'm no different from anyone else who finds comfort in the what-ifs, she thought. *Just leave it alone and try to find the good in the life you have.* Even if that seemed to be harder and harder to come by with each passing day.

"Morning," Brett's deep baritone voice intruded upon her thoughts like a masked man as he stood tall in the kitchen entryway.

"Good morning." Ella briefly surveyed her husband, dressed in his normal dark blue detective suit and white shirt with a bland, loose tie. His duty pistol was tucked inside a waistband holster. He was still handsome after nearly twenty years of marriage and worked out regularly to be in better shape than her. His graying hair was in a military buzz cut, and his stone-gray eyes gazed back at her.

Ella felt a little self-conscious about her own makeup-less appearance. Not to mention, there was nothing particularly appealing about wearing a robe and nightgown. But this was what she had morphed into at home in raising their kids and keeping things running as smoothly as possible in the household. Brett never complained, though she sometimes wished he would. Especially if there was a problem.

"I'll get you some coffee," she told him.

He checked her with a large hand. "I'll get it."

She let him, but got up anyway to begin putting food on the table. They went about their tasks in silence like strangers. Or perhaps roommates who had become so used to their particular functions that they could do them blindly and without invading the other's space.

Ella considered that Brett had been reassigned two weeks ago after being investigated by Internal Affairs of the Golfton Hills Police Department for some sort of misconduct that he had yet to fully explain to her. Was it police brutality? Evidence tampering? Or could it have been something of a sexual nature—such as sexual harassment?

Though none of these things seemed to fit the man she knew, Ella wondered if she knew her husband at all. Or if he knew her really, in the ways that counted most. She supposed that Brett would tell her what was going on when he was ready to.

"Is everything all right with the new assignment?" she asked casually.

"Yeah, it's fine," he said without looking at her as he tasted the coffee.

"Are you sure about that?" Ella pressed, studying his profile.

Brett finally turned her way. "Just trying to make the best of the situation, you know," he muttered without elaborating. "I'll get used to it." He paused. "What's on your agenda for today?"

Do you honestly even care? Ella asked herself dubiously. She lowered her eyes slightly when responding, "I'll pick up the dry cleaning and probably stop at a store to get a gift for my mother's birthday." It was still three weeks away, and she had long since stopped this practice, but it was not an unreasonable thing to say. Especially when she doubted Brett remembered precisely when her mother's birthday was.

"I'm sure you'll get her something nice," he said simply and, while still standing, scooped a spoonful of scrambled eggs from his plate and into his mouth. He gave her a perfunctory peck on the cheek. "Gotta go. Tell the kids I'm sorry I missed them this morning. See you later."

Ella watched as Brett left the kitchen, taking his coffee mug and lunch bag with him as he headed out the front door.

A moment later, as if waiting for him to leave, Ryan came bounding down the stairs, sat, and was eating in seemingly one fell swoop. At seventeen and a high school senior, Ella considered him a younger version of his father as he was already taller than him, with the same gray eyes and curly, cropped dark hair. He was dressed in his typical oversized shirt, cargo pants, and grungy sneakers.

"Did you finish your homework last night?" Ella thought to ask.

"Yeah." He wrinkled his nose. "You already asked me that before I went to bed."

"Oh. Sorry." Ella had admittedly been distracted at times, perhaps too much, though trying hard to keep her home life under control.

"People start to forget stuff when they reach their forties," Melissa remarked nonchalantly, sashaying in with her perpetual sneer. Her long blonde hair was in a side ponytail.

"I'm only thirty-nine," Ella reminded her, though sure she knew that.

"Same difference. Old is old." Melissa went to the pot of oatmeal and sniffed. "Eww. Can't you ever fix anything edible, Mom?" Her bold blue eyes narrowed.

"I see you're in good form this morning, as usual." Ella couldn't help but think that her daughter, wearing tight straight-leg jeans and an even tighter top that accentuated what few curves she had, was growing up way too fast for comfort. "You're free to make something else if you want."

"Yeah, this I've gotta see," quipped Ryan, suppressing a chuckle. "If it's not already precooked or microwaved, it would be way too complicated for her."

"Shut up, dimwit, or I'll cook something and force you to eat it," she shot back.

"You can try."

"You can try," Melissa mimicked and stuck her tongue out at him.

"Enough, you two," Ella said, raising her voice an octave. "Eat the oatmeal,

Melissa. It won't kill you."

"No thanks. I'm not really hungry."

"You have to eat something," Ella insisted.

Melissa grabbed a piece of toast and bit off a tiny piece to appease her. "See, I'm eating something. Satisfied?" She took one more bite of toast for effect, then walked away while pulling out her cell phone.

Ella didn't bother to argue, knowing now was not the time. She sat with Ryan. "Looks like it's just you and me."

He twisted his lips guiltily and stood. "Sorry, Mom, I'm outta here too. Gotta get to school early for practice."

Ryan gave Ella a wet kiss on the cheek and ran off. She knew he was on the track team at Golfton Hills High School and excelled at it. She sat back in her nook chair and sipped the now cold coffee thoughtfully.

* * *

Ella took a final look at her appearance in the full-length mirror behind the bathroom door. Her makeup was complete and complemented her hair, now coiffed perfectly. She admired the low-cut black faux wrap dress that exposed a generous amount of cleavage and matching wedges. This was accented with double-beaded drop earrings and a simple set of pearls around her neck.

She smiled at the remarkable transformation. Not bad.

In fact, I look pretty hot, if I say so myself, Ella thought while feeling a tad guilty about hiding this sexy side of herself from Brett. Would it even make a difference if he were to see her now? Or did it make him feel better about himself if she stuck to the rather frumpy-looking wife persona he was used to?

After dabbing a bit of perfume on her neck and wrists, Ella deemed herself ready to go. *I should be back in plenty of time to prepare dinner, do the laundry, and do anything else I need to do*, she thought.

Driving a Subaru Forester, Ella took the highway, heading for downtown Golfton Hills. She was meeting her lover, Mitchell Roxburgh, as scheduled.

They had settled on meeting twice a week, Tuesdays and Thursdays at ten a.m., for two hours. It was a safe time to be together without arousing suspicions.

Mitchell was married too and had been for more than a decade. Ella sometimes wondered about his wife, whom she had seen once from afar. Tori Roxburgh was tall and gorgeous, with mounds of chestnut hair and a darker complexion.

Were they alike at all other than sharing the same man? What did she bring to the table that her lover's wife did not?

Probably the same thing, Ella imagined, that he provided her that she wasn't getting from Brett—someone who allowed her to be herself sexually without the baggage of commitment, judgment, or conditions.

Ella had met Mitchell at a bookstore six months ago. They had hit it off right away, as two people who enjoyed the classics and shared that love quite naturally. The first couple of meetings were casual, at small and out-of-the-way cafes.

But the more she got to know him, a successful art dealer, the more Ella found herself enjoying his company. Though it had never been her intention to have an affair with him, when it happened, she was unable or unwilling to break away from it. Mitchell was handsome in a different way from Brett. Taller and svelte, he had a taper fade haircut, his glossy black hair bordering a square-jawed face, and deep blue eyes.

Just as importantly, he was turned on by her in a way that Brett hadn't been in a very long time. In turn, Ella was sure she, too, filled a void in Mitchell's life, though they both knew there was an element of risk—even danger—involved in their affair. While Brett had never shown a jealous streak, she had given him no reason to put that to the test. Till now.

It was on that ponderance, during the drive, that Ella began to have second thoughts as to whether it was worth possibly losing everything she had in her marriage and family life, by continuing to be unfaithful.

Maybe I need to break it off before I live to regret it, she told herself, while pulling into the parking garage of the Golfton Hills Condominiums on Twelfth Street, where Mitchell owned a condo, apart from the house he shared with his wife. Putting aside her own needs and gratification was a small price to pay to Ella for keeping her life as she knew it intact.

Was that what she really wanted?

Would Mitchell fight to keep her in his life? Or be relieved that it was over and refocus on his own marriage?

She parked the car and headed toward the elevator, still meandering as to which way to go in confronting her lover.

* * *

When Ella reached her lover's door, she had more or less decided to end their relationship. She hoped he understood. Would she, were he to have been the one to bow out? Or would she have found it difficult to walk away?

The moment the door opened, and she looked into his eyes that held her gaze intently, Ella's intentions of saying goodbye to him and their affair went out the window. "Hey," she murmured.

Mitchell, who had the whitest teeth of anyone she knew, smiled handsomely and said, "Hey, you. Come on in."

She did so, stepping onto the Eucalyptus hardwood flooring, where Ella took a sweeping glance at the interior with its open concept, floor-to-ceiling windows, and relaxed modern furniture. The walls were adorned with expensive art. She turned back to her lover, who was, as always, cool, calm, and collected, wearing a yellow polo shirt, beige slacks, and tan moc toe boat shoes.

"You look lovely, as usual," he complimented her.

"So do you," she had to admit.

He grinned. "Can I get you a drink?"

She moved closer, picking up the woodsy scent of his cologne, which had the effect of further weakening her defenses and making him that much more desirable. "I think I'd rather get right down to business," she said boldly.

"I see." He put his hands on her slender waist. "What did you have in mind?"

MYSTERIES OF GOLFTON HILLS

Ella cupped his cheeks. "This…" She began to kiss him. He reciprocated in kind, and they stood there for a while in a lip lock before she pulled away, while eager for more. "Do you want to take this to the bedroom?"

"Absolutely," he said passionately.

They walked to the primary suite, hand in hand. It was spacious and had retro furnishings. Quickly stripping naked with her lover, Ella blocked her mind from reconsidering whether or not this was a good idea and instead felt compelled to go with the flow.

Mitchell used protection, and they made love the way Ella used to make love with her husband, before they somehow went awry over the years. Leading to this moment in time.

When it was over, she fell asleep in Mitchell's arms, intending for it to only be for a short while, then they would return to their real lives. Till the next time.

* * *

They jimmied the lock, till the door was forced open. The three of them, all wearing ski masks and gloves, entered the condo. They were in search of cash and anything they could find of value to buy marijuana, fentanyl, and whatever else they needed money for.

Moving about freely, they went through drawers, cabinets, and cupboards, pocketing what they wanted. The plan was to get in and get out quickly, limiting the risks of detection or trouble otherwise.

So far, in other home invasions, this had worked like a charm. No one got hurt and they had come away with enough valuable items to make the break-in worth their while.

This time seemed like it would be no different.

* * *

Ella was roused awake when she heard a noise coming from outside the bedroom. Her first thought was that Mitchell's wife, Tori—whom he said never came to the condo—had gone against the grain and made an exception this time around.

The notion of her catching them naked in bed caused Ella's pulse to race. How would they explain the affair? Would it mean the end of Mitchell's marriage? Would the infidelity hit home with her as well, with Brett filing for divorce and wanting custody of their kids, considering her to be an unfit mother?

As she contemplated the scenarios—none of which were good—Ella realized that the sounds she heard were not footsteps. No, they were more like the noise made by opening and slamming shut drawers. And ransacking the place.

Someone had broken into the condo.

She jarred Mitchell awake. "There's someone out there..." Ella told him in a whisper, her body quivering.

Once he regained his equilibrium, Mitchell listened and, after coming to the same conclusion, said tonelessly, "Wait here..."

She grabbed his arm nervously. "Should we call 911?"

"Are you ready to come clean about us?" He peered at her, and Ella found herself speechless. "Didn't think so. I'll be fine," he insisted and hopped up. He slipped on his trousers, grabbed a bat that sat in the corner of the room and went out into the hall.

Ella tensed as she heard some commotion and verbal sparring between Mitchell and at least one other person. She could only hope that Mitchell didn't get hurt in the process, as Ella then had to consider what the home invaders might do to her if they had their way. The idea of being raped while in her lover's bed terrified her.

This can't be happening, Ella thought, panicking as everything suddenly went quiet. Had something bad happened to Mitchell?

As if the lull before the storm, she heard a male voice say, "Let's check the other bedroom..."

While Ella cowered beneath the sateen sheet on a large platform bed, she watched as two people entered the room. They were tall and slender. Both were wearing black ski masks and gloves while seemingly just as shocked to see her as she was to see them. Based on what she could assess, Ella believed that the burglars—unless they had broken into the condo for other reasons—were male.

"Please, don't hurt me," she begged them, not knowing what their plans were, but assuming the worst.

The two intruders simply stared at her for a long moment, as though transfixed by her, before the one wearing a gray fleece hoodie, denim jeans, and blue running sneakers, said succinctly to the other person, "Let's get outta here—"

The other burglar, who wore a dark green fleece jacket over a large multicolored button-down shirt, brown canvas cargo pants, and black sneakers, nodded, but said nothing.

Ella watched as the two left the room. She listened as they ran down the hall and out of the condo. But where was Mitchell? Why hadn't he come in after them? Or come in now that they were gone? Was he hurt? Or worse?

And why did the one who spoke sound so familiar, even when he appeared to make a concerted effort to disguise his voice?

Ella climbed out of the bed and quickly slipped into her clothes. In case the intruders were still there, she didn't want to give them more to see than she cared for them to. Or be any more uncomfortable than she already was.

She stepped out into the hall and saw Mitchell lying motionless on the floor in the living area. The bat was by his side.

As her heart pounded, Ella ran to him. He was flat on his back, and there was a gash on Mitchell's forehead, like he was hit with the bat or some other object.

Is he dead? she asked herself as Ella fell to her knees and tried to get him to show signs of life.

When he finally did, Mitchell asked, dumbfounded, "What happened?"

"Two people broke in, and you went to confront them," she said. "They must have attacked you."

"Actually, there were three of them," he informed her. His brows knitted thoughtfully. "Were you hurt?"

"No." Ella could see the surprise on his face, as if he had expected otherwise.

Admittedly, she was a bit puzzled as well. "Guess they got what they were after and left it at that."

He tried to sit up, but fell back down. "I'm a little dizzy."

"I'll call 911," she offered, not knowing if he had a concussion or internal injuries.

"Don't. I'm all right. I just need a moment."

"Are you sure?"

"Yeah. I have a slight headache after being hit with something. But I'll live."

Ella met his eyes. "What do you want me to do?"

"Go home," Mitchell said flatly, as he was now able to sit up. "You need to get back before your family arrives. When I report the crime, I'll say it was just me here. No reason to mess things up for either of us by exposing our affair."

She wanted to argue the point, feeling that his health and well-being were more important than holding onto their secret of being married lovers. But she sensed that he was more eager to keep his wife from finding out he was cheating on her than Ella's husband finding out about them.

"Okay, I'll go," she agreed, helping him to his feet. "If you need anything—"

"I won't." Mitchell lifted Ella's face and kissed her mouth in what she almost felt seemed like it was for the final time. "Watch your back, till you're home safely," he warned.

She nodded, fighting back an urge to cry, then left.

* * *

When Detective Brett Hampton received the call about a home invasion at the Golfton Hills Condominiums on Twelfth Street, he headed straight to the scene. Since he had been reassigned to the Golfton Hills PD's Robbery Division, Brett had become aware of a string of home invasions there in recent memory, with the thieves being apparently young offenders who were looking to steal cash and sellable items to buy drugs, clothing, or relieve boredom for the hell of it.

Was that the case here?

Brett pondered this as he drove his black Chevy Suburban down the road. His mind shifted to his previous assignment with the Homicide Division. What started as a case of a domestic violence fatality led to his being falsely accused of mishandling evidence. Though he was cleared, the department chose to move him to RD to tamp down any suggestions of favoritism.

Brett was assured that the move was only temporary and that, in fact, he was due for a promotion with the HD. He chose to keep all this from Ella, for now, while hoping the good news would strengthen their marriage at the end of the day.

He sensed that she had been pulling away from him of late and blamed this on himself. The relationship had admittedly grown stale with his being too preoccupied with work and not giving his teenage kids the time they deserved, putting much of that on Ella. But he hoped that things would soon change for the better and they could be a closer family again.

Brett reached his destination and went up to the condo to speak with the victim of the home invasion.

"I'm Detective Hampton," Brett told him.

"Mitchell Roxburgh."

Brett sized him up as he took note of the gash on his forehead, then glanced at the place that had been ransacked. "Were you alone when this happened?"

Mitchell seemed to have to think about it before he responded, "Yes, I was alone."

Brett asked directly, "Do you live here with anyone?"

"I'm married, Detective, if that's what you're asking." Mitchell looked uncomfortable. "My wife and I have a house. This condo is mainly an investment property."

"I see." Brett paused musingly. "What is it that you do for a living, Mr. Roxburgh?"

"I'm an art dealer."

Brett wondered if the burglars were somehow privy to this. Or if the home invasion was random, as the others appeared to be.

"How many perpetrators were there?"

"Three," Mitchell replied.

"Did you get a good look at any of them?" Brett asked.

"I wish." Mitchell shook his head. "Unfortunately, they were all wearing ski masks."

Brett couldn't help but notice that the man was staring at him as they stood inside the condo. Or was this his imagination? Had they crossed paths before?

"Could you tell if the burglars were old or young?"

"Young," Mitchell said confidently. "I'm guessing teenagers or young adults."

Brett nodded. "Seems to fit the characteristics of the perps in some other recent local home invasions," he mentioned.

Mitchell muttered an expletive. "Hope you can catch them."

"We will." Brett didn't see how they wouldn't. If the offenders were still in high school or even college, they weren't smart enough to know when to quit while they were ahead. Or refrain from talking about it. He eyed the victim. "Do you have security cameras?"

Mitchell stared at the question before answering, "No. But I'll definitely get a system installed after this," he promised.

"Do you have a list of the items that were stolen?" Brett asked.

"I'm still trying to determine that." Mitchell jutted his chin. "My insurance will cover my losses. But peace of mind...well, that'll take some time."

"Yeah, it probably will." Brett met his eyes musingly. "Hopefully, we can make some arrests soon and go from there."

"Okay."

"We'll be in touch," Brett told him. Gazing again at the laceration on his forehead, he said, "You might want to get that looked at."

"I will," Mitchell assured him, though Brett got a sense that this wasn't something he was truly interested in pursuing, whatever his reasons.

* * *

When she got to her house, Ella was still shaking from her ordeal. How was she to process being a party to a home invasion during a time when she was seeing another man other than her husband?

I have to find a way to deal with it as best as possible, she told herself, while taking a shower, as though to cleanse herself of the filth that came from feeling so vulnerable to the thieves who leered at her in Mitchell's bed. Even if fully covered. She may as well have been totally exposed, as could have been the case in their mind's eyes.

By the time everyone was home, Ella managed to pull herself together enough to put up a good front. She made a fresh salad, baked chicken thighs, and biscuits for dinner.

As the family sat around the rectangular dining table, Ella couldn't help but notice that everyone seemed preoccupied with their thoughts. Just as she was, considering the day she'd been through. And the guilt that accompanied it.

It was Melissa who, after only nibbling at her food, broke the silence when she asked her brother in a curious and sarcastic tone of voice, "So, what's got your panties tied up in a knot?"

That was when Ryan lifted his head and glared at Ella—or so she interpreted it this way—and responded tartly, "Nothing."

"You sure you're not just pissed at Javier for who knows what?" Melissa persisted in pushing his buttons.

Javier Gutiérrez was Ryan's best friend, and also a senior at Golfton Hills High. Ella wondered why he was suddenly weighing heavily on her thoughts.

"I'm sure." Ryan sneered at his sister. "Mind your own business."

She stuck her tongue out at him. "Make me."

"Maybe I will," he threatened her.

This prompted Brett to speak up, narrowing his eyes at his son. "No, you won't."

"I didn't mean it." Ryan grinned deferentially. "Forget I said that."

Melissa seemed to take pleasure in winning the mini battle, but offered no response as she forked a piece of lettuce.

Ryan locked eyes with Ella and asked pointedly, "What did you do today, Mom?"

She thought it sounded more like an accusation than a question, but responded coolly, "Not much, really." Could he have seen right through her? Known she was with Mitchell? How was that possible? "I ran a few errands, did some chores around the house, made dinner...what else?" She seemed stuck in trying to fill out her day with what almost seemed like a suspicious son. With an equally suspicious husband looking on. Or so Ella imagined, ill at ease.

As Ryan appeared to be digesting this, all while seeming to have a giant chip on his shoulder, Brett stopped eating and said, "My own day was interesting enough... I'm investigating a home invasion—"

Ella watched probingly as Ryan's face colored. Hers likely had as well, but she asked her husband casually, "Who's home was invaded?"

"An art dealer named Mitchell Roxburgh," Brett said matter-of-factly. "He was roughed up a bit by the burglars, who stole cash and other stuff, including apparently a couple of valuable paintings right off the walls... Seems to fit a pattern of home invasions recently in Golfton Hills, probably by some teenagers. Roxburgh, who says he was alone—but might have had some company he'd rather his wife didn't find out about—is lucky he didn't get seriously hurt. It appears, though, that the burglars are getting more brazen in their violence with each home invasion. Who knows how far they'll go, if they're not stopped."

Ella felt nauseous as she replayed in her head the words of the one burglar, wearing a gray fleece hoodie, denim jeans, and blue running sneakers, who told the other one who spotted her in Mitchell's bed, "Let's get outta here—"

She thought the voice sounded familiar but couldn't place it before now.

It was the voice of Ryan's best friend, Javier Gutiérrez.

Ella stared at her son as she went back in time to the other burglar, who wore a dark green fleece jacket with an oversized multicolored button-down shirt, brown canvas cargo pants, and black sneakers—much like Ryan was wearing at this moment.

As he held her gaze with a combination of guilt, hatred, anxiety, and defiance, Ella knew that they were suddenly at a stalemate, with both having something to hide and neither in a position to do anything about it other than remain mute in their respective corners and find a way to live with what they had done.

Unburdening His Guilt

T he man drove down the palm tree-lined street in Golfton Hills, listening to smooth jazz music on the radio. He noted that on one side, some teenagers were tossing a football on a wide lawn. The ball sailed over the head of one short red-haired boy, narrowly missing the man's black Chevy Tahoe as it passed by. On the other side, there were some old women sitting on a porch, laughing, talking, and sipping drinks.

Driving slowly, the man avoided eye contact with anyone and hoped no one crossed his path other than the intended party. A quick check of his watch told him it was a quarter past two. Timing was everything, he knew. And everyone's time came sooner or later, for better—or, in this case, worse.

He approached the house on Rosebend Lane. Like the other Mediterranean-style stucco residences on the block, it was large and two-storied, with casement windows and attractive landscaping. There was a white Mercedes sedan parked in the driveway.

He pulled up next to it, put the vehicle in park, and kept it running. Stretching a long arm to the seat behind him, he grabbed a dozen roses and took a deep whiff of the fragrance before deciding it was time for delivery.

Without drawing any undue attention to himself, the tall man took easy, looping strides to the front door and rang the bell. When he sensed someone approaching, he held the roses up so they obscured his face in the peephole.

The door opened, and a short and slender woman stood there. She was in her early thirties and attractive with short auburn hair in a shag style, while wearing casual clothing for summertime and flip-flop sandals.

"Are you Mrs. Marietta Sweeney?"

"Yes, I am." Her blue eyes lit up when looking at the roses. "Are those for me?"

"Yeah, they sure are," he told her smoothly.

She beamed again as he handed the flowers to her. "Who are they from?" she asked, as if not a clue, putting them to her dainty nose and inhaling.

"Your husband."

She flashed him a knowing look. "Douglas is always so thoughtful."

"Yeah, he sends his love—"

As Marietta took that to heart, smelling the roses once more, the man slipped a Glock 36 .45 ACP pistol from his pocket. Without giving her a chance to react, he held the barrel up to her chest and fired twice, hitting the mark both times.

The man watched as Marietta Sweeney sprawled backwards before crumbling to the hardwood floor, the roses scattering around her like a halo. He followed her inside and watched while she whimpered in agony.

"Why...?" she managed, with blood spurting from her mouth.

"Because I was paid to do the job," he responded tersely and added candidly, as though it made a difference to her at this point, "It was nothing personal."

Marietta tried to say more, but nothing would come out except horrible gasps.

For an instant, he felt the slightest remorse for what he'd just done and actually considered giving her a fighting chance to live—even if a longshot, in her bad condition—but thought better.

Holding the gun to her head, the man sighed before pulling the trigger and watched as Marietta Sweeney mercilessly expended her last breath.

* * *

"The man's got guilt written all over his face," the detective stated sharply. "Then there's the body language."

I regarded Preston Colbeck, the cold case investigator for the Golfton Hills Police Department's Homicide Division. He was African American, in his late thirties, tall and thickly built like he was a fullback in another lifetime, with jet black hair in a line-up cut and brown eyes.

Standing next to the detective, who had me by several inches, I batted my own green and gold-flecked eyes and tucked an errant strand of medium-length blonde hair, styled in a wavy lob, behind an ear. "You think?"

"What would you call a man who's been artfully dodging the murder of his wife for two decades now while hoping his hired killer would never come clean?"

I looked at the video monitor in the interrogation room. Sitting at a square wooden table, appearing cool, calm, and collected, was millionaire businessman Douglas Sweeney. At fifty-seven, he looked ten years older with thinning, graying hair swept to one side. His deeply tanned face was heavy on the wrinkles. He was of medium build, wearing business casual attire, and kept his large hands clasped as if in prayer.

Twenty years ago, his wife, Marietta Sweeney, was shot to death at point-blank range by a man after delivering her flowers. Though it was strongly suspected that Douglas Sweeney had orchestrated the murder by hiring the man so Sweeney could then be free to move on to his lover, Hayley Kapono, while saving millions in alimony and other expenses, there was not enough hard evidence to make a case against him.

That all changed two weeks ago when a dying inmate, Luther Wechsler, already serving a life sentence for murder, confessed to being the trigger man in Marietta Sweeney's death that had gone unsolved. He implicated Douglas Sweeney as his well-paying employer, providing explicit details of the hit and about the murder weapon that Wechsler had ditched and was never found.

It was more than enough to bring Douglas Sweeney in as a strong person of interest in the murder of his wife.

I had been with the Corall County State Attorney's Office for fourteen years, the last three and a half as the first assistant county attorney with the Homicide Bureau. Planning to prosecute this case myself, it was more than just a cold crime of murder to me. Keri Rohm, my best friend while attending Florida State University College of Law, had been gunned down ten years ago in a similar fashion, in a domestic violence, jealous rage situation.

So, yes, this was personal on some level in wanting to see long-overdue justice for Marietta Sweeney.

"I'll let you know later," I answered the question, squaring my shoulders on a slender frame. "For now, let's just see what Douglas Sweeney has to say for himself—or not."

"Okay," Preston muttered tonelessly. "We'll hear him out..."

We went into the holding room.

The suspect looked up with steel gray eyes that were cold as ice and practically bored right through me. I could only wonder if Marietta had even a clue as to what was coming—and by whom. Or had he managed to pull the wool over her eyes as a doting and faithful husband till the very end of her life?

Sitting beside Sweeney was his attorney, Gemma Wu, who was in her forties and petite, with brunette hair in a bun and brown eyes.

I acknowledged Gemma, whom I'd gone up against in court a few times, referring to her professionally as Ms. Wu before casting my eyes on the suspect. "Mr. Sweeney, I'm Rachelle Cavanagh, the assistant county attorney. This is Detective Colbeck. Thanks for coming in."

"I didn't get the feeling I had much of a choice," Sweeney said, frowning.

"You didn't," Preston confirmed that notion firmly.

"What's this all about?" Gemma demanded.

I sat across from the suspect and his lawyer and, eyeing him, responded without preface, "We've received some new information regarding your late wife, Marietta Sweeney's, murder."

Sweeney reacted to this, but quickly recovered. "My wife's been dead for twenty years. What supposedly new info do you have?"

"I'm curious as well," his attorney said.

"An inmate has come forward, confessing to the crime," I told them, letting this sink in for a moment or two.

"Who?" Sweeney asked keenly.

"Name's Luther Wechsler," Preston answered. "Ring a bell?"

"Why should it?"

I looked Sweeney in the eye and said bluntly, "Wechsler, who's been

70

convicted of killing another man in a barroom brawl, has implicated you in the murder of your wife..."

"What?" Sweeney's jaw set. He let out an expletive and played the innocent card. "That's ridiculous. I had nothing to do with what happened to Marietta," he insisted.

"My client has already gone through this," Gemma defended him. "Mr. Sweeney was thoroughly investigated twenty years ago and, along with having a rock-solid alibi at the time of his wife's death, was cleared of any wrongdoing."

"That's not true," I had to remind her. "As long as the case remained open, no one was given a free pass from possible guilt—including your client." I favored Sweeney with a hard stare. "We believe Luther Wechsler, who's dying from lung cancer, is very credible in pointing the finger at you as the person who hired him to murder your wife—right down to the delivery of roses to throw her off guard—in order to keep from paying her alimony when you filed for divorce to be with the woman you were having an affair with, Hayley Kapono."

Preston kept the pressure on the suspect when he said to him levelly, "If there's anything you'd like to get off your chest, Sweeney, now might be the time to do it—"

Douglas Sweeney was defiant in arguing, "I have nothing to get off my chest, Detective. What Hayley and I had ended a long time ago and played no part whatsoever in my wife's death. Nor did any reluctance to pay Marietta the alimony that she was entitled to. Any suggestion otherwise is insane." His brow furrowed. "All you've done is waste my time and yours."

"I agree," Gemma stood up for him. "Unless you've got something much more substantial than a convicted killer's lies about a murder-for-hire plot that may be some sort of desperate attempt at a mercy get out of jail free card, and are prepared to charge my client, this voluntary interview is over!"

I expected as much from them in the refusal of Sweeney to confess to conspiring with a paid assassin to murder his wife. But my gut instincts told me that Luther Wechsler was not feeding us a pack of lies, knowing that it would have no impact on his life sentence, whether he was dying or not.

"You're free to walk out the door whenever you like," I made clear to the suspect in his wife's death. Meaning, he wasn't under arrest. Yet. "But just so you know, there was no deal offered to Luther Wechsler. So he had absolutely nothing to gain in coming forward with the allegation—other than peace of mind."

"That's worth something in my book," Preston pitched in. "A lot, in fact, including some interesting details that won't be easy to run away from."

Sweeney cocked a brow unnervingly. "What details are you talking about?"

"I think we'll keep those to ourselves for the time being," I told him, wanting to make the man sweat a while longer.

"That's not fair," Gemma griped. "Let's not play games, Counselor."

"That works both ways." I held her gaze. "If your client is as innocent as he claims in his late wife's murder, then he has nothing to worry about, does he?"

She bristled and rose. "Let's go," she beckoned her client.

I got to my feet at the same time that he did and warned him in no uncertain terms, "Mr. Sweeney, I strongly advise you not to leave town for the foreseeable future—whatever your business interests may be."

* * *

I had been dating Preston Colbeck for nearly two years. He was divorced from his high school sweetheart, and I'd never been married, though I'd been in a long-term relationship with a surgeon till we both realized that we weren't right for each other and went our separate ways.

So far, things seemed to click with Preston, who had no problem with the demands of my job as a prosecutor any more than I did his as a police detective. Occasionally, our professional worlds collide, such as in the current cold case. But we mostly tried to stay in our own lanes in that regard while fully embracing the romance side of things that kept us both coming back for more. Even if neither spoke of moving the relationship to the next level, content in seeing how things played out naturally.

In bed that night at Preston's Horton Street townhouse, after having dinner together at an Italian restaurant, he said matter-of-factly, "Guess it was too much to expect that Douglas Sweeney would crack under the pressure of knowing that the man he hired to shoot his wife in cold blood was suddenly talking."

"You never know how it could have gone," I pushed back, though I hadn't thought for one moment that Sweeney would roll over. Especially with Gemma earning her retainer by fighting them every step of the way. "But, if nothing else, we put Douglas Sweeney on notice that we're onto him. If guilt doesn't eat him up first, it's only a matter of time before he has to face the consequences for what he did."

"I like the way you think, Counselor," Preston teased me.

"Is that so?" I felt his mouth tickling my cheek, chin, and neck.

"Yeah, and I like how you make me feel."

"Hmm…" I cooed, cuddling up to him beneath the cotton sheets. "We're positively on the same wavelength, Detective Colbeck."

Over the next hour or so, we put that sentiment into practice.

* * *

In the Jefferson Correctional Institution in Monticello, Florida, Luther Wechsler cringed from the pain as he lay in bed in the infirmary. This wasn't how he wanted to go out. But on the other hand, he'd put himself in this hellhole because of the poor choices he had made in his miserable life.

Now, he was paying the price.

So why shouldn't Douglas Sweeney do the same? Why should he get to go on with his life, as if he hadn't orchestrated the murder of his wife? And for what, to save some money? To be with another woman without needing to explain himself?

Luther grimaced again and then sucked in a deep breath. The way he understood it, Sweeney denied any involvement whatsoever in Marietta Sweeney's death. The bastard more or less accused him of fabricating Sweeney wanting his wife out of the picture. Now, the detective and prosecutor were at a standstill in proving the case, which was now based solely on Luther's word and his memories that weren't quite as sharp as they used to be.

The firearm he used to end Marietta Sweeney's life had long been disposed of, not wanting it to lead right back to him. Now he wished he had held onto it and found a way to tie it to the man who had given him the money to purchase it in the first place to use to kill his wife.

Douglas Sweeney.

The fact that he had sweetened the pot by seeing to it that Luther had a cool fifty grand put into his bank account made it that much easier to do what Sweeney wanted.

But now that he was dying, Luther regretted his actions in that regard. Marietta Sweeney should have been able to live a full life. Just like her husband had been able to do all these years. He was on what, wife number three now? None of which included his mistress at the time, Hayley Kapono.

Both she and Marietta had been screwed by Sweeney. So had he, Luther believed firmly. It was up to him to make things right. Before he was out of time to do so.

He winced while waiting for his pain medicine to kick in.

Once his head had cleared, Luther was able to focus his thoughts again on the desire to relieve the burden weighing down on him like a ton of bricks.

* * *

Detective Preston Colbeck sat at his desk at the Golfton Hills Police Department. If the truth be told, he'd much rather be in Rachelle's arms, as had been the case last night and early this morning, before they both had to force themselves to get up and go to their respective jobs. As far as he was concerned, she was the real deal as girlfriend material. After putting behind him a difficult marriage that had been a mistake from the beginning, Rachelle was like a breath of fresh air. Aside from being drop-dead gorgeous and just a little younger than him, she was definitely going places in the Corall County State Attorney's Office. But more than that, she didn't put the type of pressure on him that his ex, Winona, did.

Preston took that for what it was worth—which, in his mind, was everything. He was eager to see where this relationship took them down the line.

But at the moment, they were both combining their professional talents to try and put the screws to alleged wife killer, Douglas Sweeney. It didn't matter that he and his high-priced attorney, Gemma Wu, were trying to run away from the accusations just as fast as they could. What was that old saying about being able to run, but unable to hide?

The reality was that, as a cold case investigator, Preston had long suspected that Sweeney was knee-deep in his late wife's murder. Marietta Sweeney had been ambushed, plain and simple, in broad daylight. But Sweeney had covered his tracks well. As had his hired killer, Luther Wechsler.

Now that Wechsler's tongue was loosening as he faced his own mortality, Preston was determined to piece things together and nail Sweeney to the wall.

The question in the detective's mind was no longer if, but when.

* * *

I entered the State Attorney's Office building on Layden Street and was about to head up to my third-floor office to confer with my chief investigator, Dexter Guarino, on the Marietta Sweeney cold case, when I ran into Gemma Wu in the lobby.

"Hey," I said to her in a friendly tone, rather than regarding her as the enemy when doing battle in the courtroom.

"Hey," she said. "Actually, I was hoping to meet up with you." Gemma looked flustered. "Got a sec?"

Even if I hadn't, she got my attention out of curiosity. "Sure."

That second stretched out a bit longer as we wound up at a coffee shop around the corner on Earl Street.

After taking a sip of her caramel macchiato, Gemma said steadfastly, "Just to be clear, my client, Douglas Sweeney, maintains his innocence in his late wife's murder, as has been the case from day one..."

"I get that," I told her in a conciliatory tone and lifted my mug to taste my vanilla latte. "So, why are we here? What's this all about?"

Gemma squirmed. After a moment or two, she responded, "Here's the thing... I've been getting these weird vibes like something's off in this equation. Not sure what it is or if it's nothing at all."

"You mean like Sweeney's hiding something from you?" I posed across the table by a window. "Or does this pertain to your client's accuser, Luther Wechsler?"

"Maybe both," she replied, a catch to her voice. "Wechsler, who apparently has only days to live and therefore isn't likely to be around to testify against my client, should it come to that, has asked to see me."

"So, why would that freak you out?" I asked boldly, in reading between the lines. "After all, if your client is innocent, as you claim, does it really matter what the confessed killer of Sweeney's first wife has to say on his death bed?"

"It doesn't," Gemma said, seemingly regaining her normal air of composure. "I've never subscribed to the notion of a close-to-death statement somehow being synonymous with a truth serum." She paused, meeting my eyes. "On the other hand, some people tend to come clean when their backs are against the proverbial wall. In this instance, I thought it might be interesting if we went together to see what else your primary accuser wishes to spill."

I cocked a brow. "Really?"

"Why not?" she challenged me. "After all, it could just as easily go against your assumption that he will stick to his guns—no pun intended—as not. Either way, I'm in it with Douglas Sweeney for the long haul. But that may well be a moot point where it concerns his late wife's death, should you discover that you're barking up the wrong tree..."

I admired the attorney's clever angle here. She was using reverse psychology on behalf of her client while at the same time throwing a Hail Mary that Luther Wechsler would somehow recant his accusation against the millionaire businessman.

I seriously doubted there would be any persuasive reason to close the case against Douglas Sweeney pertaining to the cold-blooded assassination of Marietta Sweeney, all things considered—given Preston's investigation of the cold case and his beliefs, accordingly.

Still, I was willing to go along with this in the interest of legal unity and fairness, so I told her, "You're on, Counselor."

* * *

The man drove the dark green Toyota Highlander down the palm tree-lined Marine Boulevard, deep in thought but focused. He noted his surroundings in the upscale neighborhood before coming to the large Charleston-style home near the end of the street. Parked in the driveway was a dark gray Lincoln Nautilus and a white Genesis G80.

He pulled up along the curb and left the car running while grabbing the bouquet of yellow roses from the seat beside him before stepping outside.

Walking methodically to the front door of the house, surrounded by Florida red maple trees, he calmly rang the doorbell.

When the door opened, the person he was looking for was standing there. He was sharply dressed in a designer suit and Oxford shoes.

"Yes?" he asked casually.

The man turned the question on him by asking the older, shorter, and less muscular male to be absolutely certain, "Are you Douglas Sweeney?"

"Yes, I am. Who are you?" He flashed him a look of curiosity mixed with mild concern.

The man produced the roses, which had been held behind his back, and handed them to Sweeney and said evenly, "These are for you..."

Sweeney suddenly became even more uncomfortable, but took the flowers anyway. "Who ordered them?" He paused thoughtfully. "My wife—?"

The man took a moment to consider the irony of the question before answering in what he saw as poetic justice. Or at least for the dying man who hired him to do the job.

"Yeah, you could say that," he told Sweeney, with a hard edge to his tone of voice.

As Sweeney grappled with the meaning of the words, the man removed from inside the pocket of his zip-up jacket a SIG Sauer P320 9mm Luger handgun. He fired it twice into Sweeney's chest, causing him to sprawl backwards into the large foyer and onto the ceramic tile flooring.

While Douglas Sweeney writhed in pain and asked laboriously, "Why...?"

"Because it's time for you to pay the piper for having your wife, Marietta, taken out," the man said unfeelingly. He stood over Sweeney, glaring at him. "This last one is for Luther Wechsler, whom I owed a favor. He wanted me to remind you that it was the same way you wanted her to die, which he made happen. So long..."

With that, the man fired the final round into Douglas Sweeney's head.

Banking Crisis

"Absolutely not!" Dad's deep voice boomed. He was standing tall in the living room of our Wheyconne Street coastal contemporary home in Golfton Hills, Florida, with FBI Special Agent Terry Tauber. Dad was the supervisory special agent managing the Bureau's Resident Agency in nearby Cetona Falls.

I was peeking over the second-story balcony, watching the fireworks happening between them down below. Home for the summer after completing my sophomore year at the University of Florida, I could only imagine what it must have been like for Agent Tauber being on the receiving end of one of Dad's temper tantrums.

Admittedly, I never got to find out very often. Ever since my mom died three years ago after being diagnosed with breast cancer, Dad had treated me with kid gloves. Well, sort of. He still knew when to put his foot down, more or less, whenever I went too far in wanting my way. I simply had to avoid being stepped on with his size eleven Oxfords. Not necessarily an easy task while home, though I did continue to test his limits as any nineteen-year-old who was an only child might. Especially when boredom set in, as seemed to be the case of late.

"I can't afford to have anyone take their foot off the pedal with these bank robbers. Not on my watch!" Dad, or Supervisory Special Agent Conrad Vernon, insisted, his solid gray eyes glaring. He was six-four and had Agent Tauber by about three inches. Dad's short hair was still black, even at thirty-nine, and was cut in a masculine style, while Agent Tauber had brown hair in a comb-over cut, matching the color of his eyes that held Dad's gaze.

I knew they were arguing about the recent spate of bank robberies in Golfton Hills, where we'd lived for a year since Dad's transfer from the FBI Tampa Field Office. Seemed as though a group of masked robbers had managed to do their thing in broad daylight, almost daring the authorities to do something about it.

The last time—three days ago—they had crossed the line in a big way, and there was no turning back. A security guard at the Wacklonia Bank on Third Street had been fatally wounded in a robbery. Meaning that my dad and other law enforcement had made the case an even greater priority than before.

"No one's talking about taking their feet off any pedals," Agent Tauber insisted, though clearly intimidated. He was probably ten years younger and not in quite as good of shape as my dad, though still firmly built. "My point is that since we know we're not dealing with amateurs here—anything but—we have to be prepared for anything they might do moving forward, including kidnapping someone if they feel like they're backed into a corner. We don't want to lose any more lives, Conrad. Not if we can help it."

Dad ran a hand through his hair and seemed to calm down. "Yeah, I see what you mean. I'll make sure we have a hostage negotiator on hand when we confront these people. In the meantime, the main objective is to prevent more banks from being robbed at gunpoint by locating the bank robbers, wherever they're holed up."

"We'll get them," Agent Tauber said confidently. "It's only a matter of time."

"Yeah, well, it had better be sooner than later." Dad furrowed his brow. "Otherwise, it won't just be my ass on the line..."

Before I could duck out of sight, both Dad and Special Agent Tauber looked right up at me as if their radar suddenly went off.

I froze momentarily while my blue eyes gazed back at them before nervously flipping my long blonde ponytail and moving my tall and slender frame out of their line of vision. I suspected Dad would be royally pissed at me for listening in on his official business conversation.

On the other hand, it wasn't my fault that he chose to talk shop at our house instead of his office.

I went to my room, which had rustic furniture and two large double-hung windows with a great view, and waited for my dad to show up. He did so like clockwork five minutes later, knocking once on the door before opening it.

"Hey," he said simply, as though the calm before the storm.

"Hey." Wearing a tank top, shorts, and sneakers, I was sitting on a wingback chair with the television on, but not watching it, while fully expecting another lecture.

"Hungry?" he asked.

"Not really."

"How about a pizza? We can have anything you want on it."

"Anything...?" I looked up, forgetting for the moment that he hadn't brought up my eavesdropping.

"Well, as long as you skip the mushrooms and anchovies," he said.

"Funny." I laughed. "You know I hate those, Dad." Which was the point of getting me to give in. "Okay. Let's get one with pepperoni, extra cheese, and sausage."

"Done," he said satisfyingly. "I'll order, and you set the table."

I nodded. "Deal."

Dad paused before saying, "By the way, about what you overheard—"

"I wasn't really honed in on it," I offered lamely.

"That's not the point, Diana."

"I know." I twisted my lips. "Sorry."

"It's not your fault," he said apologetically. "I'm under a fair amount of stress right now with these bank robberies and other investigations. I don't mean to bring my work problems home."

"It's no big deal, Dad." I tried to downplay it. "I mean, it is a big deal to capture these bank robbers. But I think I understand that you're on duty 24/7."

"Yeah, that's about the size of it," he conceded. "Still, I'm your father first and always will be. I don't want you to feel that my job will ever come before you—no matter how demanding it is."

"I don't feel that way," I told him. "I'm just glad to be home for the summer so we can spend time together."

81

"Me too." He smiled faintly. "See you downstairs in a few."

* * *

We were sitting at the oval glass-top dining room table half an hour later with a medium-sized pizza between us. I couldn't remember the last time we'd had pizza. Probably when Mom was still alive.

Never too late, I supposed.

"So, how's school?" Dad asked, as if purely to strike up a conversation.

"Well, I haven't flunked out, if that's what you're asking," I quipped, as a straight-A student, majoring in business administration.

He grinned sheepishly. "Never thought that. You're way too smart. But are you having fun?"

"Yeah," I admitted, lifting a slice of pizza. "I like my friends, and the school is a great place to get an education."

"Good to know." Dad bit into his own pizza and seemed to have reconciled himself to the fact that I chose to attend UF, instead of his alma mater, Florida International University.

I frowned thoughtfully. "I just wish Mom was still around to see me attending college."

"I know. Me too." He paused. "She would have been so proud of you. Just like I am."

I fought back tears in remembering how bad things had been toward the end of her life, though she showed courage and a will to survive till the very end.

"So, are you still dating… Uh, what was his name?" Dad wisely switched the subject as he sipped his soft drink.

"Chuck Yarborough," I told him. "I actually stopped seeing him a while ago. We weren't right for each other."

"Sorry to hear that," he said, ill at ease. "But I think it's best to find that out sooner than later."

"Yeah." I had to agree, even if it was painful when we broke up, and there hadn't been anyone even remotely serious in my life romantically since.

Later, I exchanged texts with some of my college friends, who had left the campus for the summer while trying to figure out what I wanted to do with my free time for the next two months.

* * *

The next afternoon, I went out for a run on a winding trail at the nearby Golfton Hills Park, surrounded by cypress trees and lots of flowering plants. Jogging was something I used to do with my mom before she got sick. Before she died, she made me promise to never stop doing the things that I enjoyed, and I intended to keep that promise, which included jogging.

I was so wrapped up in my thoughts that I nearly ran into a guy, literally, as I slowed down and swerved at the last moment.

"I'm so sorry," I told him, blushing. "I need to do a better job of watching where I'm going."

He laughed. "It's fine. No harm, no foul, right?"

"Right." I checked him out with a quick glance. He looked to be around my age and was tall, tanned, and good-looking, with green eyes and dark hair that was textured and in an undercut. He was wearing typical jogging attire.

"So, are you in a hurry, or what?" he asked jokingly as we started running side by side down the wide path.

"Or what," I tossed back at him. "I was too wrapped up thinking about my mom."

"What about her? Or shouldn't I ask?"

"She died…three years ago," I informed him while thinking probably TMI for a total stranger. But it still felt good to get it out.

"Oh." His brow furrowed. "Sorry, I didn't realize—"

"It's all right." I lifted my chin musingly. "I miss her a lot."

"I'm sure you do." He eyed me. "I'm Andrew Keough, by the way."

"Diana Vernon."

He grinned. "Nice to meet you, Diana."

"You too."

"So, obviously, you must live around here?"

"Yeah, for the last year. Before that, home was Tampa. But I spend most of my time these days in Gainesville at UF."

"Cool." Andrew jutted his chin. "I'm in my third year at FSU. Or headed into my senior year."

"I just finished my sophomore year," I told him enviously.

"What are you studying?"

I told him and then asked, "What about you?"

"Public relations," he said. "Then there's grad school to follow, and we'll see what happens after that."

"Same here." I wondered if he had a girlfriend. Or could he actually be looking for one? "So, I take it you're home for the summer, too?"

"Not exactly. I'm visiting my brother and sister-in-law for a couple of weeks, then I'm heading to Augusta, Georgia, to hang with my folks for a bit before going back to Tallahassee."

"I see." I flashed my teeth at him and felt my ponytail bounce against the back of my neck. I decided to pick up the pace of our run, prompting him to do the same.

When we approached a clearing, we could hear some men talking. They mentioned something about stolen money and wanting to get more of it. For whatever reason, I immediately found myself thinking about the bank heists.

And that the bank robbers were still at large.

Instinctively, I grabbed hold of Andrew's muscular arm and said nervously, "Let's go back the way we came."

He must have picked up the anxiety in my voice as he asked, "What's wrong?"

He apparently had not picked up on the *stolen* part of the conversation. Before I could respond, we came into full view of two men. One was burly and looked to be in his mid-twenties. He had long, slicked-back blonde hair and a square beard. The other man was older—in his forties—taller and thinner, with gray hair in a mohawk cut.

They spotted us, and just when I was about to tell Andrew to run, fearing that these men could be the robbers, we heard a deep voice behind us say, "Just where the hell do you think you're going?"

We turned around and saw a tall African American male in his thirties standing there. He had a bleached high-top haircut and a petite goatee.

"We didn't hear anything," Andrew told him with a straight face, though obviously sensing that something wasn't right about the situation. Or was very wrong. "We don't want any trouble."

"I think it's a little too late for that," the man said sharply. A scowl formed on his face, and he pulled a gun from the pocket of his pants. I recognized the firearm as a Glock 22 40 S&W caliber pistol, similar to the one my dad carried when on duty. "You stumbled onto the wrong spot...at the wrong time—listening to something that was none of your business—"

"Please, just let us go," I begged, my voice shaking. "We won't say anything..." In so saying this, I realized I had inadvertently admitted to hearing what they were talking about and being smart enough to fill in the blanks.

"Sure you won't." The man chuckled derisively. "You're coming with us," he ordered nastily as the other two men surrounded me and Andrew.

I cringed while wondering what was in store for us, as we were apparently now seen as witnesses to the bank-robbing fugitives that needed to be dealt with.

One way or another.

* * *

At gunpoint, we were forced into the back of a red Cadillac Escalade and driven to a nearby two-story cottage on Pickton Lane. A few palm trees were out front, swaying with a gentle breeze.

There were lights on inside and two cars outside. One was another SUV— a dark gray Jeep Grand Cherokee—and the other a dark blue sedan, similar to the type of FBI-issued vehicle my dad drove.

"Get out!" the burly man directed.

We did as we were told—with neither me nor Andrew (whom I had whispered to about our abductors likely being the bank robbers on the loose) foolish enough to make a run for it and end up getting shot in the back—and were promptly ushered inside the cottage. It was sparsely furnished and painted a dull gray.

"Are you insane?" A slender, thirty-something woman with short rainbow-colored spiky hair asked as she glared at the men and then us. "What the hell are they doing here…?"

"They saw us talking in the park," the African American man responded. "We had no choice but to bring them here."

"Oh, really?" she shot back sarcastically. "That was probably the worst thing you could have done."

The older man with the mohawk defended the action. "What the hell did you want us to do, let them go?" he barked at her. "And have them report seeing some suspicious men in the park, describing us to the cops, at the same time that they're looking for bank robbers at large? That wouldn't have been very smart."

"Okay, okay, I get it," the woman relented. "What's done is done." She peered at us. "Have a seat. You're going to be here for a while…"

Or not very long at all, I told myself realistically, knowing from my dad how these things worked when criminals needed to tie up loose ends—which we were—so they couldn't be identified later.

Andrew and I sat side by side on a well-worn black leather sofa. It was hard to believe that after having barely just met on the running trail and seemingly developing a rapport that had interesting possibilities down the line, we should find ourselves being held at gunpoint by a group of bank robbers.

"Tie their hands up," the woman—who seemed to be calling most of the shots, in spite of the pushback about bringing us to the cottage—ordered. "That way, they won't be able to try something stupid."

While the African American guy kept the gun on us, the burly man cut some rope from a jute twine spool and tied our hands behind our backs as the woman began texting someone.

My eyes turned to two duffle bags on the dirty hardwood floor. Both seemed overstuffed, as if with money. Or maybe with weapons and/or drugs as part of their criminal enterprise, I supposed.

Since I hadn't checked in with my dad, I wondered if it would occur to him that I was in trouble. Or would he just assume I had simply lost track of time? Or that texting him had escaped my mind between running and then maybe hanging out at the beach afterwards?

I was certain that he could never have imagined that I would find myself right in the middle of his current investigation.

* * *

Though I was itching to tell the kidnapping robbers that my dad was the FBI supervisory special agent managing the Bureau's Resident Agency in Cetona Falls, I was smart enough to realize it might do more harm than good for some desperate criminals. So I kept my mouth shut while hoping against hope that the FBI was closing in on the robbers and ready to rescue Andrew and me at the same time.

Or was I deluding myself when maybe Dad and other law enforcement didn't even have a clue about the hideout location of the bank robbers? Much less, that my new friend Andrew and I had been brought there against our will, with the clock ticking as to how we could extricate ourselves from a terrifying ordeal before the criminals decided to cut their losses the only way they could to make sure we stayed quiet for good?

"If you hurt us, things will only get worse for you," I told our captors as desperation sank in, and I tried to loosen the rope binding my hands.

The woman laughed. "Spoken like someone who thinks she's in a position to bargain with us. Or scare us. Not sure which." She laughed again. "From where I'm standing, you need to be far more concerned about yourselves."

"We are," Andrew said daringly. "That's the whole point; we're concerned enough that we only want to forget that this ever happened. We're just college kids and more than happy to mind our own business and let you get on with yours. Let us leave, and you'll never hear from us again."

I wasn't sure if he truly meant that or simply wanted them to believe it.

My sense was that Andrew was, like me, biding for time while trying to figure a way out of this alive. But we both knew that there was no way we could keep quiet about what had happened to us if there was ever a chance to enlighten the authorities about our captors.

Of course, I hadn't had the chance to tell Andrew who my dad was. Once I did, it would be obvious that this wasn't something I could or would keep from him.

"The kid makes sense," the burly one said. "Maybe we've scared them enough that they'll keep their traps shut, if they know what's good for them."

The man with the mohawk stated flatly, "We need to keep them here till we complete one more bank job and have enough time to get away—"

"I don't like leaving any loose ends," the African American man said with snap to his voice.

"Neither do I," the woman agreed. "But we'll let the boss make the final call..."

As if on cue, we heard another car drive up, but were not able to see through the window who it was. I could only wonder how many people were involved in their bank robberies. Would they really settle for only one more bank to rob?

Or would getting us out of the picture only embolden them to continue to press their luck in targeting other local banks?

I hated the thought of my dad having to deal with my death while still coming to terms with my mom's. I prayed that it wouldn't come down to that.

When the door opened, my jaw dropped as I saw Special Agent Terry Tauber enter the cottage.

We locked eyes, and I immediately tried to avert my own while hoping that he wouldn't recognize me.

Or, if he did, I could only pray that Agent Tauber was there not as an actual real member of the group—or its leader—but working undercover as part of the operation to bring the bank robbers into custody.

He quickly dashed my hopes of his coming to our rescue as one of the good guys when Agent Tauber said in a dark tone of voice, "Nice to see you again, Diana Vernon. Too bad it's under most unfortunate circumstances for you and your friend. When this is all over, I'll be there to commiserate with your father, FBI Supervisory Special Agent Conrad Vernon, to help him get through this—just like I did after your mom's untimely death, Diana..."

* * *

"How could you?" I asked, my mouth agape with disbelief that one of Dad's agents had gone rogue.

"The short answer is money—and lots of it," Agent Tauber said unapologetically, with his firearm in full view on a waistband holster. "But you wouldn't understand, Diana. I needed my fair share from the bank heists to support my lifestyle. Suffice it to say, the Bureau was unable to accomplish that all by itself, I'm afraid."

I didn't buy his pathetic excuse for violating the law, given the position he held. "Dad trusted you," I told him as I felt the twine starting to loosen around my wrists. I couldn't tell if Andrew had made any progress in that regard. Or what we could hope to do once our hands were freed. "Not to mention the FBI itself. And this is how you repay them?"

"Shut up!" Agent Tauber blared.

"She does have a big mouth on her," the woman said, cozying up to him as if she were his girlfriend. "One that needs to be silenced permanently, so she doesn't rat you out to her father and the rest of the FBI."

"I'm for getting this over, once and for all," the African American robber agreed, still wielding the pistol intimidatingly.

Andrew, who still appeared to be coming to grips with the revelation that my dad was an FBI special agent, regarded me supportively and said, "No matter how this goes down, I'm with you, Diana, and glad that I met you, regardless of the short time we've known each other."

"Same here, Andrew," I promised him, holding back tears, as I couldn't help but wonder if this was our goodbyes forever. Or if it was possible that this entire nightmare could still end with us having the opportunity to get to know one another better as college students and beyond.

Suddenly, what happened next was like a blur.

The door burst open, and I saw my dad storm in, along with other FBI agents and law enforcement officers, in what was clearly an overwhelming and shocking show of force and determination. At the same time, my hands broke free of the rope, as did Andrew's. "Get down!" I told him as I dove to the floor, just as my dad had taught me when dealing with the possibility of exchanging gunfire.

Andrew and I protected each other as best we could, even as I heard gunshots and saw two of the bank robbers—the burly one and the female— hit with bullets. The other two robbers smartly decided to give up without much of a fight.

I watched my dad tackle Agent Tauber to the floor, even as the apparent mastermind behind the bank robberies attempted to go for his weapon. After subduing him with one solid punch to the jaw, my dad handcuffed Agent Tauber before turning him and his partners in crime over to others.

Before I knew it, I was lifted to my feet by my dad, who hugged me tightly and then asked tentatively with worried eyes, "Are you okay?"

"I am now," I told him as I watched Andrew get to his feet. He was also none the worse for wear. "This is Andrew Keough. We met while jogging on the trail at the park…when we ran into the bank robbers. They brought us here—"

"Hey," Andrew said sheepishly to my dad.

"Nice to meet you, Andrew." Dad grinned at him and shook his hand. "Glad you were there to keep Diana from having to go through this nightmare alone."

Andrew smiled and put a supportive hand on my shoulder. "Me too."

Once we stepped outside and the melee had ended, I met my dad's steady gaze and had to ask, "How did you find me?"

"I tracked your location through your cell phone," he said matter-of-factly. I was glad that I'd kept it with me for the run, even though I hadn't been able to use it with the eyes of the robbers seemingly never leaving me. "Beyond that, we were already onto Tauber as a dirty agent—and only needed him to lead us to his partners in crime, including his girlfriend, Sheila Knightley.

He did just that. Little did I know that Tauber would also be leading me to my daughter." He took a breath. "Thank goodness you weren't hurt."

"Yeah, I feel the same way," I told him gratefully.

"Me too," Andrew pitched in, offering a handsome smile to show me there was some potential there as far as us becoming closer once this episode was past us.

* * *

Three months later, I was back at school and had put the scary drama of being abducted by bank robbers behind me, more or less.

I was in my dorm room—which I shared with one roommate, Brianna McDowell—where I checked in with my dad in a video chat on my laptop. "Hey," I said while sitting on a bean bag chair.

"Hi there." His eyes lit up. "What's happening with you on campus these days?"

"Not a lot. The usual studying, hanging out with friends, and such."

"I see. And what's happening with Andrew?"

I blushed. "Oh, that…"

"Yes, that." He chuckled.

"We're good," I told him, hoping he didn't pry too much more than that. It was never an easy thing to talk about someone you were dating with your dad. I think I would have felt more comfortable had my mom still been around to confide in about a burgeoning romance.

"Happy to hear that." Dad left it at that.

We spoke briefly about former FBI special agent Terry Tauber, who had pled guilty and would be spending a very long time in federal prison. As would his ex-girlfriend, Sheila Knightley, who recovered from being shot, and the other two surviving members of the bank robbery team. Unfortunately, the burly one with the square beard didn't make it after the confrontation.

I was proud of my dad and his fellow agents for cracking the case and was happy to share this with him. As usual, he downplayed his position, but didn't shy away from being happy to have played an important role in saving me and Andrew from serious injury and probably being killed.

After we finished talking, I called Andrew, wondering what he was up to today. We had started dating long-distance, but were taking it slow. The good news, though, was that Andrew had already planned to transfer from FSU to UF to do his graduate studies next year. I couldn't have been more excited about that and the possibilities that lay ahead as his good-looking face, sporting a slightly crooked grin, appeared on the screen.

Danger in the Greenhouse

I was about to take my first trip to Golfton Hills, Florida, where my best friend from college, Jeanette Delgado, and her husband, Neal, had a farm and nursery. They had been trying to get me to come there since purchasing the place five years ago, but a busy life and timing had always gotten in the way. Finally, I decided to hell with being busy as an acting coach and inconvenient timing and took them up on an offer to spend a few days there during the annual Camellia Festival.

At forty-five, single, and living in Hawaii, I was pretty used to traveling light, as I moved back and forth from Los Angeles, California, to Honolulu on the island of Oahu, where these days I worked mostly with a repertory theater and did some occasional acting gigs as a throwback to my earlier days as an actress before going into semi-retirement two and a half years ago.

The cell phone ringing disrupted my thoughts as I stood on the lanai of my condominium enjoying a cup of Kona coffee. The caller I.D. told me it was my mother, Barbara Yung, on the other end. I debated whether or not to answer, knowing that I could be in for a long chat. Ever since my father, Albert Yung, died of a heart attack eight years ago, my mother had been in a chatty mood most of the time, whether I had other things to do or not. I figured it was just her way of escaping loneliness while living on Maui—along with a healthy dose of snooping. The latter trait I had admittedly inherited, for better or worse.

As usual, I gave in to her. "Hey, Mom."

"Hi, Lanie. Or should I say, Masako?" She laughed. "It's hard to remember what to call you these days."

Ever since I starred as Detective Masako Tomita—Chinese American like myself—in the big hit television mystery series *Honolulu's Homicide Squad* fifteen years ago, she had been playfully rotating between my character's name and real name, Lanie. The show had a five-year run and hit number one in the ratings in year two before eventually losing its steam, and the plug was pulled.

I played along with it, telling her, "Whichever name you prefer."

"Lanie, the name I gave you."

"Okay, Lanie, it is." I chuckled. "So, what's going on?" I asked routinely, not sensing that there was anything wrong in particular.

"Not much. Just sitting here waiting for my friend to show up."

My mother was seventy-two, or twenty-seven years my senior. Sometimes, I felt closer to her age than my own. Other times, I could well have been twenty-five again with more energy than I knew what to do with.

"What are you up to?" she asked curiously, as though sensing something was about to happen.

"Getting ready to go visit friends on the mainland."

"Oh…" I could hear the thoughts dancing in her head. "Not another one of your heart-pounding-on-the-dangerous-side adventures, I hope?"

"No, Mom," I assured her, but I could understand the concern. Ever since my days playing a fictional detective, I'd found that I had a knack for getting involved in real crime dramas from time to time, with murder usually at the center. Fortunately, I mostly left the hard stuff to the real police detectives. That didn't stop there from being an element of risk involved in stepping outside my lane. But the rewards from pitching in to help solve the crime seemed to justify the risks. At least up to now. In this instance, though, all I was looking to do was enjoy some leisure and fun times. "Just a sweet and simple Camellia Festival."

"Hmm…" Her skepticism rang loud and clear. "I'll believe that when I see it. Nothing seems to be that sweet and simple in your life these days."

I sensed that she was referring primarily to my recent breakup with Steve Omori, a local musician I'd been seeing for more than a year before we both decided it wasn't working and, therefore, no longer worth the investment. I think my mother had been hoping that we'd get married, with her fearing that she might run out of time before I ever got around to tying the knot. I feared the same thing, but what could I do? If the love and commitment weren't there, I had no desire to walk down the aisle with the false hope of forever.

I listened to my mother drone on a bit more about her aches and pains, this and that before her friend showed up, and we said our goodbyes.

I finished my coffee and went back inside the cozy, contemporary-furnished condo to finish packing, before my rideshare arrived.

* * *

While waiting to board the plane, Jeanette phoned me. I hoped she wasn't calling to say that the Camellia Festival had been canceled. Not that this would have prevented me from spending a couple of days in Florida with old friends.

I accepted the video chat. Jeanette had blonde hair in a stacked pixie and green eyes, while my eyes were brown, and my black hair was thick and long with wispy layers and currently in a low ponytail.

"Hi, Lanie." She seemed out of breath.

"Hi, back at you. Is something wrong?"

"Well, that depends..."

"On what?" I could only wonder.

"On whether you've changed your mind and decided not to grace us with your presence in our neck of the woods, but neglected to mention this to me."

I chuckled at Jeanette's rather melodramatic way of expressing herself. "No, I haven't chickened out. A promise is a promise—at least this time. As a matter of fact, I'm at the airport right now." I turned the phone around so she could see for herself.

"Okay, I'm convinced." She flashed her teeth. "We can't wait to see you."

I smiled back. "Same here."

"Neal still teases me sometimes that it could have been you getting your hands dirty with camellias instead of me."

I went out on one date with Neal when the three of us were undergraduates at UCLA. Though tall and handsome, he wasn't at all my cup of tea. Or coffee, for that matter. But he and Jeanette had hit it off pretty much right away and have been inseparable ever since. I couldn't have been happier for them. They have a daughter, Kara, who is attending Princeton University. I was truly honored when they named me her godmother. Since I have no children of my own, a precious godchild was the next best thing.

"Thanks, but no thanks," I told my dear friend, blushing at the idea of having taken her place in life. "Neal picked the right college roommate. I'll leave the world of camellias and the rest to you. I'm much better off coaching young actors in Honolulu."

"Hey, don't knock it till you've tried it, girlfriend." Jeanette smiled. "Still, point taken."

"I thought you'd see things my way," I quipped.

"How could I not? No one wants to get on Detective Masako Tomita's bad side."

"I only wish that were true." I chuckled. "If you watch the reruns of the series, you'll see that someone just had to piss me off every episode."

Jeanette giggled. "Yes, I suppose that is true—and it's what made you so wildly popular in taking down any villains foolish enough to mess with you."

Though I was having fun going down memory lane, I had to cut the conversation short, as it was time to board the plane and head her way.

And a date with a Camellia Festival.

* * *

Rather than have Jeanette and Neal pick me up at the airport, I chose to rent a Subaru Crosstrek for the drive, giving me a chance to take in the amazing views—though, admittedly, they were not so different than being in Hawaii, with the palm trees and other examples of a tropical environment.

It was nearly two p.m. when I spotted the sign that read: Delgado

Farm–Three Miles Ahead! I smiled, happy to see that the GPS navigation was spot-on, along with Jeanette's virtual directions.

I was soon driving through an open gate and down a long dirt road, passing rolling hills, a greenhouse, and the Delgado Nursery and Gift Shop, before arriving at the main house. In fact, I had wanted to stay at a nearby inn, valuing my own space and privacy, but not too surprisingly, neither Jeanette nor Neal would hear of it.

I noted a rather tall, thirty-something man with bushy dark hair and a medium build standing near the white fence. He was wearing a dark blue suit that seemed out of place. He was also staring at me. Or glaring at me was more like it.

Or was it only my imagination?

I did my best to ignore him and parked on a paved driveway between a blue Honda Odyssey and a white Chevrolet Silverado 1500 pickup truck with the words "Delgado Farm" on the side.

After exiting my car, I took in the residence. It was a two-story farmhouse with lots of windows and bordered by oak trees covered with Spanish moss. The front door opened, and Jeanette and Neal came out to greet me.

"Well, look who's come to town," Neal said lightheartedly. A year older than me, he hadn't changed too much since our college days—tall and slightly heavier with salt and pepper hair in a quiff style, and he now sported a short, boxed beard. His eyes were blue behind oval glasses.

I grinned. "Told you I'd make it one of these days."

"You sure did, and you're finally a woman of your word."

"Better late than never." I gave him a quick hug and pat on the back before turning to Jeanette. She, too, had changed little over the years—still slender and about my height of five-seven. We were the same age, and neither of us could turn back the clock with fifty within reach.

"You're definitely a sight for sore eyes," she said.

"I suppose anyone's eyes would be a bit sore after spending too much time staring at nothing but camellias and other shrubs," I joked.

She laughed. "Well, there is that."

We embraced and stayed that way for several seconds before I pulled away and met her gaze.

"I'm so glad you came, Lanie."

"Me too." If I hadn't known better, Jeanette's voice almost had a tenseness to it. As though there was something deeper on her mind for the invite. As with the strange man I'd seen when driving in, who now seemed to have vanished, I decided it was probably my overactive imagination, as was often the case when looking for something that wasn't there. "Wouldn't have missed this golden opportunity to step away from Honolulu and spend time with my best friend. Not to mention this annual Camellia Festival you've been bragging to me about for, well, the last five years."

"We're hoping to have our best turnout ever this year," she said, seeming like herself again, as Jeanette looped an arm around mine. "But no one could possibly be as welcome as the famous Detective Masako Tomita herself!"

I chuckled self-consciously. "Thanks for saying that, but remember you knew me before I ever set foot in Hollywood and got my feet wet as an actor."

Jeanette showed her teeth. "And it's a good thing, otherwise no one would ever believe me if I didn't have the photos to prove it."

"I'd believe anything you said, regardless," quipped Neal.

"Sounds like some things never change," I said, laughing with my two old friends.

"Whereas others never stay the same." Jeanette gazed at me musingly and again, I tried to read between the lines. I figured maybe she meant that our friendship had suffered somewhat over the years. I took much of the blame for that. Between acting, coaching, and trying to make a real life for myself, I had managed to neglect those I cared about most.

I hoped to try and rectify that somewhat on this trip.

"Why don't you go show Lanie around," Neal told his wife. "And I'll bring her bags to her room."

"Good idea," she said.

"Bag," I corrected him. "I managed to get what I needed in one bag, saving us all a little wear and tear."

"Cool." He glanced at Jeanette, before heading toward my car.

* * *

Jeanette gave me the grand tour of the house, which was pretty impressive with its open concept, bamboo flooring, a modern kitchen, plenty of natural lighting through large windows, and rustic farmhouse furniture.

My room was spacious, bright, and cheery, with antique furnishings, two windows, and its own en suite bathroom. I was told that it was Kara's room whenever she was home, but otherwise, served as one of the guest rooms.

"Kara will hate that she missed seeing you," Jeanette was saying while putting a frown on her face.

I hated it, too. After all, she was my only goddaughter. But Kara's education was far more important than seeing me this visit.

"The next time she's home, I'll have to try to come back to see her," I promised. "Or better yet, maybe Kara can pay me a visit in Honolulu to spend some quality time together."

"She'd love that," Jeanette said, her eyes lighting up at the prospect. "So long as I get to come too."

"Of course. You're always welcome to visit anytime you like."

She nodded. "I'll keep that in mind."

I waited till Neal had put my bag on the floor and left the room, before peering at Jeanette and asking her directly, "Is there something you want to tell me?"

She met my gaze and took a moment, then responded evasively, "Not really. Why do you ask?"

"No reason, in particular," I lied. "I just had the feeling you were burdened by something that you weren't at liberty to say around Neal. Or, for that matter, over the phone."

"Everything's fine," she insisted while averting my stare unconvincingly.

"Okay," I said, deciding it was best to leave this alone for the time being.

We went back downstairs, and Jeanette was about to show me the greenhouse and nursery, when the front door opened.

A tall, thin woman in her thirties with short dark hair, copper balayage highlights, and blue eyes came inside. She was wearing running attire. She looked at Jeanette and back to me before saying simply, "Hey."

Jeanette smiled and said to her, "I'd like you to meet someone... This is Lanie Yung—"

"You must be the famous actress Jeanette has been gushing over?"

"Guilty as charged." I grinned. "And you are?"

"Gayle O'Brien."

"Gayle and I met on a cruise last year," Jeanette told me, while noting that Gayle was from Louisiana.

I remembered Jeanette talking about it. She had invited me, as a ladies' only cruise, but unfortunately, I had other engagements. Perhaps I should have found the time.

"That's wonderful." We shook hands, even as I was curious as to why Jeanette had failed to mention that she had another guest. "Nice to meet you, Gayle."

"You too." She flashed a crooked smile. "And, actually, the cruise was much more than just wonderful," she claimed. "Honestly, it was quite liberating."

"Oh...?" I glanced at Jeanette and back.

Gayle ran a hand through her hair. "You see, I'd finally gotten rid of my husband—figuratively speaking—and a cruise seemed to be the perfect way to relax away from him and have fun."

"I felt the same way," Jeanette said, though it hadn't occurred to me at the time that the trip had anything to do with being apart from Neal, per se. Was there more to it?

"Do you jog?" Gayle flashed me a look that seemed doubtful, as if I'd have trouble keeping up with her.

"As a matter of fact, I do from time to time," I told her, priding myself in doing what I could, when I could, to stay in reasonable shape. "Or at least I do some speed walking."

"Great. Perhaps we can go out together one morning or afternoon while you're here."

That didn't leave many mornings or afternoons. I took the bait anyhow. "I'd like that."

"Maybe I'll join you, too," Jeanette said as if not to be left out. "As you know, Lanie, I prefer swimming, along with putting in some time on my trusty exercise bike—but it'll be less painful in the good company of you two."

"Then it's a jogging date," I told my friend and her friend.

"Well, I need to take a shower before going to pick up a few things in town," Gayle said. "See you two later."

As she walked away, I contemplated whether or not I was missing something here. I had a feeling I would find out, one way or the other, sooner or later.

* * *

I unpacked, washed my face, and put on a fresh set of clothes before sitting on the platform bed for a moment. It was soft, and I expected I'd have no trouble sleeping on it later.

I heard some chattering outside the bedroom windows, which faced the front of the house. Curiosity made me get up and take a peek out through the plantation shutters.

Down below, I saw Neal and Jeanette talking to the man in the blue suit whom I'd seen earlier standing inside the fence of the property. Since both windows were already open halfway to keep the room from getting too stuffy, I had no trouble making out the conversation.

"I strongly suggest you take what I think is a more than generous offer under consideration," the man said in a stern voice.

"I don't care if you offer us the moon, Boyle," Neal told him flatly, "get it through your thick head—we're not interested in selling our land!"

"I've already got a commitment from your neighbor, Wallace Martinez, to sell his property. These high-end homes, condos, offices, and a park are coming whether you like it or not. Fighting it is just a precious waste of my time and yours."

"Yes, it is," Jeanette spat. "You're wasting our time, Mr. Boyle. This farm is our life, and we're not going to let some real estate developer come in and sweep it out from underneath us only so you and your associates can get rich at our expense. I don't think so."

The man they called Boyle regarded Neal and cautioned him, "Maybe you can talk some sense into your wife, Delgado."

"Now, why would I want to do that?" Neal snorted. "Especially when she's made the most sense I've heard all day. Now, I suggest you get the hell off my property before I throw you off."

I watched Mr. Boyle growl at them like an animal and then retort, "Have it your way, but you've been warned."

He walked off in a huff, and Jeanette and Neal locked eyes, clearly ill at ease from the exchange, based on their body language, before heading back into the house.

It was obvious that this Mr. Boyle wanted the farm badly to convert into expensive residential and commercial properties. He had issued a stark warning and implied threat to that effect. I wondered if it was something that needed to be taken seriously. Or was he merely a creepy developer who was blowing off steam because his offer had been soundly rejected?

I intended to have a talk with Jeanette and Neal about this to make sure they weren't being pressured into doing something against their wishes. And if so, why?

* * *

A short time later, I found Jeanette in the gourmet kitchen baking chocolate chip cookies, as if that heated exchange had never occurred. There was a pitcher of lemonade on the granite countertop.

I breathed in the scent of the cookies. "Mmm, smells good."

She smiled and nodded. "I seem to remember chocolate chip cookies being your favorite item to snack on back in the day."

"Still are," I admitted, though I had also acquired some other tastes for snacks and food since then.

"Hope the cookies and some lemonade will tide you over till dinner."

I wasn't very hungry, for some reason, though I hadn't eaten anything since having a snack on the plane. "I'm sure the cookies will suffice, along with lemonade. Can I help?"

"Sure," Jeanette said. "Plates are in that cabinet, and glasses are over there." She directed me with her eyes.

I found what I needed, but my thoughts were still very much on the conversation I'd overheard.

"Where's Neal?" I asked casually.

"He went out to speak with Randy Ambrose, who supervises the workers on the farm."

"How many workers do you have?"

"About thirty-five, give or take, some of whom are seasonal."

"You really seem to be in your element here," I told her and sipped the lemonade.

She forced a grin. "Never a dull moment, that's for sure."

I watched as she put cookies on our plates before addressing what was on my mind. "I couldn't help but overhear your conversation outside with a Mr. Boyle—?"

Jeanette's brow furrowed. "That would be Emerson Boyle, local real estate developer." She paused. "How much did you hear?"

"Enough to know that he wants to buy your property—apparently, lock, stock, and barrel—and doesn't seem to want to take no for an answer."

Her shoulders slumped. "I was going to talk to you about it later."

I grabbed a cookie and nibbled on as she poured herself a glass of lemonade. "Now seems as good a time as any."

We sat on curved chairs in the breakfast nook.

"So, tell me exactly what's going on here?" I asked intently.

Jeanette sighed. "Boyle has this grand scheme to gut the entire area to build luxury residences and upscale offices that he expects to fill with employees and their families of the high-tech firm that will be coming to Golfton Hills next year, as well as other well-paid young people moving into the area." She nibbled on a cookie. "Apparently, Boyle has already sold our next-door neighbor Wallace Martinez on it, making him an offer he couldn't refuse. But he was about to retire anyway and move to New Mexico. But this is our livelihood and we're not interested in selling for a quick buck and loss of what this amazing community has stood for ever since we've lived here."

"So don't sell," I told her tersely, in what seemed the obvious answer and pushback of the would-be buyer. "No matter what threats he makes, this Boyle character cannot force you to do anything you don't want to. Besides, aren't there zoning laws against the sort of thing he has in mind?"

"Seems like the city council is leaning more and more towards expansion in the name of profits at the expense of rural property owners," Jeanette replied. "There are also rumors that Boyle has one or two council members in his hip pocket."

"Even if he does, I'm sure that your farm—with the annuals and perennials, greenhouse, nursery and gift shop, online sales, and more—is bringing in plenty of business. That has to count for something." Or at least I hoped so.

"It does, but not nearly enough." Jeanette moaned and made a face. "The truth is, Lanie, business has not been very good the last couple of years. The Camellia Festival still packs them in, and the online business is going fairly well, but our month-to-month sales are slower than any of us would like. We're sure that with aggressive advertising and expansion of international sales, things will improve. However, that could take another couple of years... I'm just not sure we can wait that long—"

"And you feel that if Boyle is able to strong-arm the right people, you could actually be forced out of business before things can turn around...?"

"Exactly."

"Maybe I could talk to Emerson Boyle," I suggested. I knew very little about real estate development and even less about farming. But I did have pretty good instincts and better than average business acumen—and would do whatever I could for people I cared about.

Jeanette and Neal Delgado definitely qualified on that front.

Jeanette shook her head as if she had fleas. "No, that won't be necessary," she was adamant. "I don't think that even Masako Tomita would have much pull with the likes of Emerson Boyle, determined as he is to get his way. Besides, I didn't want you to come here to solve all our little problems. We'll be fine."

I wasn't so sure about that. Indeed, it seemed to be just the opposite, as they were clearly in trouble, trying to keep their heads above water while fending off a greedy land developer. But I decided not to press the issue. "All right," I relented. "Just know, Jeanette, that I'm always there for you—and Neal. Not to mention Kara. So don't think you have to go it alone for any battles you face. Uphill or otherwise."

Jeanette forced a smile and touched my hand gratefully. "I'll remember that. Same goes for you, should you ever need a helping hand. Now, enough of this, frankly, rather depressing stuff. Let's go meet some of the workers, see the nursery and gift shop and, of course, take a look at the greenhouse."

"Sounds like a wonderful idea." I finished off the cookie I had been munching on and stood up.

I was worried about my friends and hoped that they were able to weather the storm of Emerson Boyle or whatever else they faced that could endanger their farm and livelihood.

* * *

"I'd like you to meet Randy Ambrose," Jeanette said. "Randy, Lanie is one of my oldest and dearest friends."

"But not too old," I stressed and shook his hand, which felt warm and clammy.

Randy was African American and in his late thirties, with deep brown eyes and dark hair in a flat-top style. Dressed in work clothes, he was solidly built and tall. He grinned and said in a friendly voice, "Welcome to Delgado Farm. If there's anything you want to see or know about the way we operate around here, just ask, and I'll be happy to fill you in with any details you like."

I smiled at him. "I'll remember that."

"Good." Randy favored Jeanette and gave a nod. "Well, I'd better get back to work. The camellias and more are calling my name."

She smiled. "Then by all means, don't keep them waiting."

"Bye, Randy." I waved at him. "Seems like he fits right into your down-to-earth world here, Jeanette," I told her once we had moved on.

She chuckled. "Yeah, Randy's definitely a down to earther."

"How long has he worked for you?"

"Two years in October." Jeanette gave me a knowing look. "Are you interested in getting to know him better? He's single, last I heard."

Randy was a handsome man, I had to admit. But as much as I wouldn't mind getting to know him better, I wasn't there to find romance. At least not when my attention was much more focused on trying to find a way to help Jeanette and Neal dig themselves out of a hole they seemed to have fallen into. Beyond that, I didn't do particularly well with long-distance relationships, from experience. And it didn't get much farther than between Hawaii and Florida, no matter the temptations.

"I'm good," I told her, leaving it at that.

"All right. But if you change your mind, I'll be happy to play matchmaker," she said with a mischievous grin. "No pressure, though."

I felt none whatsoever. If only she and Neal could say the same.

* * *

I was introduced to other employees and saw a bit of the rich land the farm sat on before we went into the Delgado Nursery and Gift Shop, which was next to the main house. It had everything from supplies to interesting varieties of plants and floral arrangements and even snacks.

At the nursery sales counter, I met Veralyn Muldaur, the new girl on the payroll. She was in her early twenties and petite, with curly mid-length brunette hair and side-swept bangs.

"It's been really busy today," she said while wiping some dirt off the counter.

I wasn't sure if this was merely an observation or a complaint. "I think that's a good thing."

She didn't respond, but Jeanette said with a catch to her voice, "I know it is! Knock on wood."

I could tell that she was still concerned with the real possibility of losing this wonderful farm, as I would be if something or someone were trying to push me out.

Turning toward the gift shop, I spotted Gayle O'Brien. She seemed to be having a heated exchange with none other than Emerson Boyle.

"Isn't that your friend Gayle?" I asked Jeanette, already knowing the answer.

"Yes." She seemed surprised.

"Did you know that Gayle knew Boyle?" I asked.

"No, I didn't." Jeanette looked annoyed.

We stood there as Gayle walked out of the gift shop and headed straight toward us. "Hey," she said nonchalantly while holding a bag of items.

"What were you doing talking to Emerson Boyle?" Jeanette demanded.

Gayle made a face. "Who?"

"The real estate developer you were just with," I put in my two cents. "The same one who wants Jeanette and Neal to sell him their land—"

Gayle turned toward the gift shop, and Jeanette and I did the same, just in time to see Boyle glare at us before storming out of the nursery.

"That man tried to hit on me," Gayle said. "Before that moment, I never saw him before in my life. I told him in the clearest terms that he wasn't my type and that I was not interested." She took a breath. "But he didn't seem to want to take no for an answer—actually grabbing my arm before I threatened to make a real scene if he didn't let go. That's when he released me, and I got out of there. End of story!"

"That bastard," Jeanette cursed. "How dare him." She frowned. "Guess I should have warned you when I invited you to visit to be on the lookout for any first-class creeps trying to hit on you."

"It's okay. I'm fine," Gayle assured her. "Sorry you thought I was going behind your back or something with him. I would never do that."

"I drew the wrong conclusions," I defended my friend, "before knowing all the facts. Sorry."

"Me too," Jeanette voiced apologetically. "It's been a bit stressful around here lately. Didn't mean to take it out on you."

"I understand, and we're good." Gayle gave her a gentle smile. "If it's all the same to you, to be on the safe side, I think I'll just stick with you guys till we get back to the house."

"Good idea," Jeanette told her.

I concurred, as it now appeared that Emerson Boyle was a scoundrel in more ways than one. We headed to the greenhouse to check out the camellias that would soon be on display at the Camellia Festival.

* * *

That night, when Jeanette had already gone to bed, I got to spend a few minutes with Neal. We sat on the terrace under a full moon, drinking red wine while fighting off mosquitoes that seemed to be in definite attack mode.

I held off talking to him about my overhearing the conversation he and Jeanette had with Emerson Boyle and how concerned she was over their state of affairs and the pressure from Boyle to sell, deciding it wasn't my place to do so. But it was clear to me that Neal was just as uneasy on both fronts.

"Everyone I've spoken to seems pretty excited about the Camellia Festival," I commented.

"Yep, it's our big event every year," he agreed. "And this year should be no different, with people coming in from all over. Actually, I guess it will be different this year with you in town, something Jeanette has been very much looking forward to. Me too."

I colored. "I'm happy to be here."

"We'll know in a few days if the Festival proves to be everything it's cracked up to be," Neal said, sipping the wine. "Best case scenario is that we'll beat last year's sales."

"And the worst case...?" I glanced at his profile.

He faced me and sighed. "I'm sure Jeanette has told you that things could be better all the way around for us?"

"Yes, she did mention that you were having some difficulties," I admitted, sipping the wine. "Do you think you can get through them without having to give up the farm?"

Neal stared at the question. "I'd like to think so. But who knows how things could end up, even with the best-laid plans?"

I knew the feeling all too well, with the ups and downs of my own career choices. "I have a bad feeling about Emerson Boyle and hope you don't succumb to his seemingly desperate attempt to buy the farm and questionable tactics in that regard."

"I have no intention of doing that," Neal insisted. "Yes, we're not where we want to be, but Jeanette and I will do our best to see this through and come out ahead on the other end."

"Good." I smiled at him, feeling somewhat relieved. "If there's anything I can do to help..." I offered sincerely, even to the point of lending them some money I'd socked away for a rainy day if it meant saving Delgado Farm.

"You already have, Lanie," he assured me, then reiterated, "just your presence in Golfton Hills is more than enough. Obviously, Jeanette really appreciates it—and so do I."

"Thanks for saying that, Neal," I told him. "You and Jeanette have always been like family to me. I only want the best for you."

"We feel the same way about you, Lanie. Always have."

For an instant, I wondered what my life might have been like had I wound up marrying Neal instead of sending him in the direction of my best friend. I'd never know, but had little doubt that I made the right choice for myself and for them.

I finished the wine and got to my feet. "Well, I guess I'd better call it a night. Jeanette and I have taken Gayle up on her offer to go jogging in the morning before another busy day."

I thought about mentioning to him how Boyle was causing more headaches with unwanted advances toward Gayle, but didn't want to make matters any worse than they already were.

"I'll stay out here a bit longer," Neal said. "I always do my best thinking when the moon is out in force. Good night, Lanie."

"Good night, Neal."

I left him on the terrace, wishing there was more that I could say or do, but recognizing my own limitations.

By the time I hit the sack, I felt exhausted and looked forward to some needed sleep; as well as making the most of my remaining time in Golfton

Hills.

* * *

I got up at the crack of dawn for the run with Gayle and Jeanette, but decided at the last minute to let Jeanette enjoy her beauty sleep instead of joining us, knowing that running had never been her thing.

When I saw no sign of Gayle downstairs at the agreed-upon time, I wondered if she had overslept. Or perhaps chose to get a head start as a warmup.

I went back up to check her room, but found it empty and the bed made. *Looks like she went for a run without me or Jeanette*, I told myself.

I headed out to see if I could catch her. It proved to be a tall order, as there was neither sight nor sound of Jeanette's friend. Given the open spaces and inviting trails on the property, I conceded that Gayle could be anywhere.

What started out as a run turned into a power walk, with my settling into going it alone, while wishing I had awakened Jeanette to accompany me.

As I came upon the greenhouse, I could hear the sounds of two people talking inside. I recognized one shaky voice as that of Gayle. The other voice sounded a lot like Emerson Boyle. His tone was decidedly hostile.

I went inside the greenhouse and followed the voices till coming upon rows of annuals and perennials, where I spotted Boyle attacking Gayle. I yelled at him to stop. But, after momentarily halting his aggression, while giving me the evil eye as though possessed, Boyle ignored me and continued to try to have his way with her.

I watched, horrified, as she fought back. Gayle then grabbed a pair of pruning shears and stabbed Boyle in the chest. Only then was she able to push him off of her. Boyle stumbled backwards, as if in shock, before losing consciousness.

I ran over to Gayle, helping her to her feet. "Did he hurt you?"

"Not so much," she contended, "but not from lack of trying. He followed me during my warmup run and caught me totally off guard in the greenhouse, hoping to resume where he left off at the gift shop. Thankfully, Boyle couldn't complete what he started." She was trembling. "If you hadn't found us, Lanie—distracting him just long enough for me to regroup—there's no telling how this might have ended for me..."

I had to agree with her, having witnessed firsthand just what the real estate developer was planning.

"I'm glad you were able to stop him in his tracks, Gayle," I told her, happy to take credit for any role I may have played in that regard.

Gayle's eyes watered. "Me too."

Glancing at her fallen attacker, who was still out and in need of medical attention, I said, "Though he doesn't deserve it, I think we better get Boyle some help."

I took the cell phone from the back pocket of my running shorts and called 911. Afterwards, I rang Jeanette and Neal to apprise them of the situation and let them know that Gayle and I were unharmed, more or less, during the unsettling ordeal with Emerson Boyle.

* * *

Boyle survived his injuries, only to be charged with the attempted sexual assault of Gayle O'Brien, along with other attacks on women. Turned out that Emerson Boyle was the culprit in some local unsolved rapes, with DNA evidence connecting him to the crimes. With Gayle being one of the prosecution's star witnesses, Boyle would now have to face justice for his crimes and an undoubtedly long stint behind bars when all was said and done—his overzealous plans for building some expensive housing and offices in the area having blown up in his face, literally.

In spite of this unexpected turn of events, the Camellia Festival was a smashing success and more than enough—along with a small loan from me and an aggressive online marketing campaign—to keep the Delgado Farm up and running for some time to come.

Jeanette, Neal, and Kara managed to find time from their busy schedules to visit me in Honolulu, where I'm still an acting coach and currently involved in a hot new relationship with a great guy. I have already made plans to return to Golfton Hills for next year's Camellia Festival. But, hopefully, minus the drama, this time around that nearly cast a shadow over the last Festival and threatened to ruin things for the Delgados.

Gayle has already booked a flight there too, undeterred by her brush with disaster. Like me, she's determined to keep the tradition going and make the annual Camellia Festival a big success for Jeanette and her family.

One Life for Another

After being acquitted of criminally negligent homicide two weeks ago, Maude Rodriguez was still trying to come to grips with taking the life of a woman who tried to rob her at gunpoint. It didn't seem to matter that, in her mind, Maude honestly feared for her life and would have done just about anything to save herself. No, in the eyes of those who tried to make an example out of her for all the wrong reasons, she should not have grabbed the first weapon she could find—a ten-inch butcher knife that was sitting on the counter—and stuck it in Sydney Krause, which eventually resulted in her death.

Never mind the fact that Sydney, a twenty-nine-year-old known meth addict who was desperate to find an easy mark to steal from, got much more than she bargained for when Maude surprised her by putting up a fight. She hadn't intended to kill her—only hold onto what was rightfully hers. Whereas the victim, as they referred to Sydney Krause, had made it perfectly clear that unless Maude handed over the hard-earned money she'd pocketed from her waitressing job in Orlando, Florida, Sydney had no qualms about killing her with the Taurus GX4XL Standard 9mm Luger pistol she accosted Maude with inside her own apartment on Conway Road.

A battle ensued between them, and somehow, Maude was able to knock the gun out of Sydney's hand and grab the knife while Sydney, in her haste, determination, and mind fog, ran smackdab into the knife. Or at least it seemed that way to Maude at the time. All she knew was that the blade wound up in Sydney's stomach, and she died from the combination of blood loss and internal injuries.

Had her actions truly amounted to Maude being criminally negligent in the death of Sydney Krause, as the prosecution would have you believe? Or had it been a matter of self-defense and a reaction to a tense moment in time, as Maude's lawyer argued?

The jury sided with the defense, and Maude—a month shy of turning thirty-two years old—was let off the hook for taking the life of Sydney Krause, tragic as it was for all parties concerned. Now, she was left to try and pick up the pieces in her own life, however difficult that might be.

* * *

Ralph Padalecki ached inside as surely as if he'd been poisoned and was dying a slow death. The death of his stepdaughter had been damn near the most painful experience of his life. Probably even more painful than when he lost his wife to cancer five years ago. Why hadn't he seen this coming? Why hadn't he done more to get her help when she was the closest thing he had to a daughter of his own?

He turned his attention to the person he blamed for his stepdaughter dying. If not for that bitch, she would never have reached the point of no return.

So why shouldn't the person responsible for his stepdaughter's death pay the price, too, with her own life? Wouldn't that be fair? A way to even the score?

Ralph sat at the bar, nursing the shot of whiskey before him. He downed it in one gulp and had another. At the same time, his mind continued to swirl around the need for revenge as the only way his stepdaughter could rest in peace. Something she never had in life and deserved.

Yes, it was up to him to make that happen. Suddenly, he found himself determined to do just that.

* * *

Maude stood at the door of her sister's Queen Anne Victorian on Fisher Avenue. When it opened, Lynetta Steward regarded her with warm brown eyes, the same color as Maude's, and said, "Hey."

"Hi." Maude forced a smile and briefly studied her sister, who was two years older and much more settled in her life. Lynetta was slender like her and an inch taller and had dark hair in a V-cut layered style. Maude's own hair was longer and blonde, while in a razored shag style. Lynetta was married and two months pregnant with their first child. By comparison, Maude was currently single and had nothing but bad luck when it came to men and romance. She gave Lynetta a hug, fighting back the need to cry.

"It's okay," Lynetta comforted her. "This is all behind you now."

"Not so sure of that," Maude said, ill at ease, as she separated in her mind the legal decision from the real-time reckoning of taking another person's life.

"You have to try," her sister pleaded as they went inside. "It's the only way to get on with your life."

"I know," Maude conceded, taking a look around the place Lynetta had purchased with her husband, Ivan, three years ago. It was spacious, with bay windows and traditional furnishings. They sat on a white sectional.

"So, what do you want to do now?" Lynetta asked her directly.

It was a question Maude had asked herself more than once since the verdict. Now, she needed to look at it squarely. "I really don't know," she spoke truthfully. She had lost her job during the course of the trial amid mostly negative publicity, for whatever reason, and her lease had expired, leaving her with no permanent address. "Dad's allowing me to stay at his rental house in Golfton Hills that's currently vacant—till I can figure things out."

"Good." Lynetta flashed her an approving smile. "That house is on a golf course and is the perfect place for you to unwind and retool."

"Yeah." Maude ran a hand through her hair musingly. She wondered if she could actually find a way back to becoming a productive member of society. Or would she continue to languish in self-pity?

As if reading her mind, Lynetta said, "What happened is not your fault. You do get that, right?"

"She's dead because of me." Maude lowered her eyes. "How is that not my fault?"

"You know what I mean. None of this would have ever happened had she not tried to rob you at gunpoint." Lynetta made a face. "You only did what anyone would have done had they been in your shoes. If you hadn't acted to protect yourself, you're the one who would be dead now...and I would be without my sister and best friend."

"I know," Maude said tenderly, grabbing her hands. "I love you, too, and don't know how I would have gotten through this without your support."

Lynetta squeezed her fingers. "That's what big sisters are for."

Maude nodded, knowing she could have counted on the same, had the situation been reversed. Now the trick was to learn how to forgive herself and find some way to make amends, even if this was seemingly all but impossible to do when the person you owed was no longer alive.

* * *

Lynetta watched through the window's venetian blinds as Maude hopped into her blue Honda Civic, started it, and drove off.

She couldn't help but think just how brave Maude had been through all this. Having your life turned upside down by circumstances totally beyond your control was horrifying. Lynetta knew in her heart of hearts that Maude only did what became necessary when it came down to her life or the life of the drug-addicted home invader.

Lynetta could well imagine that, had Sydney Krause managed to take the knife from Maude or regained possession of the gun that she used to force her way into the apartment, things very likely would have ended much differently.

Then Lynetta believed she would have had to bury her sister, and the aftermath would have been even more difficult to digest. She could only pray that Maude—now a free woman again—would be able to turn things around and discover whatever it was she was looking for to make her feel whole again.

Maybe the first step was getting out of Orlando and spending some time in Golfton Hills to recharge her batteries.

At least this was how Lynetta envisioned things going with her younger sister—and it was equally supported by their father as well as Lynetta's husband, Ivan. With a little one on the way, Lynetta wanted Maude to be there for her niece or nephew as well—and vice versa.

One step at a time.

* * *

Maude pulled up behind her father's silver Ford Ranger pickup truck at his craftsman bungalow on Spartan Street. She wondered if he might have second thoughts about letting her stay at his rental home. Or was she merely questioning herself for wanting to get away from where her life was blown up in ways she never saw coming?

Till faced with death down the barrel of a gun.

Maude could hear her father's dog, Racy, barking as company arrived. Unfortunately, she wouldn't be staying long, not wanting to get stuck in rush hour traffic with a six-hour drive ahead of her.

Before she could get to the door of the modest home Maude had grown up in, it opened, and her father stood there. Sam Rodriguez was a tall and sturdily built, sixty-two-year-old Mexican American with short salt and pepper hair with the sides shaved and brown eyes. Apart from owning several houses in Florida as investment properties, he ran a successful landscaping company.

"Hey, Dad."

"Hey, yourself." He offered her a sporty grin. "You about ready to head off to the rental?"

"As soon as I get the key," she said, eager to begin her escape of sorts. She had offered to pay rent, even if she could barely afford gas to get there, but he would hear none of it.

Racy, a black Lab, slipped past his owner and nearly bowled Maude over while trying to jump up and lick her face as a show of love. Her father had rescued the poor dog from an animal shelter three years ago, quickly becoming his companion and seemingly the most important thing in his life since her mother's death.

"Nice to see you too," Maude told the dog while gently pushing him away and trying to get in the door.

"Leave her alone, boy!" Sam ordered, and Racy obeyed instantly, running back into the house.

"Thanks," Maude said. "The last thing I need before heading off is to have Racy's saliva all over my face."

Sam laughed. "He just gets a bit hyper at times. I seem to recall you used to be the same way."

"Oh really?" She smiled, remembering her childhood when she was a bundle of energy.

They went into the sunken living room, which was still pretty much the way Maude remembered it through the years, with dark leather chairs and maple furniture. A framed landscape painting hung on the wall.

"You want something to eat?" her father asked.

Maude waved this off. "I'll pick up something along the way."

He nodded. "The house was professionally cleaned after the last tenant moved out, so you should be all set."

"Okay, and thanks again, Dad, for giving me a place to chill."

"It's the least I can do to help you get back on your feet," Sam offered. "If you need anything else, let me know."

"I will." Maude gave him a hug and was handed the key to the rental, before she headed off to her temporary residence.

* * *

Ralph Padalecki was still incensed over the unnecessary death of his stepdaughter and vowed to do something about it. He couldn't just sit around and let her get away with what she did—while his stepdaughter lay in a casket buried in the ground.

No, he needed to hunt her down and make things right. Or, at least, make it so it didn't feel so wrong. As was the case at the moment, while his stepdaughter was deprived of getting the help she needed. Instead, all she got was a short life span and no chance to get past her demons and make a decent life for herself.

Ralph drove his red Lincoln Corsair down State Avenue, his mind working overtime in coming up with a plan of action to finish what he'd made up his mind to do.

In the back seat was his Ruger American Predator 6.5 Creedmoor Bolt-Action loaded hunting rifle with a Vortex Crossfire II 4-12x44 scope. It would prove useful in going after his target.

* * *

It was five-thirty p.m. when Maude drove down the palm tree-lined Pineberry Street. She passed by the Golfton Hills Golf Course and expensive coastal contemporary homes, before turning onto Chestnut Lane with a string of ranch homes. She found the one she was looking for and parked in the driveway in front of the attached garage.

Inside the house, Maude was surprised to see that it was more spacious than she realized. She set her bags down and checked out the place. It had an open layout with high ceilings, plenty of windows, porcelain tile flooring, and rustic furnishings. She opened the sliding glass doors and stepped out onto the back patio. It offered an unobstructed view of the golf course, and she could see a few golfers at play. Though she didn't play golf, Maude imagined she could learn someday. Assuming she stuck around there long enough.

She went back inside to unpack and decide what to do about dinner.

* * *

Quentin Blakely sat at the corner desk in his office, wishing for all the world that he was on the golf course adjacent to his house, teeing off. Instead, he was working overtime, as were the members of his team. As the head of Blakely Builders, a construction company in downtown Golfton Hills, it was his job to make sure everyone was on the same page in securing contracts and building accordingly. Right now, they were working on a huge shopping complex in a renovated part of the downtown area.

As far as Quentin was concerned, staying busy was what kept him going, and he wouldn't have it any other way. Having lived in Golfton Hills for nearly two-thirds of his thirty-five years of life, he appreciated as much as anyone the laid back, feel-good environment and active lifestyle that came with living in the coastal community. He was happy to do his part to add to the conveniences afforded residents and visitors alike.

Quentin only wished he could do more for his sister, Carrie-Anne. A historical romance author and five years younger, she was still reeling over the death of her ex-girlfriend, Krysten, who took her own life. Carrie-Anne, having ended the relationship, was putting up a brave front. Knowing she wasn't at fault didn't stop her from feeling guilty and wondering what she might have done differently were she able to have a redo.

All Quentin could do was offer her a shoulder to cry on whenever Carrie-Anne needed it. And know when to back off whenever she needed her space, which seemed to be the case at the moment. He had to respect that, even if he feared that this might be doing more harm than good.

His phone buzzed, snapping Quentin out of his reverie. It was his assistant, Meredith Osaka.

"The meeting will start in five minutes," she informed him.

"I'm on my way," he said and was on his feet to head for the conference room to bring everyone up to speed on relevant information.

Quentin walked out of his office, still thinking about his sister and what, if anything, he could do to ease her burden at this moment in Carrie-Anne's life.

* * *

Maude stood on the patio, sipping coffee while ignoring the pesky mosquitoes hovering around in the air. She was grateful that her father had let her stay there for the time being, believing that the idyllic setting might be just what she needed to take her mind off Sydney Krause's death.

She gazed across the golf course and could see houses on the other side. What were the life stories of the ones who lived there? Did she really want to know? Perhaps they were no better than her own sordid tale. Maybe even worse.

Out of her periphery, Maude spotted movement. She turned and saw a slender and attractive woman around her age, with long crimson hair in a high ponytail, step out onto the patio of the house next door.

The woman, who was holding a half-filled wineglass, turned her way and forced a smile.

"Hi," Maude felt compelled to say in a neighborly way.

"Hey." She stared for a long moment and then looked away.

Maude wanted to say something more but wasn't sure she was receptive to conversation.

The woman finished off her wine, gave another little smile, and went back inside her house.

Maude was curious about her, but didn't dare pry, knowing she had her own troubles and wasn't exactly ready to share them with a total stranger.

She went back into the rental and grabbed her handbag off the coffee table, ready to go find a place to eat dinner, as she was suddenly starving.

* * *

Quentin drove into the parking lot of the Golfton Hills Diner on Flakerton Road, his eye catching a car that had just pulled into an empty spot. It was a Honda Civic. He'd had one just like it a few years ago before upgrading to his current car, an orange BMW 228i Gran Coupe, which was a much better fit for him. He parked on the opposite side and glanced through the rear-view mirror, curious as to who owned the car.

A tall and slender woman with long blonde hair got out and headed toward the restaurant. He wondered briefly if she was a local. Seemed like the area had been attracting more and more young professionals in recent years, as new businesses moved in and more areas were developed for both residential and commercial use.

Guess I should just mind my own business, Quentin told himself, emerging from his own car and stretching his legs before going into the diner.

He wound up sitting at a table next to the one with the blonde-haired woman. While studying his menu, Quentin couldn't help but study her as well. She looked to be in her early thirties and was attractive. But was she single and available like him? Or was that asking too much for a total stranger who likely had more than her fair share of suitors to be interested in him?

* * *

Maude sat at the table near a window. She could literally hear her stomach growling as she studied the menu. Though nothing in particular stood out to her, at this point, she felt that almost anything would do. Maybe she should have grabbed something from a fast-food restaurant during the drive in Golfton Hills.

"Try the braised short ribs with mashed potatoes," she heard the deep male voice say in a confident tone.

Maude turned to look at the man sitting by his lonesome at the table next to hers. She guessed him to be in his mid-thirties. He was solid in build and tall, with interesting gray eyes and thick dark hair in a tapered cut. Not bad looking. In fact, if she was honest about it, he was quite handsome. She wondered if this was his pickup line for a newbie in town? Was it that obvious?

She smiled, happy to take her mind off her woes. "Why not."

He grinned. "I was hoping you weren't a vegetarian, meaning I would have totally misread you and made a fool of myself at the same time."

Maude laughed. "I wasn't the last time I checked." She smiled faintly. "So, no, you didn't make a fool out of yourself."

"Good." He smiled back and waited for her to order before saying, "I'm Quentin, by the way."

"Maude."

"Nice to meet you, Maude."

"You too." She was glad they didn't exchange last names, otherwise she might have had to use a fake one—in case he kept up with the news, and she had to try to explain her recent run-in with the law and court system—which was no way to begin a conversation with a handsome guy. Maude regarded him as he sipped water. "So, I take it that you come here often?" Or was that being too presumptuous?

"Probably more than I should," he conceded. "I have a good excuse this time, though. After working late, I had no desire to go home and cook. Beyond that, I've never been much for eating alone."

"I see." Maude had gotten used to eating alone in recent times—though she had also been roped into having more meals with her sister and brother-in-law, and even her father, since her ordeal had ended.

"I thought about inviting my sister to join me—or dropping in on her—but, right now, she's going through some things, so neither seemed like a good idea."

At least it was somewhat comforting for Maude to know that she wasn't the only one carrying a burden, even if she wouldn't wish what she had just been put through on anyone. Including Quentin's sister. Or him, for that matter.

"Guess you'll just have to be stuck with me," Maude half-joked, even if the prospect of getting to know what he was made of was an intriguing distraction.

Quentin flashed straight teeth. "Sounds like something I can live with."

Maude smiled, too, but wondered if she might bring too much baggage with her for any man.

* * *

Ralph had driven around town, drinking beer and sulking over what he believed was a terrible injustice that his stepdaughter had to die way sooner than she ever should have. He blamed that bitch for everything that went down. It shouldn't have ended this way. But it did and now he was left to

123

try and pick up the pieces. Again.

He had never been one for dealing with grief well. This time was no different.

He gulped down more beer, giving him the liquid courage to do what had to be done.

Now it was time to give his stepdaughter the peace of mind in death that she never seemed to have in life.

Then, and only then, could he come to terms with the fact that she was gone and wouldn't ever be coming back.

Ralph drove his car toward the residence located on the golf course, where he knew she was living.

* * *

Maude knocked on the door of the ranch house next to hers. She wasn't sure this was such a good idea, but felt compelled to do it anyhow.

When the door opened, the woman she had seen earlier on her patio stood there. This time, her long red hair hung loose. Her pretty eyes were ocean blue.

"Hey," Maude spoke tentatively. "I'm your next-door neighbor. Thought I'd drop by and introduce myself. I'm Maude."

"Carrie-Anne," she responded evenly.

"I could use a friend," Maude told her honestly. "And I was hoping you could, too." She lifted the bottle she was holding. "I brought wine."

"I'd say that's a good icebreaker." Carrie-Anne chuckled. "Come in…"

The house had an identical layout to the one Maude lived in. Only the coloring was brighter with more contemporary furnishings. She couldn't tell if Carrie-Anne lived alone or not.

"So, did you move next door by yourself?" Carrie-Anne asked, just as curious as she was.

"Yeah," Maude told her honestly. "My dad owns the place and usually rents it out. He's letting me stay here for a while. Not exactly sure for how long."

"Well, enjoy it while it lasts," she said, handing her a goblet of wine. They sat at a pub table in the kitchen.

"Have you lived here for long?" Maude asked her.

"Just a few months." Carrie-Anne tasted her wine thoughtfully. "In case you're wondering, I live alone." She paused. "Used to have a roommate." Another pause, and her voice choked up when Carrie-Anne uttered, "She took her own life a week ago."

Maude reacted to this unsettling news. "I'm so sorry to hear that."

"A week before that, we broke up after I decided that it just wasn't working anymore," Carrie-Anne said, her voice trembling. "I guess it was more than she could handle—"

Maude furrowed her brow. "You can't blame yourself for someone deciding to commit suicide," she said with a catch to her voice while hoping she wasn't overstepping with her bluntness.

Carrie-Anne sipped more wine. "That's what everyone keeps telling me, but I can't help but feel that maybe if I had approached things differently, it might have made a difference."

"Or might have made no difference at all," Maude thought out loud. "Usually, it takes more than a breakup to end one's life. Was she depressed or...?"

"She didn't use drugs," Carrie-Anne answered what Maude was about to ask. "As for depression, I suppose between our relationship ending and the recent loss of her job—it was just more than she could take."

"You couldn't have known it would go that far," Maude was sure as she took a sip of the wine. "We often never know just how depressed someone was till something like this happens. But it still wasn't your fault, as no one should be forced to remain in an unhappy relationship—no matter what."

"I know." Carrie-Anne finished her wine and poured more into the glass. "It still hurts, though."

"I understand where you're coming from," Maude had to confess and drank wine musingly. "My story is just as bad...if not worse—"

"Oh...?" Carrie-Anne met her eyes. "Tell me..."

Maude hesitated, but knew she needed to let it out to someone other than family and her attorney. She had come close to revealing it to the man named

Quentin, whom she met at the restaurant, but held back for fear that it could derail from the start something that seemed like it had potential between them.

"I killed a woman—" she began, finishing off the wine and refilling the glass as her chilling words sank in.

"Killed...?" Carrie-Anne's eyes danced with uncomfortable curiosity.

"It was self-defense," Maude told her levelly. "It happened during a break-in at my apartment. One moment, the meth-addicted intruder was holding a gun to my head, and the next, I was fighting to stay alive and grabbed a knife to that effect. She ran right into it and later died at the hospital."

"I'm sorry about that." Carrie-Anne's voice cracked. She put a sympathetic hand on hers.

"It gets worse," Maude hated to say, but wanted to get it off her chest at the same time. "I was charged with criminally negligent homicide."

"What?" Carrie-Anne's mouth stayed open in disbelief.

"I know, right?" Maude still had trouble digesting it herself. "I went to trial for it. Two weeks ago, a jury found me not guilty, thankfully—even if deep down inside, I'm still trying to make myself believe that. I mean, I took her life..."

"You were defending yourself during a home invasion." Carrie-Anne's eyes narrowed. "That was your right—and very likely ended up saving your life."

"That's what I keep telling myself," Maude muttered, tasting the wine. "Just wish it had never happened."

"As do I with my ex," Carrie-Anne contended. "But some things—okay, many things—are outside our control. We just have to deal with them as best as possible. No matter the difficulty."

"I suppose." Maude nodded, knowing deep down she was right and that they could relate to each other's emotional baggage. She was glad to have Carrie-Anne as a new friend.

* * *

Quentin had enjoyed his chat with Maude at the Golfton Hills Diner. Apart from being very nice on the eyes, she seemed like someone who was easy to get along with. He gathered that she was new in town and between jobs, but appeared to be holding back. Maybe he was guilty of that too, to some extent, in not opening up about his love life—or lack thereof—and the difficulty of finding someone who got him and vice versa. Or what his sister was going through that had an impact on him.

Quentin had managed to get Maude's phone number and promised to give her a call and see if they could maybe pick up where they left off. And then some, if he read her correctly, about being open to whatever could happen between them.

After swinging by his place for a bit, he decided to head over to the other side of the golf course, where Carrie-Anne had been living with her girlfriend, before asking her to leave and going it alone. Quentin felt he needed to be there for his sister, whether she wanted to push him away or not. She didn't need to go through this alone, losing someone she cared about, even if they had gone their separate ways.

* * *

Maude was enjoying some girl time with her new neighbor, both having been traumatized recently and left to try and pick up the pieces of their lives. She probably could have stayed and talked with Carrie-Anne all night, but felt it was time to go. Maybe they could hang out together tomorrow, and Carrie-Anne could show her around Golfton Hills. Beyond that, Maude was hoping that Quentin would call her and ask her out.

Just as Carrie-Anne walked her to the door, Maude was shocked when it opened, and they both saw a tall, slightly overweight man standing there. He was in his fifties and had slicked-back gray hair in a men's undercut and blue eyes. The man was holding a high-powered rifle and pointing it at them, an angry look to his countenance.

Oh no! Maude told herself, feeling a sense of déjà vu. Was this another home invasion?

Then she heard Carrie-Anne say with alarm in her voice, "What are you doing here...?"

The man wrinkled a crooked nose and responded menacingly, "Back inside!"

They obeyed his command. After he followed them in and closed the door behind him, Maude looked at Carrie-Anne and asked, after sensing this, "Do you know him?"

"His name is Ralph Padalecki," she answered, ill at ease. "He's the stepdad of my ex-girlfriend, Krysten Gilsig." Carrie-Anne peered at him. "What do you want, Ralph?"

"Retribution," he said tartly, still aiming the rifle at them.

"You can't blame me for what Krysten chose to do all on her own," Carrie-Anne insisted.

"But I do blame you." His lips pursed. "If you hadn't chosen to end things with her, Krysten wouldn't have been driven to kill herself. You could have worked things out."

"Believe me, I tried," Carrie-Anne argued. "It just wasn't working any longer. I'm sorry."

"Not as sorry as you're gonna be," Ralph spat, and Maude could smell the alcohol on his breath. "You have to die, just like Krysten. If you can't be together in life, I'm here to see to it that you are in death."

In that moment, Maude froze, believing that Carrie-Anne's fate was sealed. And hers, too. But then Maude reached back to the last time when she stood at death's door and found a burst of adrenalin she didn't know existed inside her. She had to fight back, not allowing herself the time to have second thoughts after what happened in her deadly confrontation with Sydney Krause.

Maude surprised Ralph Padalecki by grabbing the barrel of his rifle and fighting him for control of it. That distraction allowed Carrie-Anne to get in on the fight, climbing on Ralph's back and getting him in a headlock. Maude slammed the heel of her sandal into his ankle as hard as she could.

As he howled like an animal from the pain, mixed with profanities, Maude kneed him between the legs and thought that might do the trick. But he managed to shake off Carrie-Anne and still maintain possession of the rifle, which he turned on Carrie-Anne, who had fallen to the floor.

Just as Maude fought to catch her breath and look for something heavy to hit him with, out of the corner of her eye, she watched with astonishment as the man she'd met earlier, Quentin, seemed to come out of nowhere and tackled Ralph, just as the rifle went off. The bullet lodged into the ceiling.

Quentin was on top of Ralph and gave him one solid shot to the jaw that was more than enough to render him unconscious.

"How did you find me—?" Maude had to ask Quentin as he took the rifle out of Ralph's hands and got to his feet, wondering if Quentin had followed her from the restaurant.

He gave her a crooked grin and gazed at Carrie-Anne, who got to her feet. "Actually, she's the one I came to see… Carrie-Anne is my sister—"

"What?" Maude was trying to piece this together in her head. "Since when?"

"We never got around to talking about family," Quentin noted accurately.

"True," Maude conceded.

Carrie-Anne ran into her brother's arms. "Did he hurt you?" Quentin asked her.

"Not as much as we hurt him," she said toughly. "Krysten's stepfather wanted me dead as his way of getting revenge for her suicide."

"What a jerk!" Quentin furrowed his forehead, peering at the still-unconscious would-be killer.

"Thanks for showing up when you did," Carrie-Anne told her brother.

"No problem," he said in a gratified tone.

"I feel the same way," Maude expressed. "If you hadn't come at that exact moment…"

"Don't even go there," Quentin cut her off. "Timing is everything, as they say. And I think you both deserved a break. Don't you?"

"Absolutely," Maude could hardly argue the point, believing that, on some level, this was the redemption she had sought in moving past her ordeal with Sydney Krause.

"Definitely," Carrie-Anne seconded.

Quentin pulled out his cell phone and called 911 to deal with the likes of Ralph Padalecki.

After the police came and arrested him and they gave their statements, Carrie-Anne looked from Maude to Quentin and back quizzically and asked inquisitively, "Now, would one of you like to fill me in on exactly how you two know each other?"

Quentin grinned. "You want to tell her, or should I?" he asked Maude with expectation.

Maude flashed her teeth at the two new people in her life and said lightheartedly, "I think we'll need to open up another bottle of wine to get to the root of it and beyond. Are we all in agreement?"

Graveside Chat

It was a lovely Saturday afternoon in Golfton Hills, Florida, under the circumstances, with nary a cloud in the sky and the temperatures in the low eighties. A small gathering stood on a hill at the Orchards Cemetery on Jake Boulevard to say goodbye to Vincent Frost, a local businessman and prominent figure in the community. He had been murdered just before turning seventy, and the killer remained at large.

Eliza Frost could barely believe her father was dead—the one man who had always been there for her, through thick and thin. Unlike the one-time boyfriend who had inexplicably bailed on Eliza five years ago, leaving her heartbroken and alone. She'd once thought Will McDougall practically walked on water as the love of her life, ignoring what her father said was a big mistake when she began seeing Will. As far as Eliza was concerned at the time, it didn't matter that Will had been strangely evasive when it came to his background, family, and how he made a living. For whatever reason, she trusted him, believing his heart was in the right place—giving it to her.

Until seemingly out of the blue, Will pulled a vanishing act, and the hot and steamy fairytale romance abruptly ended almost as soon as it began.

A few weeks later, Eliza found out she was pregnant with Will's child.

Her green eyes watered as she looked down at her son, Gabriel. He was four years old and didn't know the man he was the spitting image of on a pint-sized level—with blue eyes and dark hair in a skin fade with a textured short top. Instead, it was Eliza's own father who had been a surrogate dad to Gabriel. Now, he had lost two fathers, in effect.

Eliza, who was tall like her own late father and slender, had long black hair that was currently in a tight chignon, as opposed to when loose and in waves while parted in the middle. She squeezed her son's small hand and got a squeeze back. Gabriel had cried when he first learned of his grandfather's death—though unaware of the brutal nature of it, in being shot to death at close range—but since then had refused to cry, as if determined to remain strong for her.

In turn, Eliza had to somehow muster that same strength now in order to give her son the best life she could. She glanced over Gabriel's head to her sister-in-law, Kim, a leggy redhead who had been part of the family for four years now and had become a good friend. Next to her was Eliza's brother, Carter. At thirty-three, tall and lean, with blonde locks in a quiff hairstyle, he was two years her senior. He hadn't always seen eye to eye with their father, but at the time of his death, they seemed to have come to an understanding.

She would need her brother more than ever now to help fill the void in Gabriel's life as his only uncle. But that could be a tall order, considering up to this point, Carter had seemingly only pretended to like Gabriel, as if he resented the fact that she'd given their father a grandson before Carter could.

Eliza would not apologize for bringing her son into this world. Even if it had to be as a single parent, much like her own father—after losing her mother when Eliza was around Gabriel's age. Wherever Will was, she didn't need him to make her life whole. He'd deserted her, and she wouldn't waste any energy wondering what might have been.

She could only deal with the present, beginning with the sorrow and pain of having to bury her father—even as the authorities tried to solve the suspected case of a drive-by shooting thought to have been gang-related in possibly targeting the wrong person. Eliza wasn't so sure about that. She knew that her father was having financial difficulties before he died and borrowed money from a less-than-reputable lender that was overdue. Could that have had anything to do with his death?

Eliza felt a comforting arm around her shoulders. She turned to the man she had only recently begun dating, Sergio Hutchison. In his thirties, he was tall and fit, with brown eyes and brown hair in a low drop fade cut and smooth-shaven. A car dealer, he was a nice guy who liked hanging out with Gabriel and seemed content to take things slowly, as she preferred. She appreciated that he'd wanted to be there with her for the funeral, though they had barely gotten to know each other. At least it showed her that Sergio cared.

Eliza couldn't help but wonder if that had ever been the case with Will.

* * *

The drive down this stretch of winding road, dotted by royal palm trees, wasn't exactly as Will McDougall remembered, as he navigated it in his Dodge Durango SRT Hellcat, and his blue eyes took in the surroundings. Had things really changed that much in the last five years since he'd been in Golfton Hills? Or was it more about him and the changes he had gone through over that span of time?

Something told him that he wouldn't exactly be welcomed with open arms. And could he blame anyone for that—especially Eliza Frost—considering the way he left things?

Not one day had passed over the last five years that Will didn't regret the choices he'd made that impacted his personal life for the good of his professional existence. In the process, he had destroyed any chance he had with the one woman who had totally sold him on what it meant to want someone so badly that he could practically taste it.

Will was sure it was love he felt for Eliza, and she made it perfectly clear that she felt the same way toward him.

But what she didn't know was when they met, he was deep undercover on a drug trafficking case as a special agent for the Florida Department of Law Enforcement's Investigations and Forensic Science Program. Continuing their romance would only have placed Eliza in danger, not to mention risk compromising his true identity and the integrity of the assignment.

So, when he requested to be pulled from the investigation, Jared Evigan, the special agent in charge—his boss at the Pensacola Regional Operations Center in Pensacola, Florida—granted the request. Will was reassigned and moved on with his life.

Now, at age thirty-four, he had returned to Golfton Hills to face the music. He missed Eliza more than he cared to admit and wanted to come clean to her at last. But just as important, as it concerned them both—and no longer working undercover—Will was back in town to investigate the death of Eliza's father. Vincent Frost had been in the FDLE's crosshairs recently in relation to a broader statewide investigation into money laundering. Contrary to some members of local law enforcement who were focusing on a turf war between rival gangs, with Frost inadvertently caught in the crossfire, the FDLE and the feds had a different take. They believed that Vincent Frost's death was directly tied to a case of laundering illicit drug money.

Will needed to get to the bottom of it while trying to repair the fractured relationship he had with Eliza. Or was that even possible at this stage?

I have to try, he told himself while approaching the cemetery where Vincent Frost's funeral was currently underway. He owed Eliza that much. Not to mention how he, too, could be impacted if he were able to get a second chance with her once the investigation was completed.

* * *

Eliza wept as the pastor spoke graciously about her father's generous contributions to local charities and his willingness to give the shirt off his back if someone needed it. She certainly wouldn't argue with anything that had been said, with him being even more caring to the members of his own family. Even if her father wasn't perfect, Eliza loved him and believed that her parents would find their way back to one another now that they were in a distant place where neither would ever again feel pain.

She caught movement out of the corner of her eye and looked in that direction. A tall and well-built man in a dark suit and loafers was making his way toward the gravesite. He walked with an air of confidence, then stopped just short, hands clasped, as if not to disrupt the funeral.

Eliza held the gaze of his blue eyes on her. It took only a moment for her to recognize the face—broad-featured and tanned, with a three-day stubble beard—beneath wavy raven hair in a crop cut, even though he was five years older.

Will McDougall.

Her heart skipped a beat. Maybe two beats. Eliza could barely believe that after all these years, he had chosen this time of mourning to show up.

Why?

She couldn't imagine Will all of a sudden wanting to pay his respects to a man he never particularly seemed to get along with, in spite of Will's best efforts. Eliza was acutely aware that her father sensed that something was off with Will and, as such, felt she could do a lot better than him as a boyfriend, though she believed otherwise.

Until the day Will walked out of her life and made her seriously question everything she had felt for him.

Eliza tightened her grip on Gabriel's hand, as if Will somehow knew he was his son and wanted to take him from her. That would never happen. Not over her dead body. He'd given up the right to wish that a long time ago.

She had sought to locate Will right after learning she was pregnant but had no luck. It was as though he had vanished off the face of the earth. No working phone number. No forwarding address from the condo he'd stayed at in Golfton Hills on Junner Drive. Not even a clue from those at the seafood market where he'd worked on Pepton Street.

It became painfully clear to Eliza that the man had no desire to be found. Certainly not by her. As such, she felt no guilt in keeping his child from him, since it was obvious Will wanted nothing to do with either of them.

"Who's that incredibly hot-looking man standing all by his lonesome?" Kim whispered in Eliza's ear.

Eliza blinked back more tears. The last thing she wanted to do was confuse Gabriel, who already had enough to deal with losing his grandfather. Suddenly gaining a dad out of the blue, who had seemed like he was out of the picture for good, might be too much to handle right now.

"Someone I once knew." She left it at that, though Eliza suspected that

Carter, whose relationship with Will had been lukewarm at best, would surely fill her in on their history later.

Kim fluttered her fake lashes. "Looks like he still knows you—or wants to—the way he's staring, as though he can't take his eyes off you."

Eliza bit her lip. "I seriously doubt that."

Much had changed in her life over the last five years. After finally getting him out of her system and beginning to find some semblance of happiness again, she had no intention of allowing Will to disrupt that, even if her feelings for the man had never gone away entirely.

She averted her watery eyes, first turning to Sergio and offering him a reassuring look before refocusing on Pastor Muriel Forlani, an attractive gray-haired woman in her fifties, as she said a final few words.

Once the attendees began to disperse, Eliza expected some of them to come to the post-funeral reception at the house. While Gabriel had run off to play with a friend, she couldn't help but think that the brightness of the afternoon was perhaps a sign that her father's death needn't be the end of her own life, per se. After all, she had Gabriel and her work as a curator at a museum, giving her hope for a bright future on both fronts.

She looked up, expecting to be approached by Will, but he seemed to have vanished—again. Why was she not surprised? Some patterns never changed.

In this instance, Eliza felt that it might be for the best she not go there with Will in rehashing their past.

"It was a nice service for your father," Sergio said, getting Eliza's attention. "I'm sure he would have appreciated it."

"I agree." She smiled at him, imagining her father's spirit giving his approval.

Sergio took her hands. "Just so you know, I'm here if you need anything."

Eliza took solace in hearing those words. She needed him as a friend right now more than anything else. "Thank you, Sergio."

His cell phone suddenly rang, causing his brow to furrow, as if irritated at the timing. "I should probably get that."

Eliza didn't object, sliding her hands from his. From what she understood, the car dealership Sergio co-owned was one of the busiest in town, commanding much of his time. She wasn't sure how that would affect their dating in the long run, as she needed someone who was able to at least meet her halfway, if it were to work at all. Something that Will had evidently been incapable of doing.

She glanced around for Will again and then smiled when Gabriel ran up to her. "Can we go home now, Mom?" he asked impatiently, tugging on her hand, after his best friend Andy Granger had left.

"In a few minutes," she promised.

He pouted. "Why do we have to wait?"

"I have someone I need to speak to." Eliza still saw no sign of Will. "It won't take long."

"Who?" Gabriel asked curiously.

Eliza realized it was almost asking too much to restrain an active boy at a cemetery. But could she forever avoid the man who had fathered him, even if she wanted to? Or would Will simply show up at her house, causing even more problems?

And how could she explain to Gabriel that the man Eliza truly thought she'd never see again—who had left her with a gift of a lifetime in Gabriel—had suddenly and inexplicably returned?

She looked up and froze as she saw Will standing there.

* * *

Eliza hadn't changed a bit, as far as Will could tell. Including her long black hair in an updo. She was still just as beautiful and slender as he remembered. He noted she was holding a boy's hand, while a little earlier, a man had his arm around her in a proprietary way before he went off to talk on his cell phone. Had Eliza married him and given him a son?

Though not surprising after five years, the notion that someone else had stolen Eliza's heart was almost too much for Will to bear. He should never have let things go as far between them as they had. Only to pull the proverbial rug from beneath her feet and pay just as high a price himself.

But he could only deal with things as they were today. If Eliza was no longer available, he had to take it like a man. At the very least, Will believed he would be able to make his peace by giving back what was owed to her.

An explanation. Along with doing what he could to help solve her father's murder.

Will had waited till the funeral ended, quietly making himself scarce so as not to be a distraction to Eliza or other mourners, before approaching her and the boy. Will noted there was no ring on her finger, giving him hope that Eliza wasn't married to the other man after all—at least not yet.

Though he'd replayed this moment in his head at least a thousand times, now that it had come, Will suddenly felt nervous. What could he possibly say that didn't sound like a hollow—too little, too late—apology?

"Hello, Eliza."

She flashed him an uneasy look. "Will... I honestly never expected to see you again."

He hadn't expected it either. Death and regrets had a way of making one reassess what—and who—was truly important in one's life.

"I get that," he muttered lamely.

"What are you doing here?" Eliza demanded.

There will be time to get into the details later, Will thought. "Heard about Vincent." He straightened his shoulders. "I'm sorry about your father," he expressed.

She frowned. "I can't believe he's gone...not that way—"

I'm here to help give him justice, Will thought. But with the boy standing there, hanging on his every word, he told Eliza, "The authorities will get to the bottom of it—"

She nodded while seemingly more uncomfortable in his presence than he wanted her to be. Was his unwanted appearance messing things up with the boyfriend?

Will directed his attention to Eliza's son. He guessed that he was about four or maybe five.

"And who might this be?" Will asked, intrigued as he studied the small boy's features.

"My son, Gabriel," Eliza responded tersely.

"Hey, Gabriel." Will grinned at him musingly.

"Who are you?" the boy asked, gazing up at him.

"I'm Will McDougall."

"Hi, Will. Are you friends with my mom?"

"We used to be friends," he answered, eyeing Eliza. "But we haven't seen each other in a few years."

"Did you know my grandpa?" Gabriel asked him.

"Not well, but we did meet." Will gazed at Eliza again and recalled that her father had given him the cold shoulder—believing, and rightfully so, that he would only end up hurting Eliza in the long run. Her brother, Carter, was friendlier toward him, but also had his qualms that he was a keeper for Eliza. Will only wished he could have proven them wrong.

Was it too late to do so now?

Will watched as the man Eliza was with came up to them. Putting his arm around her slender waist, he said equably, "Hey."

Eliza gave him an ill-at-ease grin, glancing at Will and back, before saying, "Hey."

The man flashed Will a hard stare and asked coldly, "Who's he?"

She regarded Will and introduced him. "This is Will McDougall, an old friend," Eliza said with a catch to her voice.

"Sergio Hutchison," the man said stiffly, extending a hand to shake.

Will reluctantly shook hands with him, feeling jealous, even while having absolutely no right to. "Nice meeting you."

"You too," Sergio said and turned to Eliza. "Are you ready to go?"

"Give me a minute," she answered hastily. "Do you mind taking Gabriel to your car?"

Sergio glanced at Will suspiciously before telling her, "Sure, no problem. We'll wait for you there."

Eliza put a hand on her son's head. "Go with Sergio. I'll be there shortly."

Will watched the boy furrow his brow and say, "Okay. Bye, Will."

"See you later," Will said routinely while wondering if he would get that chance. He watched Gabriel obey his mother and leave with Sergio Hutchison. Once some distance had been put between them, Will faced

Eliza and asked hesitantly, "Do you think we could go somewhere to talk...?"

She folded her arms petulantly. "It's a little late for that, don't you think?"

He took a breath, reading the ire coming from her pores. "If I can just explain—"

"Say what you have to say, Will," Eliza stated bluntly. "Only make it quick. I have to go back to the house with people dropping by to pay their respects— and to be with my son. I'd rather not have you there. So, let's get this over with here and now, and I'll be on my way. And you can be back on yours, wherever you've been for the past five years..."

* * *

Eliza didn't feel at all like she was being unreasonable here. After what he had put her through, Will couldn't honestly just show up at her father's funeral after being completely absent from her life for five years—and somehow expect her to simply melt in his arms, as she once had.

He met her gaze with one that seemed to be a mixture of determination and sympathy, then said solidly, "Look, I owe you an explanation. Here goes..." She watched as he took a deep sigh, before removing something—an identification—from the inside of his suit jacket. "I'm a special agent for the Florida Department of Law Enforcement's Investigations and Forensic Science Program."

"What?" Eliza's eyes widened as she studied his credentials that had his name—Will McDougall—and the official title with the FDLE. "Since when?"

"Since before we first met," he said calmly. "I was working undercover at the time while investigating drug trafficking in Golfton Hills. Unfortunately, I couldn't blow my cover—not even to you. The work to get illegal drugs off the streets was just too important..."

While processing this shocking news, Eliza stared at him and asked dubiously, "So you led me on and made me fall for you—all as part of your undercover assignment?"

"It wasn't like that," Will insisted. "I never meant to get involved with you...or anyone. It just happened." He drew a breath. "I certainly never intended to hurt you."

"But you did, Will," she shot back. "You had no right to play with my emotions when you knew it was deception on your part."

"What I felt for you—still feel—wasn't deception, Eliza," he told her with a straight face. "Yeah, working at the seafood market was part of my cover—but our romance in and of itself was very real to me."

"So real that you just left me, high and dry, with no explanation whatsoever?" she challenged him. "I deserved better."

"You did," Will acknowledged. "Better than I was able to give you, which is why I had to go. It had become too dangerous to stay and risk having you get caught up in the drug trafficking probe. So, I walked away without jeopardizing the investigation—even while knowing I couldn't come clean with you. I felt you'd be better off just getting on with your life and putting me in the rear-view mirror. If I could go back in time…"

"You'd do the same thing," Eliza finished for him, if she was reading him correctly. "After all, your mission would have repeated itself, and your reasoning for keeping me in the dark wouldn't have changed any." She wondered if he meant he would have avoided a romance with her, which would have meant that Gabriel would never have entered her life.

"Maybe you're right." Will looked down at his shoes. "This is probably way too late, but I'm truly sorry about everything."

So am I, Eliza told herself. Except for their son, who she loved more than life itself and couldn't imagine not having been brought into this world had Will been able to change their history. "What's done is done," she said, trying hard to forgive him. She eyed Will with curiosity. "So, why did you come back now?" She sensed there was more to it than attending her father's funeral.

Will took a moment or two to seemingly collect his thoughts and responded, "Apart from the opportunity to see you again and set the record straight, I'm here in a non-undercover capacity, looking into money laundering…" He paused, regarding her directly. "The FDLE believes that your father's death may not be gang-related…or accidental—"

Eliza frowned. "What are you saying?"

He scratched the hair on his chin. "That we think it was no case of mistaken identity, but part of a money laundering operation. Vincent Frost borrowed money from them—and when he was unable to pay it back with heavy interest, he ran out of time to do so. He was apparently killed as a result and to make an example of."

Eliza was at a loss for words, stunned at the allegations, even as part of her had believed her father's death was related to his financial problems.

"I know this isn't what you wanted to hear," Will told her. "I'm sorry to have to be the one to tell you—especially at your father's gravesite. I just want you to know I'll do everything in my power to bring his killer to justice."

"I don't know what to say," she told him, as he had given her almost too much to process.

"Don't say anything—right now. I'm sure you need time for all of this to sink in." Will met her eyes and asked, "So, how long have you and Sergio been together?"

Eliza returned his gaze. "Not long," she replied tartly, seeing no reason not to admit that she and Sergio hardly knew each other and certainly were not yet an item. "Not that it's any of your business. You gave up that right years ago."

Will twisted his lips. "Fair enough." He shifted his attention to where they could both see Sergio and Gabriel standing by Sergio's blue Mercedes-Benz sedan. "I just have one more question…"

"What's that?" she hesitated to ask, reading his eyes in speculating what was coming next.

Will peered at her. "Is Gabriel my son?"

Eliza swallowed thickly, knowing she could no longer keep the truth from him any more than he had in being straight with her in his uncomfortable truths.

* * *

Eliza tried to pretend that she wasn't rattled by Will's reappearance. She'd wanted nothing more to do with him and the awful hurt he'd left her with.

His sudden departure had left her with a permanent scar on her heart. But there was no denying he was Gabriel's father, and she knew that would've had to be dealt with sooner or later, whether she wanted to acknowledge it or not.

Beyond that, the revelations that Will was a special agent and had been working undercover when they met threw Eliza for a loop. As did his re-emergence in town and assertions that her father's death was tied to a money laundering operation. Yes, she had suspected that her father's money issues might come back to haunt him. But was that the reason he was killed?

For now, she just wanted to get through the funeral reception in one piece. It was being held in the great room at the Edwardian home Eliza grew up in. She'd moved back there a year ago, hoping to provide Gabriel with a more stable environment by having his grandfather as a positive influence, knowing Gabriel's father was out of the picture.

Now that her father was gone, Eliza wondered if Will was up to the task of being a real father to Gabriel. Or would Will leave again once his assignment was over, shirking his responsibility to his son, if not to her?

They had left this unresolved once she had admitted to Will that Gabriel was his child. Will had honored her request that he not come to the funeral reception. Or try to speak to Gabriel till she'd had a chance to do so. Beyond that, Eliza was still trying to sort out her feelings about the one-time love of her life and if it was even possible to recapture those feelings, all things considered, with his deception and questionable motives, then and now. Or was it best not to let her guard down and, in the process, risk history repeating itself at her—and Gabriel's—expense?

Especially when Sergio was now in the picture and seemed like someone she might be able to establish a future with in time.

"Eliza…" The voice got her attention.

She looked at Karin Webb, a woman whom Eliza's father had recently been romantically involved with, before things ended abruptly between them earlier in the year. It had been rumored that she had turned her attention elsewhere, much to his chagrin. The attractive divorcée, was sixty-something, petite, and had a blonde bob.

Eliza offered her a respectful nod. "Thank you for coming."

Karin touched her round glasses and said, "How could I not have come? Your father was a wonderful man. Vincent will be sorely missed."

"Yes, he will be."

Karin patted her hand. "Feel free to call me anytime you like if you need to talk or..."

"I will." Eliza didn't see that happening anytime soon. Though she was curious as to whether or not Karin may have had any further insight into her father's money woes.

Karin's blue eyes crinkled as she smiled warmly. "Good."

Eliza politely excused herself to greet others. As she headed across the hardwood flooring amidst traditional furnishings, she was intercepted by Carter. He wrinkled his nose and muttered, "Looks like you're having about as much fun as I am."

"Funeral receptions aren't supposed to be fun," she reminded him.

"Now I see why." He glanced at Karin, who was shaking hands with other attendees as though on a campaign stop. "I can't believe she had the gall to show up."

Eliza didn't want to go there. "She had every right to, since she and Dad used to be an item."

"Until Dad decided he didn't need a two-timing woman in his life."

"Whatever happened between them was their business." Eliza chose to take the high road, knowing that it made little difference at this point.

"If you say so," Carter said, but clearly seemed to feel otherwise.

"What do you know about Dad's business dealings?" Eliza asked him, figuring this was as good a time as any to do so after learning about Will's investigation into money laundering in relation to their father's murder.

"No more than you do," her brother replied with a straight face. "Dad never talked to me much about what was going on in his professional life. Why do you ask?"

"Dad was having financial issues when he died," Eliza said candidly. "He went to a loan shark for money."

Carter cocked a brow. "I didn't realize things had reached that point."

"They had, unfortunately." She paused, then said to him in a conspiratorial undertone, "And it may have had something to do with his death—"

"What?" Carter's eyes narrowed. "And you know this how?"

Eliza hesitated, but felt that she couldn't and shouldn't keep bottled up inside what he needed to be aware of. "Will's back in town..."

"Since when?"

"He showed up at Dad's funeral."

Carter reacted with irritation. "What did he want? If he thinks he can just waltz back into your life—"

"Will is a Florida Department of Law Enforcement's Investigations special agent," Eliza told her brother without preamble. She watched the shock on his face before proceeding. "Without rehashing our past, this was apparently why he left five years ago. More importantly, it's why Will has returned. He seems to think that Dad's death is linked to a money laundering operation..."

"And you believe this?" Carter's thick brows knitted. "From a man who didn't have the guts to stick around—leaving you to raise his kid alone?"

"He never knew about Gabriel," she reiterated and assumed it would have made a difference on some level as to how things might have turned out between them.

"That's beside the point. Even so, you're better off without him—and Gabriel definitely is," Carter insisted. "The man clearly can't be trusted, no matter his lame excuses for then...or his accusations now." He licked his lips. "The police believe Dad's death was gang-related and that he wasn't the intended target. Unless we hear differently from them, I wouldn't put too much stock in whatever Will has to say—whether he's an FDLE agent or not..."

Eliza was somewhat taken aback by her brother's position regarding Will. Though they had hardly been confidantes when Will was around, she sensed even more animosity this time around. Was Carter really more concerned about what was in her best interests? Or his own, now that they were both left to deal with their father's estate?

"Hey," Eliza heard Carter's wife Kim utter, as she walked up to them.

"Hey." Eliza gazed at her, wondering how much she'd heard of their conversation.

But Kim cupped an arm beneath Carter's and appeared to be oblivious to it as she asked, "Everything okay?"

"Yeah, we're fine." Carter peered at Eliza. "Better get back to our guests. We'll talk more about this later."

"All right." Eliza nodded thoughtfully and saw them walk one way as she headed another while wondering if Will was truly onto something regarding the nature of her father's death. Or was Carter right to imply that Will was barking up the wrong tree—perhaps as a sort of back door way to reenter her life?

Beyond that, Eliza knew deep down inside that no matter which way the pendulum swung with Will, things were not going to work out between her and Sergio. The sooner she told him this, the sooner they could both be free to move on with their lives—while hopefully remaining friends.

* * *

Will was still thinking about his brief but eye-opening reunion with Eliza at the cemetery a couple of days ago as he sat in the conference room at the Golfton Hills Police Department. The joint task force members—which included local detectives, FDLE investigators, and FBI and DEA special agents—were discussing the money trail through shell companies of fentanyl and methamphetamine traffickers.

Will was floored with the knowledge that he was a father—and had been for nearly five years. The moment he first laid eyes on the young boy, Will knew instinctively that he was his. The similarities between their features made it all but a given. But he kept open the slimmest of possibilities that Gabriel just might be Sergio's son—till Eliza confirmed that her son was, in fact, Will's flesh and blood. He wanted to kick himself for bailing on Eliza and, unknowingly, their son—at a time when she likely needed him most.

His career had always come first—only this time, it had come at a high price. For he had lost years with Gabriel and being a father to him that every boy needed. Having been without his own father, who abandoned Will's mother when he was only a boy, he would never have allowed history to repeat itself had he known about his own son. Now, it was up to him—if Eliza would let nature take its rightful course—to try and make up for lost time and be the father that Gabriel deserved.

Whether or not this meant that Will could worm his way back into Eliza's life and bed remained to be seen. His read on her relationship with Sergio Hutchison was that it wasn't serious. But what if it was? That would mean that Eliza might well be lost to him for good.

Will had to believe that there was still a chance for them to right the ship before it was too late. Unfortunately, to do so meant not only being able to get beyond Eliza's involvement with Sergio—but more importantly, Will would have to win her over despite needing to come down hard on her brother, Carter Frost.

The money laundering investigation had pinpointed the ringleader as Eliza's own brother. He and his partners in crime had successfully been able to conduct a drug trafficking business in Golfton Hills and across the state, without Eliza being the wiser. Carter had used Vincent Frost's financial vulnerabilities to rope him into borrowing laundered money—not realizing it was coming from his own son.

By the time Vincent figured it out and tried to extricate himself from a bad situation, Carter had become far more interested in saving his own neck. Even if it came at the expense of his father. The shooter, Larry Narducci, a nineteen-year-old gang member, was picked up two hours ago and fingered Carter as the one who hired him to murder his own father. The evidence backed this allegation and left Will with no other choice than to place Eliza's brother under arrest.

While hoping that Eliza didn't hold that against him in the interest of solving the murder of her own father.

Will could only pray that they could get to Carter without his attempting to take Eliza or Gabriel hostage. Or use them as human shields as he sought to elude capture.

* * *

Eliza walked into the car dealership on Bogue Road and past the shiny new vehicles on display, straight toward Sergio's office. She had been on the fence as to whether to meet at a restaurant or another public setting, before settling on his place of business, wanting to give him the courtesy of a face-to-face chat rather than by phone or text as the right thing to do in ending things between them.

Unlike the way Will had managed to keep her totally confused with his silence and disappearing act five years ago.

Sergio looked surprised to see her when she walked into the huge office with high-end modern furnishings. "Eliza..."

She smiled thinly as he started to stand up from his desk. Lifting the palms of her hands, Eliza said earnestly, "Please, don't get up..."

"All right." Sergio did as she requested. "What's going on?"

Eliza wasted no time in getting right to the point. "I don't think it's going to work between us," she told him straightforwardly. "You're a great guy, Sergio, and Gabriel thinks you're cool—"

"But just not the right person for you," he said, as if resigned to this.

"Yes." She met his eyes. "I'd like to still be friends."

"I'd like that too," Sergio surprised her by saying. "I just want you to be happy, even if that happiness comes from the old friend you ran into at Vincent's funeral..."

Eliza colored as his intuition impressed her. She didn't know if things could ever go back to where they once were with Will, but at least she wanted to keep the door open to any possibilities. "Thank you," she told Sergio, her eyes twinkling, before heading home to her son.

* * *

When Carter stepped outside the house that Eliza lived in and Will had spent time at when they were together, the team waited till he approached the gold Acura Integra parked in the driveway—before converging upon him.

Carter looked shocked as he stared Will down. "You..."

Will held his gaze. "Yeah, it's been a minute, Carter." Having already removed the Smith and Wesson M&P40 M2.0 pistol from his shoulder holster, Will feared that Eliza's brother might be packing. He aimed the gun at the suspect and said in a harder tone of voice, "Carter Frost, you're under arrest for the murder of Vincent Frost—"

Carter furrowed his brow and dropped his lower lip with dismay. "You can't be serious?"

"I wish I weren't," Will said smoothly, "but I'm afraid I'm as serious as a heart attack, Carter. You killed your own damn father and will have to pay for it." He slapped the cuffs on the unarmed suspect, and Carter was led away by law enforcement without incident.

As though on cue, Will saw Eliza emerge from the house and race past others up to him, demanding an explanation. He hated to have to give it to her, but he also wouldn't have wanted it to come from anyone else. Other than maybe her brother Carter, who would at some point need to explain how he came to choose blood money over his own bloodline.

* * *

Eliza could barely believe that Carter had been responsible for the death of their father. If she hadn't been presented with the hard, cold evidence, she would never have thought him capable of such a barbaric action. Even if he didn't pull the trigger of the Colt Python .357 Magnum revolver that Will noted was the firearm used to kill her father, Carter may as well have pulled the trigger himself as the one who set the assassination in motion.

Almost as disturbing to Eliza was that Carter was involved in both drug trafficking and money laundering. How could she have not suspected any of it? Had Kim been privy to his criminality? Or had she been in denial?

No matter how Eliza sliced it, she had now lost her father and brother, in effect. And Gabriel no longer had a grandfather or an uncle, with Carter betraying him and her in the worst way and would undoubtedly be put away for a very long time.

But Gabriel did have a mother who loved him dearly and would do anything to help him deal with the losses that would be a major adjustment for a four-year-old.

And a father, who had reentered the picture in Eliza's world, for which she was still assessing its implications for both her and their son as the three of them looked toward the future and whatever possibilities it presented to them.

Eliza turned to her son as they walked hand in hand and barefoot down the beach toward the tall and handsome man standing there. Once they reached him, a smart grin playing on his square-jawed face, she met his eyes briefly, a glint of hope in her own—and then turned back to her child and said warmly, "Gabriel, there's someone I'd like to introduce you to..."

Fatal Reconnection

Rosamunde Remick scrolled through her inbox routinely on the laptop till her bold turquoise eyes landed on an email with the subject, Golfton Hills High School Ten-Year Reunion, and opened it to see the official invitation.

Ten years? Had it really been that long since she graduated from high school?

In her mind, Rosamunde whisked through the years that seemed like a blur. Graduated as an honor student at age eighteen, got her undergraduate degree from the University of Central Florida, then a master's from Yale University. Along the way, she got involved with more than one wrong man, including one who fathered her only child. She then moved a number of times around the country and abroad before settling into her current Spanish Colonial home in the French Quarter in New Orleans, Louisiana, where she had become a bestselling romantic suspense author.

All in all, I suppose my life could be a lot worse at age twenty-eight, Rosamunde thought honestly as she sat on the Queen Anne chair in her living room, where she was surrounded by antique furniture. The beamed ceiling, original bay windows, and parquet hardwood flooring gave the place the charm she'd wanted since purchasing it three years ago.

Rosamunde mused briefly about the little girl she'd reluctantly decided would be better off being raised by stable parents rather than a struggling nineteen-year-old college student once the father had turned his back on both of them. She had prayed often that her daughter had a good life with a family who loved her as much as Rosamunde knew she would have had the right circumstances presented themselves at the time.

She blinked back tears and turned her thoughts back to the class reunion. It was being held at the Golfton Hills Hotel on Willman Lane on Saturday, August 24th. That was three weeks and several states away in Golfton Hills, Florida. She hadn't been to a single reunion. At first, it was because she hadn't had any reason in particular for wanting to see people whom she hadn't kept in touch with. Later, her life had become too busy for trips down a memory lane that was mostly forgettable.

Who am I kidding? Rosamunde asked herself. There was only one reason to ever go—or not. Or should she say one person?

She brushed an errant lock of her stylishly cut, shoulder-length blonde hair with brown highlights from her brow as her mind homed in on the man who once made Rosamunde's heart flutter wildly.

Aiden Wolf was her first love and quite possibly the only man she'd ever loved from deep within her soul. Handsome beyond words and so full of life and ambition, she couldn't help but fall hard for him. But their budding high school romance ended when they graduated—both deciding to attend separate universities and establish themselves in life apart from each other and the teenage love they had professed for one another.

As far as Rosamunde knew, Aiden never made it back to the five-year class reunion. Maybe he wouldn't show up at this one, either. Not that she would blame him one bit. Why go back to where it all began when, presumably, there was so much ahead to look forward to for both of them?

Rosamunde's reverie was broken when she heard the chime of her cell phone. She grabbed it from beside her on the chair and saw the video caller was Beatrice Neeson, her best friend since high school when both were cheerleaders. She anticipated why Beatrice was calling as Rosamunde accepted the chat request.

"Hey." Rosamunde smiled as she saw Beatrice appear on the screen. African American and gorgeous with big brown eyes and long brunette hair styled in Senegalese twists, she was still as slender as she was in their high school days. As was Rosamunde. Beatrice lived in Los Angeles, where she was a successful fashion model and social media influencer, and seemed to have a different romantic partner every other month.

"Did you get the invitation to the class reunion?" Beatrice asked her expectantly.

"I was just looking at it," Rosamunde confessed.

"So, are you going? Please say yes."

"I really haven't had time to think about it," Rosamunde lied. "I'm just so busy these days between working on my new novel, planning the next book tour—"

"Oh please..." Beatrice gave an exaggerated sigh. "We're all busy, girlfriend. Still, I think I'm going to go."

Rosamunde cocked a brow. "Really?"

"Yeah. I think it would be fun to hang out with the old crowd for a bit of fun and bragging about my life these days," she said immodestly. "But I'd like it even more if you were there."

I'll bet you would, Rosamunde thought. So they could both live to regret it. Misery loved company and all that. "Let me think about it."

"What's there to think about?" Beatrice persisted. "It's our ten-year class reunion. We need to be there. Maybe this will give you some added incentive..." she said with a catch to her voice. "It's been rumored that your ex-boyfriend, Aiden, might actually show up..."

"Oh really?" Rosamunde's lashes fluttered at the prospect, which, honestly, she would have to see to believe. Though they had not stayed in touch through the years, she had checked him out from time to time on social media. Last she knew, Aiden was living in Atlanta, where he was an entrepreneur and apparently still single. She wondered how that was even possible while fantasizing that he was waiting to reconnect with the one who got away. Herself. *Dream on*, she mused, coming back down to earth.

"Why not?" Beatrice said. "Maybe he thinks the time is right, too. Or maybe he just wants to step away from his life and go back to a simpler time when the only thing on his mind was you—"

"I doubt that." Rosamunde colored while remembering how he made her feel in what seemed like so many years ago. But she wasn't eighteen anymore, and neither was he. There was no going back for either of them, even with all the wishes in the world. How could there be?

"Hey, don't underestimate chemistry," Beatrice argued. "It never dies, and you two definitely had it—no matter what twists and turns your lives have taken since then."

"Hmm…" Rosamunde couldn't deny that. Even if she wanted to try and forget. But they did break up for a reason. Could either of them so easily toss that away and rekindle what they chose to turn their backs on a decade ago?

"We won't know one way or the other unless we go—" Beatrice kept the pressure on. "Just say you'll go!"

"Okay, okay, let's do this," Rosamunde relented.

"Cool." Beatrice's face lit up. "You won't regret it."

"If I do, you'll be the one I blame," she joked.

Beatrice chuckled. "Duly noted."

After Beatrice ended the call, Rosamunde looked again at the invitation. She surprised herself by getting goosebumps at the mere prospect of seeing Aiden Wolf in familiar territory. Even if it was too much to expect that they might magically reconnect and bring all the feelings they had for each other as teenagers back into the fold, it didn't mean they couldn't open up a new chapter of camaraderie. Making it all worthwhile. Right?

* * *

Aiden Wolf sat at his ergonomic desk on the twenty-fifth floor of the office tower on Peachtree Street in midtown Atlanta, a window wall offering a nice view of the landscape. The owner of a string of upscale restaurants across the city, he was admittedly enjoying the good life, as he had always envisioned would be the case when graduating from Golfton Hills High School a decade ago and then getting his degree in marketing from Florida State University three years later.

The one thing missing in his life at twenty-eight and a half was someone to share this with. He'd had a few flings over the years, but nothing that stuck. Certainly not like with his high school sweetheart, Rosamunde Remick.

They sizzled when they were together their junior and senior years, but chose to go their separate ways, not trusting enough that what they had could survive in the real world. Or maybe part of them wanted to see what—or who—else was out there.

Now Aiden wondered if the right person for him had been staring him in the face a decade ago—only to let her slip from his grasp for another man to discover and cherish. *Maybe Rosamunde and I should have tried harder to stay together*, Aiden thought. Or was he speaking only for himself? It wasn't for him to say, whether or not she had any regrets that they broke up. After all, it was a mutual thing, and she may have gone on to have a happy life on the personal front. Though they had not kept in touch since high school, he'd heard through the grapevine that Rosamunde had never been married. Beyond that, he'd discovered a few years back that she had become a bestselling author and actually read a couple of her novels as a way to keep tabs on what she was up to from afar. In looking at her photograph on the back of books and Rosamunde's website, it was obvious to him that she was still as gorgeous as ever.

Aiden leaned his tall and firm frame back against the leather swivel executive chair and homed in with deep blue eyes on his iPad at the invitation to his high school's ten-year class reunion. He had it on good authority that Rosamunde would be attending. Along with her old high school bestie, Beatrice Neeson.

Though his first instinct had been to pass on the invite, just as he had the one-year and five-year reunions, this time around Aiden felt inspired to attend. He needed to see Rosamunde again in a comfortable space in their hometown to determine if the spark they had was still there. Or realize, once and for all, that there was no turning back the clock. No matter how appealing it was to have a second chance with the only woman Aiden had never been able to get out of his system.

What do I have to lose? he asked himself while believing, on the other hand, that he potentially had everything to gain if things were to click again with Rosamunde.

Aiden went online to make airline and hotel reservations that would bring him back to Golfton Hills and, hopefully, face-to-face with Rosamunde Remick.

* * *

With less than two weeks to go till the class reunion, Rosamunde flew to New York to meet with her editor and now close friend, Helen Navarro. Helen was in her late forties, Cuban American and petite, with a blonde layered bob and brown eyes behind horn-shaped glasses.

"The sales of your last book have been solid," Helen pointed out as they sat in upholstered armchairs by a large picture window in the associate editor's office.

"That's great!" Rosamunde beamed, always happy to hear that her hard-fought efforts as a writer had paid off.

"But, still...not as good as your previous book, I'm afraid," Helen said, touching her glasses.

The smile vanished from Rosamunde's face. She should have sensed there was a catch to this news. "So do I need to do more book tours, virtual and in person, work harder on getting readers to sign up for my newsletter, or what?" *Surely, she's not suggesting the quality of my writing is slipping?* Rosamunde thought with dread.

"That might be something to consider down the line, though the publisher is actually thinking of cutting back on in-person book tours—as a cost-cutting measure in today's economically strapped times." Helen tasted her cappuccino. "Maybe some fresh ideas to revitalize your storylines would do the trick."

"I can work on that," she readily agreed.

"Good." Helen leaned forward. "Perhaps this class reunion you have coming up might serve as the inspiration for some romantic suspense plots or subplots..."

"You think?" Rosamunde arched a brow while imagining she would hear one or two stories that might make for interesting frameworks for future novels.

"Why not? I know from my own experience in attending high school and college class reunions that people have some wild stories they're only too happy to share—especially once they have a few drinks in them."

Rosamunde laughed. "I'll keep that in mind."

"So, are you looking forward to seeing your old boyfriend, or what?" Helen asked directly.

Rosamunde tasted her latte musingly. "Yes, I think I am," she told her flatly, even if she had no expectations of reuniting with Aiden, who was now confirmed as being an attendee at the class reunion. "It should be fun to catch up with him after ten years."

"If you play your cards right," Helen told her with a wicked grin, "you might be able to rekindle those old feelings and whatever might come after that."

Rosamunde blushed. "Not much of a gambler, I'm afraid. As for rekindling a past romance, that rarely works out in real life. We'll see how things go." She wasn't closing any doors but was wise enough not to open any prematurely, at risk of having her heart broken. Again.

Helen flashed a soft smile, seemingly content to leave it there while keeping her own focus on whatever Rosamunde could do to come away from the experience refreshed and ready to work hard on her next novel.

* * *

Aiden studied the list of class reunion attendees as he nursed the Bloody Mary that he'd grown a predilection for through the years while sitting by his lonesome at the Limmy Bar in Downtown Atlanta on Edgewood Avenue.

He saw a few names that rang a bell—some that he had stayed in contact with since high school.

The name that caught his eye was Rosamunde Remick, confirming what he had already ascertained. A slow smile spread across Aiden's mouth. Thoughts of their long-ago romance, when it was all fresh and exciting, flooded his head. Truthfully, he'd never really wanted things to end between them. But life had other plans, and the rest was history.

Wasn't history always repeating itself?

Or was it more often than not just a one-off that had little chance of being any more successful a second time around than the first?

He was more than ready to test the theory. Assuming Rosamunde was up to playing ball and allowing the chips to fall where they may. Could be that reconnecting after ten years and living happily thereafter was the way it was meant to be. If so, it was up to them to take the opportunity and run with it.

Aiden finished off his drink and resisted the urge for another one. Instead, he ran long fingers through his dark, medium textured hair with tapered sides before getting up and leaving.

* * *

Arriving in Golfton Hills the day before the class reunion, Rosamunde was happy to spend it hanging out with Beatrice. They sat at a table in Lily's Café on Brussels Avenue, where they'd spent so much time while in high school.

"This place hasn't changed a bit," Beatrice remarked, sipping on iced coffee.

"True," Rosamunde had to agree. She stuck a fork in her Greek salad and eyed her attractive friend. "Not to say that we've changed much either—except for the better."

"Ditto!" Beatrice flashed her teeth. "So, do you think Aiden is here?"

"I don't know." Rosamunde felt butterflies in her stomach as she mused about her ex-boyfriend. "If so, I haven't run into him yet at the hotel—assuming he's staying there for the reunion." She recalled that his mother lived in Golfton Hills a decade ago, as had her own parents before they relocated to the Florida Keys.

"Have you thought about what you want to say to him?" Beatrice asked while lifting her veggie wrap.

"Hi," Rosamunde quipped and chuckled. "Seriously, I'll play it by ear. Just as I'm sure you will if your old boyfriend Lester Hornsby shows up."

"Point taken." Beatrice laughed. "Not exactly the same, though. What Lester and I had was only puppy love, if that. You and Aiden went well beyond that—even if you were too young at the time to process it properly."

Here's a chance to see if it's still there to start up again."

Rosamunde chuckled. "Slow down, Ms. Matchmaker. Let's not get ahead of ourselves. Right now, I just want to make the most of reuniting with our class—including Aiden—and go from there."

"Got it," Beatrice said. "No pressure."

"None," Rosamunde agreed, even if, for some reason, she did feel pressure on some level to get through the weekend in one mental piece, whichever way the pendulum swung where it concerned Aiden.

* * *

After paying his mother a visit on the day the class reunion was to commence and meeting the new man in her life these days, Aiden was happy that she seemed happy. As a single mom—having lost his father to a drunk driver early in the marriage—her life had seemed anything but happy when Aiden was growing up, with her working two jobs and still struggling to make ends meet. Maybe now things were starting to turn around in her life.

Aiden invited his mother and her partner to visit him in Atlanta, promising to show them a good time every step of the way.

He drove his rented red Mitsubishi Outlander Sport to the Golfton Hills Club to meet up with a couple of old friends for drinks. As they joked about old times and commiserated about the ups and downs since then, they drank tequila shots. When chatting about failed relationships and future prospects, or the lack thereof, more shots of alcohol followed.

By the time he was ready to head back to the Golfton Hills Hotel—where he had checked in that morning for his eagerly awaited opportunity to see Rosamunde again at the class reunion—Aiden had gulped down a couple of Bloody Marys, adding to the alcohol already in his system from the tequila shots. He left the bar and stumbled to his vehicle before climbing inside and taking a moment to clear his head.

Aiden started the car and drove off, Rosamunde occupying his thoughts as he wondered if it was even possible that they could somehow find their way back to each other ten years later. Or was that asking too much with so much time having passed and the different directions their lives had taken since?

* * *

At Beatrice's prompting, Rosamunde acquiesced and decided to do some last-minute shopping at the Golfton Hills Mall on Frandower Avenue for outfits to make an entrance at the high school reunion.

"What do you think?" Beatrice asked as she showed off a pink strapless bow-bodice evening gown she had tried on to go with strappy dress sandals.

"Wow!" Rosamunde marveled at the gown on her amazing slender frame. "What's not to think? You look gorgeous."

"Thanks." Beatrice was all smiles. "Your turn."

Rosamunde went through a few dresses, ultimately choosing a fuchsia off-the-shoulder cocktail dress that flattered her figure and went well with her designer evening pumps. "How do I look?" she asked her friend enthusiastically.

"Absolutely fabulous." Beatrice declared. "You'll have them eating out of your hands. Or at least one person, in particular."

Rosamunde chuckled. "I'll settle for the two of us looking amazing when we enter the ballroom."

Beatrice smiled. "In that case, we've already won the battle before the reunion begins in earnest."

"So, let's do this and show everyone who we've become over the past decade," Rosamunde tossed at her, as they changed back into their original clothes and paid for the items.

They headed for the hotel in the white Toyota Corolla that Beatrice rented. Rosamunde sat in the passenger seat, each caught up in their own thoughts while she took in the sights of the town Rosamunde once called home. *So familiar, yet so much like foreign territory in some respects,* she told herself. She wondered which might prove to be truer when she had the chance to chat with Aiden. Would it be more for old times' sake? Or the possibilities of good times ahead?

Just as Rosamunde turned her head to glance at Beatrice behind the wheel as they drove down Golfton Hills Road and across the intersection of Terry Street, with the light green, Rosamunde barely had time to scream as the Toyota was T-boned on the driver's side by a red SUV.

Suddenly, everything went black.

* * *

When she opened her eyes, Rosamunde felt groggy and in discomfort. For an instant, she wasn't quite sure where she was or how she got there. Then, it all began to come back. She'd been in a car accident after someone rammed into Beatrice's vehicle.

As though on cue, Rosamunde heard a deep voice say, "She's awake..."

Turning her head with some effort, Rosamunde gazed first at a very tall and lanky man in his thirties, with a brown masculine haircut, wearing a dark blue suit. She shifted her eyes to the slender female beside him. Wearing a white lab coat, she was forty-something with a crimson feathered pixie and rectangle eyeglasses.

With a dry throat, Rosamunde swallowed thickly and asked her for clarification, "Where am I?"

The woman regarded her ill at ease and said, "You're in Golfton Hills General Hospital. I'm Dr. Kressley. Do you remember what happened...?"

Rosamunde nodded. "We were in the car...and then someone hit us..."

"That's right," Dr. Kressley said evenly. "It happened three hours ago. You were very fortunate to come away from it with only a concussion, bruised ribs, and a few cuts."

Rosamunde was grateful to be alive, as would anyone who had been T-boned. But what about Beatrice and the driver of the other car? How badly were they hurt?

Rosamunde eyed the doctor and asked tentatively, "Where's my friend, Beatrice Neeson?"

Dr. Kressley glanced at the man in the room and back to her before responding in a contrite tone of voice, "I'm sorry to have to tell you that Ms.

Neeson suffered very serious injuries." She paused. "I'm afraid she didn't make it..."

Rosamunde's heart sank. Beatrice dead? This couldn't be happening. As she tried to process the unthinkable—and at a time in Beatrice's life where she was at the top of her game on various levels—Rosamunde had to ask, "What about the other driver?"

The doctor deferred this to the man beside her. He furrowed his brow, took a step toward the bed, and said equably, "I'm Detective Vogel of the Golfton Hills PD. The other driver is recovering in another room from minor injuries. He's being charged with DUI manslaughter and vehicular homicide, along with additional charges—when it was determined that he had a blood alcohol level well above Florida's legal limit. The accident was captured on surveillance video."

Rosamunde felt tears flow down her cheeks as she thought about the class reunion being totally ruined. Certainly, for her. And even more for Beatrice. She hated to think that her best friend's precious life had been snuffed out so suddenly. Meaning Beatrice would never again have the opportunity to attend any more high school reunions, marry, and finally settle down, have kids, or anything else that came with living a long and fulfilling life.

And why? Because some jerk decided to drink and drive. Only to survive himself. His paying the price for taking away Beatrice's life—and effectively ending his own—by going to prison gave Rosamunde some solace. But not nearly enough to compensate for the tremendous loss she was left to deal with.

Rosamunde fixed the detective's face and asked curiously, though unsure if he would answer, "What's the other driver's name?"

Detective Vogel ran a hand across his mouth and, after a moment or two, looked her right in the eye and responded, "Aiden Wolf. From what we've gathered, he was in town to attend a high school reunion..."

Predisposed to Kill

T he old woman died in the Golfton Hills Nursing Home on Plakerville Road under what could best be described as suspicious circumstances. She choked to death while in bed. There was some indication that she may have been helped to her demise.

Or was frightened to the point of dying.

I pondered this as I watched the dead woman's body being carted away by the medical examiner.

Now, why would someone want to off an eighty-four-year-old who already had one foot in the grave? I had to ask myself, as a homicide detective for the Golfton Hills Police Department.

The first thing that came to mind regarding the motivation for murdering the woman was the best reason around: money. Elderly folks were perfect prey for violent con artists and property predators, who view them as easy marks to take advantage of and don't have many qualms about making sure no one's left to squeal on them once they rid the victims of their entire life's savings.

In that vein, I also had to at least consider the bloodline angle as an equally strong possibility—especially in this case. It wouldn't be the first time that family greed took center stage when it became more lucrative to expedite grandma's death when it seemed to take way too long for it to occur naturally.

Trouble was, as far as I could tell, the dead woman named Betty Huffman was not up to her neck in riches. Far from it. Records indicated she lived on a fixed income after years as a pediatric nurse. Since entering the nursing home, the old woman had juggled Social Security and a modest pension as her sole means of support.

Without an obvious financial incentive, I knew I had an intriguing investigation on my hands. So much for hoping to take it nice and easy on this one, in what was to be my last case before going into retirement at the relatively young age of fifty-seven. Not that I was ready to be put out to pasture, per se, after logging in more than thirty years of my life with the force. But cutbacks in the department's budget and incentives to walk away, while more or less being told that my services would no longer be needed, gave me all the motivation I needed as a widow—still mourning the death of my cop husband, Manuel Elizondo, who died in the line of duty more than a decade ago—to believe that maybe the time had come to hand in my badge.

Though not just yet.

There was still Betty Huffman's disturbing death to deal with.

I trained my big brown Latina eyes on the long-term care bed where she had spent much of the last days of her life. The bedding was crumpled and smelled of disinfectant, which did little to mask the pungent mixture of urine, vomit, and blood. I wondered exactly how things unfolded during the last moments of the dead woman's life.

I left the room, my five-foot-eight-inch frame on the slender side in detective casual attire and comfortable flats. In the corridor, I ran a hand through my choppy blonde hair in a pixie cut and tracked down the director of the nursing home.

Ruth Windom was about forty-five and a little on the heavy side, with short auburn hair. I flashed my identification at her that read Homicide Detective Mariah Elizondo, voiced this routinely, and asked in earnest, "What can you tell me about Betty Huffman?"

Ruth touched her square eyeglasses, pursed her lips, and replied bluntly, "To be perfectly honest, Detective Elizondo, though she was of relatively sound mind, Betty was not the easiest resident we've ever had here. Sometimes, she had fits and had to be sedated. Other times, she seemed to think she owned the place, barking out orders left and right like a four-star general." As if she realized that her comments might be misconstrued, Ruth turned a smile and said in a nicer tone, "But she was still like family to all of us here and will be missed—"

"Not by everyone," I begged to differ respectfully. "It appears as if Betty Huffman was murdered."

"I get that." Ruth's brow creased. "But it's hard to digest. I mean, why would anyone want to kill her?"

"I was hoping you might be able to tell me that," I turned the onus back on the director. "Someone decided Ms. Huffman was better off dead. Any idea who that might be?"

Ruth batted her lashes. "None whatsoever," she said firmly. "Certainly, no one on staff would do such a thing."

Had I really expected her to say differently at this point? She was trying to cover for the nursing home, its reputation, and any potential criminal or financial liability for the death. But how far was she willing to go to possibly protect someone? Would she knowingly withhold information on a killer?

"How often was the patient checked on?"

"Every hour," she said without hesitation. "Even less than that, if needed."

"I'll need a list of all the employees," I told her evenly. "Especially those who were on duty yesterday."

"No problem." She wrung her hands. "I can have that for you later this afternoon."

"Good." I glanced at my notepad, where I'd scribbled a few things that needed to be addressed. "Did Betty Huffman have any family?"

"Just a daughter and grandson, I believe," Ruth answered.

"How often did they visit her?"

"The daughter never visited Betty," she said, as if a mortal sin. "The grandson only visited sporadically and not very recently."

Sounds like a close-knit family, I thought sarcastically, and asked, "Did Ms. Huffman have *any* visitors lately?"

Ruth mused. "Not that I recall. She seemed to have no friends to speak of, aside from other residents." She gave a loud nasal sigh. "I'd have to double-check that."

"Please do." I favored the director with a hard stare. "Apparently, someone did pay Betty Huffman a visit during the night and—unless it's proven otherwise—killed her." I let that sink in, then added candidly, "If that someone didn't come from inside, then he or she came from outside..." I was still on the fence that it could go either way at this stage.

As if for the first time, Ruth appeared shaken at the notion and was thoughtful.

I left the nursing home, admittedly still with more questions than answers. Just another day in the life of a detective on her last leg, so to speak, as far as the police department powers that be. That being the case, I was determined to go out with a bang.

If only for the sake of allowing Betty Huffman to rest in peace, by finding out how her life came to an end and why.

* * *

The autopsy on Betty Huffman was performed that afternoon. I went to the Corall County Medical Examiner and Coroner's office to learn the official cause of death. The partially covered body was still on the autopsy table as I stood across from the medical examiner, Doctor Len Yamamoto. He was a razor-thin Asian man in his early forties with black hair in a faux hawk style.

"So, what do we have?" I asked eagerly.

Yamamoto surveyed the deceased woman's remains. "Betty Huffman died from strangulation," he said without preamble. "Her windpipe was crushed in the process, probably by the killer's bare hands. Or, in other words, we're talking about a homicide here."

I nodded glumly. "Any other injuries?"

"There was some bruising about the face on the right side," Yamamoto explained, demonstrating this with his nitrile gloved hand. "As if she had been punched with a fist. Contusions also appear on her wrists and legs... likely from attempting to resist her attacker."

"Was she sexually assaulted?" I almost hated to ask, but I had no choice but to cover all the bases. It seemed insane to imagine that anyone would rape someone her age. But this was not unfathomable, unfortunately.

"No," Yamamoto stated. "There was no indication that she suffered from any type of sexual trauma."

I studied the corpse and then looked at Yamamoto's face curiously. "So, what's your take on this, Doc? Why would someone kill her? Bottom line?"

Yamamoto's bushy brows contemplated this, and he responded evasively, "I'm not a psychologist, Detective, so I can't really get into the head of the killer." But he chose to do so anyway. "However, if I were to take a stab at it, my guess is this was personal."

"You think so?" I pressed him.

"Seems to fit with the autopsy and circumstances of her death," Yamamoto argued. "The decedent appeared to have been killed by someone who must have hated her very much, for whatever reason. Or, at the very least, had an intense dislike—"

An intense dislike for old women in general? I mused. Or this one, in particular?

* * *

What was undoubtedly the hardest part of my job was notifying next of kin of one's death. Unfortunately, this came with the territory. The address I had been given for Jackie Huffman, Betty Huffman's daughter, was an apartment building on Wentington Street.

Why hadn't she visited her mother at the nursing home? I couldn't help but wonder about this as I drove my duty vehicle, a white Dodge Charger Pursuit. Would her death come as a total surprise? Or did the daughter simply not give a damn about Betty languishing in a nursing home?

I arrived at the Ferrine Apartments in a seedy part of the city, parked, and climbed three flights of stairs before reaching apartment 326.

A couple of knocks on the door went unanswered, though I could hear loud music inside the apartment. I was about to leave my card with a note to call me as soon as possible, when the door opened—bringing with it the distinct sickly-sweet scent of marijuana emanating from inside.

A stocky man in his mid-fifties with a graying-brown rocker shag haircut stood there, eyeing me suspiciously. "Yeah?"

"I'm looking for Jackie Huffman," I told him, wondering if I could have been given the wrong address. "I was told she lived here."

"What do you want with her?" he demanded.

"It's police business." I showed my I.D. "Is she home?"

His eyelids closed, as if they'd been pulled down like a window shade, before opening again, when he sighed and said bleakly, "She was killed last night—"

For a moment, I almost thought he was referring to Jackie's mother, Betty Huffman. "What?"

"She's dead," he reiterated, peering at me.

"How?" I asked curiously.

He shrugged. "The police haven't told me nothin', other than she was murdered."

Murdered?

The word admittedly gave me a start. That old saying, like mother, like daughter, came to mind, giving it a whole new and disturbing meaning. How was she murdered? By whom?

Was it entirely coincidental? Or was there a connection between the two homicides?

I gave the man blocking the doorway like a security guard might at a nightclub, the benefit of a hard stare, asking him, "What's your name?"

"Roy Brown."

"Mind my asking, Roy, what your relationship is...was...to Jackie Huffman?"

"We lived together," Brown said matter-of-factly. He added, as if to leave no doubt, "I was her boyfriend." A scowl grew on his face. "Now, what the hell type of police business did you need to talk to Jackie about—if you really didn't know she was dead?"

It was a fair question under the circumstances. And one I almost hated to answer in compounding the situation. But he did ask.

"I came to inform Jackie that her mother, Betty Huffman, was the victim of a homicide also last night," I responded straightforwardly, watching his stunned reaction. "Guess I came a day too late..."

Once he recovered, Brown muttered, "Mother?" He rubbed his nose. "Didn't know she had one. At least not someone that Jackie ever talked about."

"Maybe she had her reasons for that..." I gave the dead daughter the benefit of the doubt. But it made me think about the grandson that Ruth Windom indicated that Betty Huffman had. "Did Jackie have any children?" I asked the man she lived with, knowing that Betty might have had other offspring that Ruth knew nothing about.

Brown shrugged. "Not that I know of. But she never talked much about her background, and I never asked. Maybe I should have..." He scratched his jaw thoughtfully. "Why do you ask?"

"Just part of the routine investigation," I answered elusively.

He met my eyes. "So, did someone have it out for both Jackie and the mother, or what?"

"That's something I definitely intend to find out," I answered, while wondering just where this was headed and whether or not I might find myself needing to pay Roy Brown another visit.

* * *

I headed to the police department, wondering what the chances were that Betty and Jackie Huffman would both be killed on the same night. Unless the deaths were anything but disconnected.

My mind wandered to my late husband, Manuel, whose untimely death over ten years ago as a police officer—after being shot at point-blank range while confronting a fugitive during a traffic stop—still played on my emotions to this day. I wouldn't wish that kind of gut-wrenching pain on anyone.

Double the pain was even worse.

Yet, this was precisely what Betty's grandson would have to deal with. Assuming he didn't already know that she and presumably his mother, Jackie Huffman, were dead.

Detective Stephen Heinle was sitting at his desk, piled high with police reports, when I walked up to the cubicle. Heinle was in his mid-forties, thickly built, and had short brown hair in a comb-over style with a deep part on the left side.

He looked up at me inquisitively. "What's up?"

"What can you tell me about Jackie Huffman? I understand she was killed last night..." And I had learned that the case had been assigned to him.

Heinle cocked a crooked brow. "That's right. A woman by that name was D.O.A. at Golfton Hills General last night. So, what's your interest?"

"Her eighty-four-year-old mother, Betty Huffman, was found murdered in a nursing home this morning—having been killed the night before."

"That's odd." Heinle contorted his face. "You think the two are somehow connected?" he questioned.

"Maybe." That was the best I could offer at this point. "How did Jackie Huffman die?"

Heinle riffled through some notes on his desk like a deck of cards, before coming up with what he was looking for. "The fifty-two-year-old victim was found in a convenience store parking lot, where she apparently was dumped. According to the preliminary autopsy report, Jackie Huffman was suffocated to death." He sighed. "How did the mother die?"

"Strangulation." I leaned against the side of the desk, while continuing to stand.

"You got a suspect?"

"Not yet," I told him. "Just a gut feeling."

"What is it?"

I paused before replying in earnest, "That the two are, in fact, connected, and the killer is almost certainly trying to tell us something—"

Heinle leaned forward. "Such as...?"

"Haven't figured that out yet," I admitted reluctantly, not quite ready to step out on any limbs just yet. "Once I locate the grandson of Betty Huffman— Jason Sean Huffman, according to records from the nursing home—and, I suspect, the son of Jackie Huffman, perhaps he can supply some answers— assuming he's still alive..."

"You're saying you think someone may have gone after *three* generations in the family?" Heinle's mouth hung open as if trying to digest this notion.

I contemplated this for a long moment and responded bluntly, "I'm saying someone *inside* the family may have done this."

Heinle slanted me a dubious look. "So you think this guy did in his own mother and grandmother?"

I found myself equivocating for some reason. "Someone sure as hell did," I offered. "Wouldn't be the first time that family violence went way too far. My working theory is that the killer of both women hits very close to home, till proven otherwise."

"There was no indication that Jackie Huffman was robbed," Heinle remarked. "Her purse appeared to have been left untouched. And no witnesses to speak of, though we're looking into surveillance cameras at and around the location where the deceased was discovered..."

Betty Huffman was also killed without the killer being seen, I considered. Or at least where the perpetrator could be identified as such.

Was the unsub that clever? Or just damn lucky? Maybe a combination of the two, I was starting to believe.

* * *

I was at my own desk to see what I could find out about Jason Sean Huffman. It didn't take long to make some interesting discoveries.

White male, age thirty-five, six feet, two inches in height, with an arrest record a mile long for everything from drug-related offenses to identity theft to assault to fraud to disorderly conduct.

Huffman had been known to use at least one alias: Joel Sackhoff.

Digging deeper, I learned that Huffman had twice been committed to a psychiatric institution and had a checkered life as far as employment, working mostly in low-paying jobs.

The last known address for Jason Huffman was on Pier Lane. I headed over there to pay him a visit and inform him of the deaths of his mother and grandmother, assuming he wasn't already privy to this.

The stone cottage had a couple of palm trees in the front, along with overgrown weeds. A gray Volkswagen Atlas was parked in the driveway.

Sitting on the front porch was an attractive, slender, twenty-something African American woman with blonde box braids. I approached her, showed my ID, and said, "I'm looking for Jason Huffman."

She rolled her big brown eyes. "He's not here."

"And your name?"

"Lenora Watson."

"Do you know where I can find him, Lenora?"

"I wish," she muttered. "Jason took off over a month ago and left me to deal with paying the bills for this place. Haven't seen him since."

"So, you two were together?" I asked to be sure.

"Yeah, till he decided he could do better." She frowned. "Or whatever."

I had no reason to believe she was covering for Huffman. Or hiding him, at the moment. I handed her my card and said, "If he happens to show up, give me a call. It's important."

Lenora nodded, glancing at the card. "Is he in trouble?"

"That's still to be determined," I told her candidly while sensing that Huffman could well be trouble himself. But I needed to locate him to determine if he was a victim of a double tragedy. Or the perpetrator of such.

* * *

With Jason Huffman missing, I headed back to the Golfton Hills Nursing Home for some follow-up questions. Though he had apparently only visited Betty Huffman sporadically, maybe someone there had information on her grandson that could lead me in the right direction to discover his whereabouts.

Beyond the specter of Jason Huffman being a possible killer, I had to consider that as a member of the Huffman family, he, too, could have been a victim of foul play.

Inside the nursing home, residents were being wheeled about, or aided by use of a cane or walker by staff that genuinely seemed to give a damn. Something I'd want to feel, were I ever unable to care for myself at some stage, with retirement looming.

I'd been informed by Ruth Windom that the staff member on duty yesterday and caring for Betty Huffman was head nurse Vera Gallo. She was pointed out to me when leaving a patient's room.

In her early forties and of medium build, Vera had light blonde hair in a blunt cut. I showed my badge to her and said, "Detective Elizondo. I understand that you were on duty when Betty Huffman died?"

"That's right, I was," Vera acknowledged. "Such a tragedy."

"Yes, it was," I agreed.

"How can I be of assistance to you, Detective?"

"Did you see or hear anything unusual during your rounds last night, as it related to Ms. Huffman?"

"Not really," Vera claimed. "When I last checked on Betty, she seemed fine." She paused. "There were no signs of anxiety...or danger—"

"I'd like to take another look at her room," I told the nurse.

"Not a problem," she said. "Follow me."

We walked side by side down a narrow hallway, and I asked, "Who was present when it was discovered that Betty Huffman was dead?"

"I was," Vera answered, "along with one of the orderlies."

"How did you come to know that something was wrong with her?"

"It was time to check on Betty. That's when I noticed that she was unresponsive."

We entered the room. The bedding had been changed, and everything was cleaned, as if the previous occupant's stay had been erased from memory in preparation for the next patient's stay.

I felt a knot in my stomach, hating to think that Betty Huffman was now dead and damn near buried and, apparently, there was no one to mourn her.

With the possible exception of her grandson, Jason.

I regarded Nurse Gallo with a sideways glance. "So, someone should have seen a stranger lurking in the halls, given these regular visits to patients' rooms?"

"Yes, it would seem so," Vera voiced hesitantly. "But it doesn't mean an outsider couldn't have slipped into Betty's room without staff being the wiser...and killed her—"

"True," I conceded. My eyes narrowed thoughtfully at the nurse. "Unless Betty's killer was someone who worked here and knew exactly when she would be unattended."

Vera reacted defensively. "The staff here is carefully screened," she insisted. "It had to be a visitor that came in and—"

"Doesn't say too much about your security, does it?" I scoffed, cutting her off.

She glared at me. "We're not an armed guard camp here, Detective Elizondo! And we do not have a staff large enough to be with all patients at all times." She took a deep breath. "Whoever went after Betty could well have done the same to a patient at any other nursing home in town."

I conceded as much. Problem was, I didn't believe for one instant that this was a random attack. Or just for kicks. My sense was that Betty Huffman had been targeted by her killer.

I walked to the window of the first-floor room. It was halfway open. Undoubtedly to relieve the stuffiness inside. The screen, I noted, was sticking out in one corner, as if it had been removed altogether recently and put back on hastily and sloppily.

Had the killer come in through the window? And escaped the same way? Unnoticed like a homicidal thief in the night?

Nurse Gallo had remained at the foot of the bed ever since we entered the room, almost as if to go any further would kill her. I faced her and asked curiously, "What can you tell me about the orderly who came into the room with you to discover Betty was dead?"

Vera stared at the question and shrugged. "Not much, I'm afraid. Just an average guy. He's worked here for a few weeks and had no problems that I'm aware of. In fact, he took it hard what happened to Betty, having taken a liking to her. Said that she reminded him of his own grandmother."

"What's the orderly's name?" I asked interestedly.

"Joel Sackhoff," she responded evenly.

Joel Sackhoff? I recalled that this was an alias of Jason Huffman's, but I didn't remember seeing the name on the list of staff supplied by Ruth Windom.

Why would Huffman use a moniker to work at his grandmother's nursing home under false pretenses?

"I need to speak with this Joel Sackhoff," I told Nurse Gallo. "Where can I find him?"

She hesitated. "Well, that's the thing…you can't. Not here, anyway. Joel never showed up for work today—"

* * *

I showed Jason Sean Huffman's mug shot to Ruth Windom and identified him as Joel Sackhoff while also noting the evidence supporting this conclusion. The director was stunned and mystified that someone she hired should prove to be a fraud.

I wasn't as shocked, but equally disturbed that Huffman had used his alias to gain access to his grandmother. Had she ever recognized him? If so, was this what set him off? Or was it his intention to go after her all along?

At my desk later that afternoon, I compared Huffman's latest booking photo with his employee photograph at the nursing home where he was pretending to be Joel Sackhoff. Aside from his deep blue eyes and square face, in his mug shot, Huffman had short blonde hair in a mullet cut and a goatee. In his alter ego, he had died the hair black and changed the style to a crew cut with a side part and had a chin strap beard, while wearing horn-shaped glasses, as an obvious attempt to conceal his true identity.

"What have you come up with on the investigation into the old woman's death?" I was asked by the deputy chief of the Golfton Hills PD, Bradford Paxton, as I stepped inside his office.

At thirty-eight, he was African American, tall, and muscular, with black hair in a closely cropped fade style. Though I had the utmost respect for him, I only wished he'd fought the bureaucracy a little harder to keep me and a couple of other older cops from being shoved out the door. Or if he had, it wasn't something I was privy to.

175

"I think Betty Huffman was murdered by her grandson," I answered without preface.

"Really?" Paxton's dark eyes bulged as he sat at his wooden desk.

"Fingerprints from Betty Huffman's room at the nursing home confirmed that Jason Huffman, posing as Joel Sackhoff, had been in the room. Beyond that, I believe that he may also have killed his own mother, Jackie Huffman, who was found suffocated to death in a parking lot the same night Betty Huffman died. I can't tell you what the motive might have been," I stressed. "Still trying to figure that out."

"Is he in custody?" Paxton asked, peering at me.

"Not yet."

"Why the hell not?"

I swallowed thickly, then admitted, "Huffman's disappeared. I think he may be on the run..."

Paxton's thick brows bridged. "Well, find him—whatever hole he's crawled into," the deputy chief warned in no uncertain terms. As if my job depended upon it.

It honestly didn't at this stage of my long journey. I responded anyway, even-voiced, "You can count on it, Sir."

A BOLO was issued for Jason Huffman and the black Ford Bronco Badlands he was believed to be driving.

* * *

I sat across the table from Detective Stephen Heinle in a dimly lit club on Minden Street in downtown Golfton Hills. We were both drinking mugs of beer.

"Turns out that Jackie Huffman's old man may have killed her," Heinle remarked.

I raised a brow in hearing this. "Roy Brown?"

"Yeah, looks like it. Not only did he not have an alibi for the night she was killed, but Brown was arrested twice—actually, three times—for domestic violence. Each time, she refused to press charges."

"So, if that's the case, why would he kill her?" I asked with healthy skepticism, though not at all discounting the man's penchant for violence that may have gone too far. To say nothing of the battered woman syndrome that had Jackie Huffman willing to stay with a batterer.

"Why does any violent person kill?" Heinle shrugged. "Maybe Brown's temper got the better of him this time around. Or maybe Huffman had had enough of him beating her up and threatened to file charges—or perhaps worse, leave him—and Brown retaliated by killing her."

Though this made sense, and the dynamics seemed to support it on its face, I was having a hard time buying it, all things considered. Not unless Roy Brown also murdered Betty Huffman, whom he claimed to have not even known existed. Was he lying?

"Brown didn't do it," I said boldly.

Heinle regarded me intently. "I'm listening..."

"I think Jason Huffman killed his own mother," I said candidly. "Then he killed his grandmother, Betty Huffman." I laid out the alias Huffman used to gain employment at her nursing home.

"Hmm..." Heinle uttered musingly.

I stated sharply, "Huffman's our killer. I can feel it with every fiber in me."

"You may be onto something," Heinle muttered, putting the mug to his lips. "Be that as it may, we simply can't go on hunches. The fact is, as of yet, we've found nothing to tie Jason Huffman to Jackie Huffman's death. No incriminating fingerprints, DNA, or eyewitnesses. There's no proof that she was even in contact with her son before her death." He sat back. "On the other hand, we know that Jackie Huffman was a drug addict who sometimes turned tricks for a living. Semen taken from inside her may or may not have belonged to Roy Brown, pending DNA tests. My guess is that if it wasn't Brown who killed her, Huffman may have been killed by a john."

I pondered the theory while drinking beer, prompting Heinle to say sardonically, "Unless you're trying to tell me that Jackie Huffman got it on with her own son the night she died—?"

Though I knew that incest was often one of a family's most guarded secrets, I dismissed the possibility out of hand in this instance. Assuming Jason

177

Huffman knew that Jackie Huffman was his mother. *But how could he not know?* I asked myself. Especially since he knew about the grandmother and most likely killed her.

I had to at least consider that there may have been two killers here. Could Huffman have had an accomplice in taking out Jackie Huffman?

I looked at Heinle while finishing off the beer and said thoughtfully, "At this point, I suppose all possibilities have to remain on the table—at least till we can bring Jason Huffman in for questioning."

* * *

While my number one suspect in the murders of Betty Huffman and Jackie Huffman remained at large, I decided to pay Roy Brown a return visit.

I found him in the parking lot of the apartment complex, leaning against a gray Buick Envision and smoking a cigarette.

"You again." He frowned.

"Afraid so," I said. "Have some follow-up questions for you."

He drew on the cigarette. "So, what is it this time?"

"I need to talk to you about Jackie Huffman."

"I told the cops all I'm going to," he argued.

"Not yet, you haven't." I glared at him. "Now we can either do this the easy way, or I can take you in as a person of interest. Your call." I carried a Glock 42 .40 S&W service pistol, but kept it tucked inside my linen blazer, in a waistband holster.

He seemed to weigh his options before saying, "All right, all right. What about her?"

I peered at him. "I understand you liked to get rough with Jackie?"

Brown suddenly looked uncomfortable. "I got as much as I gave."

"We both know that isn't true," I told him flatly.

"We got into it like all couples do," he alleged. "Just some pushing and shoving. No big deal."

"Domestic violence is always a big deal," I made clear, and then asked point-blank, "did you kill her?"

"No way." He raised his voice.

"Honestly, I want to believe that," I said. "Unfortunately, the detective handling Jackie's case seems to think otherwise. It happens that way when you have no alibi for when she was murdered."

"Can I help it if I fell asleep by myself?" Brown dragged on the cigarette once more before tossing it to the ground and squashing it with his foot. "I still didn't kill Jackie," he insisted.

Given that I was with him on this one, believing that the killer lay elsewhere, I asked, "Were you aware that she was a part-time prostitute?"

He rubbed his nose. "Yeah, I knew."

"And you were okay with that?"

"It was how we met," he admitted. "Who was I to judge? She did what she wanted."

"Jackie may have been with a john when she was killed." I thought he should know this and tried to read his body language as a possible killer.

Brown bristled, but seemed to take this in stride. "Okay. So, maybe he was the one who killed her."

Or not, I thought. "We'll see what the investigation turns up." I paused and informed him, "Jackie had a son."

Brown looked taken aback. "That's news to me."

"His name is Jason Sean Huffman. He may have had something to do with her death and is suspected of being involved in the death of Jackie's mother, Betty Huffman."

"That's crazy," Brown said, shaking his head in disbelief.

"Yeah, tell me about it." I wondered why Jackie Huffman would keep her son—and her mother—a secret from her lover. What was up with that? Could she have been afraid to tell him? Or were there other legitimate reasons? Had the mysteries been buried with the mother and daughter? I regarded Roy Brown and said seriously, "For your sake, I hope the evidence to prove the contrary doesn't make its way back to you."

* * *

The following morning, I drove to the Coastview Psychiatric Hospital in nearby Bay County in the Panhandle, where I learned that Jason Huffman had spent some time.

I had an appointment with Doctor Malcolm Fujita, hoping to gain more insight into the tripartite relationship between Huffman, his mother, and his grandmother that might have led to murder.

After showing my I.D. at the reception desk, I was let in through a buzzing door and then met by a tall, thin man of about sixty with gray hair in a slicked-back style. He wore oval eyeglasses that hung low on an aquiline nose.

"Detective Elizondo, I presume," he said in a gravelly voice.

"Yes," I confirmed.

"I'm Dr. Fujita." We shook hands, and I couldn't help but notice that the doctor's hand was trembling. "Parkinson's disease," he said matter-of-factly. "I've had it for the last ten years. Not very fun, that's for sure. But I've learned to live with it for as long as possible. Why don't we go into my office—?"

I followed him into a large, clean office with a picture window that looked out over palm trees. A bookshelf lined with academic texts and other books stood behind a huge L-shaped birch desk and high-backed leather chair. Two swivel armchairs were on opposite sides of a circular glass table.

"Have a seat," Fujita said and proffered a trembling arm toward one of the chairs. I sat down and watched him sit in the other. "So, how can I help you, Detective?"

"I'm investigating one of your former patients, Jason Huffman, in relation to two homicides," I spoke frankly.

Fujita jutted his chin thoughtfully. "Is that so? Tell me more..."

"I believe that Huffman murdered his grandmother, Betty Huffman, and his mother, Jackie Huffman, two days ago—suffocating one, strangling the other." I leaned forward. "The suspect is still at large, even as we speak. I'm trying to make some sense out of a senseless act, even by the standards of the mentally unstable. Or, in other words, I need to know why Jason Huffman would go after them like that, as it's obviously not the normal way of dealing with family issues."

I watched the psychiatrist react, not seeming to be entirely shocked at the allegation. Knowing that the HIPAA Privacy Rule didn't apply for law enforcement requests pertaining to a criminal investigation, I waited for his response.

"Sometimes there is no sensible explanation, per se, for why some people do the things they do, Detective," Fujita said, as if resigning himself to this reality. "But, in this case, there may be some method to Jason Huffman's apparent actions, if you will—"

"I can hardly wait to hear it," I voiced sarcastically.

Fujita adjusted his glasses. "To be quite honest with you, I'm not surprised that Jason has perpetrated these actions, allegedly. In fact, I predicted long ago that something like this might happen..."

"Maybe we could cut to the chase here, Doctor," I said impatiently, "and you can tell me what you know about Huffman?"

"All right." Fujita wrinkled his brow. "Jason Huffman's mother, Jackie Huffman, abandoned him as an infant. She was scarcely more than a child herself at seventeen, running away with the boy's father. It was her own single mother, Betty Huffman, who was left to raise the child." He paused as if reliving the painful memories. "Jason's grandmother, bitter and vindictive over her daughter's promiscuity and abandonment, unfortunately, took it out on the child. She abused him by denying him food, keeping him locked in closets or the cellar, and other equally hideous forms of maltreatment. I suspect that she may have done the same things to her own daughter—which apparently led to Jackie Huffman running away from home as fast as she could..."

"How the hell did she get away with it—over two generations—if Betty Huffman did as you say?" I could only wonder out loud.

"By doing it behind closed doors at a time when people didn't ask as many questions about how one chose to raise children," Fujita suggested straightforwardly.

As I grappled with these revelations, I had to ask, "So, how did Jason Huffman wind up here?"

"The usual things." Fujita angled his face. "Jason began acting up in and out of school…temper tantrums, delinquency and criminality, substance abuse, etc. Authorities finally realized that there was a serious problem at home. But by then, the damage had already been done." Fujita sighed. "To make a long story short, as it relates to psychiatric care, Jason has spent time at our facility on two separate occasions—and has also received outpatient therapy."

I took note of this and asked, "Was Betty Huffman ever held accountable for what she did to him?"

"As far as I'm aware, Jason's grandmother received little more than a slap on the wrist from the authorities," Fujita answered. "I don't think that Jason ever forgave his mother for leaving him in the care of his grandmother—or his grandmother for the hell she put him through…"

"So, he makes up for it by waiting until years later to murder them both?" I scratched my head quizzically.

"It's called post-traumatic stress disorder, Detective," Fujita said. "Jason was also dealing with borderline personality disorder," he explained. "Sometimes it takes years before something triggers the repressed painful memories, the negative self-image, and other symptoms of this disorder—till, finally, it triggers a violent or otherwise destructive resolution."

I regarded Fujita while weighing his words and asked directly, "Based on what you've said, Doctor, if Jason Huffman killed his own grandmother and a mother that he apparently never got to know—now that he's tasted blood, so to speak—do you think Huffman might go after his father if he's still around and can be found? Or, for that matter, is a threat to anyone who may have crossed him in one respect or another?"

Fujita returned my gaze and replied contemplatively, "As to the first part of your question—yes, I believe that Jason could possibly seek revenge against his father for abandonment, which led to child maltreatment and such." He sucked in a deep breath before continuing. "Regarding Jason being a threat to anyone who's wronged him—assuming he's gone over the edge in his homicidal tendencies—this is entirely possible and, as such, Jason has to be considered extremely dangerous…"

With two dead bodies left in his wake, I needed no convincing that Jason

Huffman was a danger to society after the system failed him in a major way, so long as he remained on the loose. Having more than enough to work with in assessing this psychological blueprint to a double homicide, I stood up.

"Thanks for your time, Dr. Fujita," I told him sincerely.

He stood, too, nodding. "It was my duty to give you what you wanted, considering the circumstances."

After being walked to the exit doors, I turned to Fujita and asked out of curiosity, "One other thing... If, as you believe, Jackie Huffman may also have been abused by her mother, why on earth would she leave her son with Betty Huffman, only to get the same treatment?"

Fujita removed his glasses and slid them into the pocket of his poplin shirt, and responded candidly, "I wish I could give you a simple answer, Detective, but I cannot. Generally speaking, my professional opinion is that Jason's mother—burdened with self-loathing, guilt, and fear—abandoned her child to an abusive mother to punish herself, her mother, and maybe even the child."

If this was indeed the case, I mused sadly, then Jackie Huffman certainly succeeded on all counts.

My fear, though, was that Jason Huffman was not through with his campaign of retaliation and murder—making it all the more important to stop him in his tracks sooner rather than later.

* * *

That afternoon, I met with my former partner, Odessa Jumper, at Golfton Hills Park on Golf Lane. The forty-one-year-old member of the Seminole Tribe of Florida had quit the police force three years ago to become a full-time private investigator. It surprised many in the police department, but not me. I could see that she wasn't happy playing by rules other than her own and had the courage to do something about it.

"Thanks for meeting with me," I told her as we sat on a park bench and watched some mallard ducks milling about near a pond.

Odessa, who was slender, attractive, and divorced, with a brown-blondish jaw-length bob with bangs, smiled and said, "It sounded urgent."

"It is," I stressed. "I need your help."

"Sure. What's up?"

Knowing that Odessa was good at what she did was good enough for me, even if it meant stepping outside the department to solve my final case. As such, I got right to the point when I told her, "I'm looking for a man who I believe murdered his mother and grandmother."

Odessa's brown eyes widened. "Sounds like a real piece of work."

"Yeah, with a sordid family history to match," I told her and outlined it briefly while handing her a picture of Jason Huffman. "Looks like he may have gone underground, assuming he's still alive. Apart from his real name, he's been known to use the alias, Joel Sackhoff."

"Okay." Odessa studied Huffman's picture. "Send me any other relevant info you have, and I'll see what I can do to discover his whereabouts."

"Thanks, Odessa."

"No problem." She met my gaze. "I owe you, Mariah. I still use the things you taught me when we were partnered in my private eye business."

I smiled at her. "If you can help me track down Jason Huffman, I'll consider us even."

"I'll be in touch," she said after we stood up.

"Okay."

We headed in opposite directions as I worked on other leads in pursuit of Jason Huffman, wanting badly to take him into custody before he set his sights on anyone else.

* * *

I lived in an elevated beach house right off the water. It was the same home I'd occupied since Manuel and I purchased the place as our dream home when it was new, five years before his death—with its open concept, high ceilings, natural stone tile flooring, and big windows everywhere.

Though I had considered moving when faced with the reality of living there alone as a widow, I decided to stick it out. I believed in my heart of hearts that this was what Manuel would have wanted.

Now it seemed as if I was soon going to have a lot more time to hang out there, with the beach house style furnishings, ceiling fans keeping the place cool, and access to the water.

Still, I'd give it up in a hot second to have Manuel back among the living. Since that wasn't happening, the next best thing would be to wrap up my career as a police detective in style by bringing in Jason Sean Huffman to answer for what I believed were two homicides he perpetrated.

* * *

"What have you learned?" I asked at my desk when Odessa called the next day, with Huffman still managing to elude the authorities.

"Got a good lead on your person of interest," she said, almost as a teaser, in the video chat.

"Don't keep me in suspense," I uttered snappily.

"All right. If you can believe this, the guy actually left a forwarding address when he worked at the nursing home as Joel Sackhoff. It's a different address from his last known address as Jason Huffman. It's still in Golfton Hills, on Sapple Road. Guess he didn't figure anyone would come looking for him there." She cleared her throat.

"What's the address?" I asked.

Odessa gave it to me and said, "Beyond that, it appears as though Huffman has been using a second alias—Daniel Lafferty. I believe this is the name he's currently using while holed up at the Sapple Road cottage."

"I'll check it out," I told her.

"Need backup?"

It was tempting to go one more round with us as partners, but I turned it down in favor of doing the rest by the book.

"Thanks, Odessa," I said appreciatively, "but that won't be necessary. You've done what you needed to. The rest is up to me."

"Okay, if you say so."

"Be sure to bill me for what I owe you," I insisted, not wanting to deprive her of what she was owed for the work, our history notwithstanding.

"Will do," she relented.

"We'll speak soon," I told her and disconnected before getting on the phone with Detective Stephen Heinle to apprise him of the situation with respect to our concurrent homicide cases.

* * *

The black Ford Bronco Badlands registered to Jason Huffman was found parked about a block from the address where he was believed to be hiding out.

With my weapon drawn and accompanied by Heinle, officers, and members of the Golfton Hills PD's SWAT Team and K-9 Unit, the one-story craftsman-style cottage was surrounded.

When Huffman, aka Joel Sackhoff and Daniel Lafferty, refused to come out with his hands raised in surrender, we went in after him.

Using a battering ram to force open the door, none of us were quite sure what to expect from the man wanted for a double homicide.

What we got was a dead suspect. Jason Sean Huffman was lying on the hardwood floor of a furniture-free living room in a pool of blood. Beside him was a SIG Sauer P365-XMacro 9mm compact pistol and a handwritten note.

Huffman had taken his own life while confessing to the murders of his grandmother, Betty Huffman, and mother, Jackie Huffman—whom he blamed for his terrible childhood and all the poor choices he'd made in his life ever since.

Pending any surprises down the line in my final case, the investigation into the death of Betty Huffman had been cracked, more or less, with only some paperwork left to complete the process.

What sent Jason Huffman over the edge at the time it happened might never be known. There could be no argument, though, that three lives in three different generations of one family had been tragically lost, with plenty of blame to go around.

I would leave that to others to try and figure out as I turned in my badge and gun, invited Odessa to attend my retirement party, and reflected upon a long career in law enforcement with its mostly ups and a few downs to ponder on the way out the door.

As I walked barefoot along the beach while trying to keep up with my new companion, an Airedale terrier—I felt the spirit of Manuel with us, encouraging me to make the most of the rest of my life, and I intended to do just that.

The Arsonist's Revenge

She peeked inside her parents' large and traditionally furnished bedroom and saw, as expected, that they were sound asleep. Or at least they were quiet while cuddled together beneath the comforter. Just then, she saw her mother stir a little at about the same time that her father began to snore lightly.

Neither awakened.

She watched them a moment longer before closing the door softly.

Fully dressed but barefoot, she quietly walked down the straight staircase and into the U-shaped kitchen. There, she pulled open a drawer and removed the box of matches. Studying it for a moment, she imagined what would happen when she lit some of the matches before calmly doing just that.

First, she set the paper towels and cloth towels in the kitchen on fire.

Then she went into the great room and lit the bespoke curtains that were floor-length, and then the fluffy pillows on the sectional sofa and a recliner chair.

After watching the flames erupt and begin to spread like wildfire, she wondered if her mommy and daddy would be mad at her for doing this. Much like when she had what her mother called a temper tantrum last summer at her birthday party. Would they wake up? Or keep sleeping as the house burned?

She headed for the front door and walked out of the house, as if an ordinary day.

She moved down the stone pathway, which felt cold to her feet and toes, to the sidewalk, then turned to watch as the flames shone brightly through the large windows. They quickly began to fill the downstairs and make their way upstairs, just as swiftly.

It gave her a sheer sense of excitement that tickled her fancy as much as anything she'd experienced before during her six years of life.

In what almost seemed like a blink of her small green eyes, the entire house was engulfed in fire, and she felt impassive, even with her parents helpless while trapped inside.

By the time the fire department arrived, she wondered if there was anything they could possibly do to save the house. Or, for that matter, those who were still inside and now surrounded by the colorful flames.

* * *

Twenty years later, Amber Knight stood among a group of onlookers as the two-story coastal contemporary house nestled amongst palm and oak trees in Golfton Hills went up in flames, destroying the multimillion-dollar home and all the custom-made Italian furnishings and expensive paintings decorating the shiplap walls within.

Even the shiny black Rolls-Royce Ghost was not spared, engulfed into what looked like a fireball with flames shooting out from the shattered windows.

Though she wanted to feel remorse for the man trapped inside the home, Amber felt none whatsoever. Quite the contrary, she felt a surge of adrenalin that she hadn't experienced in years. Or ever since she set her parents' Spanish-style house in Miami on fire and watched it burn.

Miraculously, they both somehow managed to escape with only a few superficial burns and total befuddlement as to why she would have done such a thing.

Amber choked back tears as it related to her mother and father. She'd been in a bad place at the time. Or as much as any six-year-old could be who was angry that she didn't get her way. She'd wanted to make them pay for this and at the same time, succumbed to the strong urge that came from within her for starting fires.

Over the next few years, she went to therapy to deal with the pyromania that poisoned her mind and distorted reality. The treatment had worked. Her once overpowering need to be a pyromaniac subsided, and she was able to live a normal life in adulthood, where Amber was a classical musician and made a good living, doing concerts and traveling around the country. She'd even been dating the man of her dreams, Elliot Weigel, and believed him to be the one she would someday marry and have children with.

Till that all changed, and she saw him for what he truly was. Someone who was only after her body and musical talents—and had no qualms getting it any way he saw fit.

Afterwards, having succeeded in his conquest, he'd tossed her out like garbage and quickly replaced her with another attractive and naïve talented and younger woman—only to eventually discard her the same way.

Amber couldn't allow that to happen. Elliot needed to be stopped from making a fool out of people like her—and she was the only one with the guts and knowledge to do just that.

She sucked in a deep breath, breathing in the humid air mixed with the scent of a house burning, while her bold apple-green eyes gazed at the place Elliot felt he was most at home. And untouchable.

He thought wrong. Oh, so very wrong.

His place of refuge and conquests had proven to be his undoing. A trap from which there would be no return for him.

Amber felt a tickling sensation within her tall and slender body. Inside her head, covered with long and voluminous dark hair with retro bangs, she wanted to believe that the pyromania was but a one-off, and that would be that. The last thing she wanted was to return to fire setting as a way of life.

But who was to say whether or not she could control this. Or be controlled by it once again.

Amber wrinkled her delicate nose and thought back to when she first met Elliot a year ago and how things could have been so different.

* * *

Amber had moved to a nice beachfront condominium on Harper Lane in

Golfton Hills six months ago, having left Miami, where she'd had and dished out so much pain. She hoped to escape the memories by having a different landscape to lead her life and continue to establish her career.

Though she had dated off and on through the years, no Prince Charming had emerged. There seemed to be more losers than not in the men Amber had romances with. Even with that, like others, she still felt there was someone out there for her. This prompted her to give online dating a try.

An agency matched her up with Elliot Weigel, a successful and wealthy music promoter who was based in Golfton Hills. He was thirty-one, five years her senior. Like her, he had never been married and was seemingly serious about being in a committed long-term relationship.

Amber was on pins and needles with nervousness, for whatever reason, as she sat at the bar in the Golfton Hills Club on Sherman Street while waiting to meet Elliot face-to-face for the first time. Would he like her in person? Would she like him?

Or would they both be turned off by the other and run as far away from the situation as they could?

She sipped on the vodka gimlet and calmed down a bit when Amber heard the smooth and masculine voice say, "You must be Amber...?"

Turning, she looked into the most enchanting blue eyes of a familiar and quite handsome square face. "I am," she uttered. "And you're—"

"Elliot Weigel," he finished before she could.

Amber gave him the once-over and was even more taken by his good looks than what she saw on her cell phone and laptop. His dark hair was cut in a drop fade pompadour style, and he had a long stubble beard. He was tall and in great shape while looking stylish in a white polo shirt, brown linen pants, and moccasin boat shoes.

"Nice to finally meet you in person, Elliot," Amber admitted honestly.

"You too," he told her, showing straight white teeth as they locked eyes. He extended a hand, which she shook, as Elliot said coolly, "You're gorgeous."

Amber blushed. "Thanks. You're pretty amazing yourself."

Something told her that he was probably even more used to being complimented than she was. Not that this changed the equation any.

Grinning at her, Elliot said, "Do you want to get a table?"

"I'd love to," Amber told him and stood up. She picked up her drink and said anxiously, "Lead the way..."

* * *

Elliot Weigel meant it when he told Amber Knight that she was hot stuff. While sipping on a dirty martini, he eyed her as they sat at the table. With black hair well below her shoulders, green eyes that sparkled on a diamond-shaped face, a small chin dimple, and a slim body with nice-sized breasts in a cute little blue asymmetrical dress worn with slingback sandals—what was not to like?

Not much, as far as he could determine.

That being said, there were lots of good-looking women in Golfton Hills and elsewhere in Florida. He was not exactly a one-woman type of man. Quite the contrary, he enjoyed playing the field. Online dating made this almost too easy. But he couldn't complain about the results. His job was to have as much fun as he wanted. Then, move on to new and interesting conquests.

He conceded that not all the women he bedded would be okay with this. But that was their problem. Like him, they were free to be with whomever they wanted.

First, though, he needed them to want him and then take things from there. To him, that meant getting what he needed from them before showing them the door.

In the case of Amber, he hoped she didn't take it the wrong way when that time came. After all, with her classical music talent and his being a successful music promoter, he saw this as a perfect business opportunity that could benefit both of them. But even that could only go so far at the end of the day.

At which point, they needed to go their separate ways and not look back, as he never did.

* * *

It took Amber two weeks after that initial meeting to visit Elliot's beachfront contemporary house. To say she wasn't impressed would be an understatement. It was enormous with an open floor plan, two stories, an abundance of windows with solar roller shades, ceiling fans, Brazilian cherry hardwood flooring, custom furniture, a wet bar, oil paintings on the walls, a heated pool, and so much more. That included his primary suite with a large sleigh bed as the centerpiece.

"This is incredible," Amber told him downstairs, wishing she weren't gushing over everything. But she couldn't help herself.

"I get that a lot." Elliot laughed. "Glad you like the place. Make yourself at home, and I'll fix us a drink."

"Sounds good to me." She did take it upon herself to wander about while wondering curiously just how many other women he had brought there. Not that it mattered, at least not too much. She was the one Elliot wanted to be with right now and was crazy about—he had certainly told her this enough—so why not just embrace it and see if they could turn what they seemed to have into something truly special?

They had sex that night and many times in the days and weeks that followed. Each time seemed that much more satisfying to Amber than the last. Even more importantly, Elliot seemed generous to a fault, showering her with lots of gifts and his apparently undivided attention.

The relationship extended as well to the connections he used in getting her bookings to play her music locally, across Florida, and around the country.

It wasn't hard for Amber to have fallen in love with Elliot Weigel.

He intimated he felt the same about her, if not in so many words.

As far as Amber was concerned, she had found a man she wanted to partner up with for the rest of her life.

That was until things turned sour.

* * *

"It's over," Elliot told her coldly after they'd just had sexual relations.

For an instant, Amber was sure she had misheard him. Surely he wasn't breaking up with her? Not now. "What?" she asked, wide-eyed and naked atop the luxury sheet on his bed.

"We're through," Elliot reiterated as he climbed out of the bed. "Put your clothes on and get out."

She sat up, stunned. "But I don't understand... Why are you doing this? What have I done? Or haven't I done?"

He stood before her in the nude, gazing at her thoughtfully, before responding coldly, "This was never intended to last forever, Amber. Not for me anyway."

"Oh, really?" She pursed her lips, fighting back tears. "I thought we were on the same page."

"We were good together," he said, softening his tone a bit. Then he became cruel again. "But truthfully, it's grown stale of late. On top of that, I can't do much more for you as a promoter than I've already done."

"You mean you don't want to?" Amber countered. Yes, bookings had slowed down. But she was still good at what she did and in demand. Somewhere.

"Whatever." He rolled his eyes. "It's not working anymore."

"And you tell me this right after we made love?" She glared at him, filled with anger and humiliation. "You bastard!"

"I'm sorry." His tone made it clear that he wasn't anything of the sort. "Just leave." He turned away from her while grabbing his clothes off the floor.

After getting out of bed, Amber had to ask the obvious question, even if she didn't really want the answer, "Is there someone else?"

Elliot waited a beat, faced her, and responded flatly, "Yeah, if you really want to know, I have met another woman. She's great and an aspiring singer that I'm working with."

"So, you've been sleeping with her, too?" Amber demanded, hands on her hips as jealousy and betrayal raged within at the prospect.

He wrinkled his nose dismissively. "Yeah, we've hooked up a few times. No big deal. Don't make it one."

She got in his face. "How could you?"

"It happens, Amber," Elliot snorted. "Deal with it and get on with your life. We're done. You can let yourself out..."

Amber watched as he walked out of the room, not having the guts to look back at her. She gathered her clothes and took them into the bathroom before getting dressed and crying her eyes out. How could she have not seen this coming? She had instantly gone from being in love and feeling loved to hating him and feeling used and abused.

She couldn't get away from that monster fast enough.

And he obviously had already kicked her to the curb, even before taking her to bed. This only added to Amber's overwhelming fury.

It was the type of anger that made her feel he couldn't be allowed to get away with this.

She wouldn't let him.

Two months would pass by before she had gathered the courage to carry out her ultimate revenge.

Now it would be his turn to deal with it.

Only then would she be the one to come out on top.

* * *

Wearing a blonde balayage pixie wig, Amber put on a red cap-sleeve cocktail dress and evening T-strap heels before heading out. Ten minutes later, she showed up at Elliot's front door, a pretty smile painted on her face, while holding a half-filled bottle of Cabernet Sauvignon with a leather hobo bag strapped across her shoulder. She had waited for his latest girl toy, a voluptuous blonde dancer and pop singer named Heida Muñoz, to leave.

Elliot cocked a brow. "You changed your hair."

"I wanted a different look," she said simply.

He frowned, clearly not expecting to see her again. "So, what are you doing here, Amber?"

She flashed her pearly white teeth innocuously and uttered nicely, "I'm moving back to Miami tomorrow and thought we could enjoy a night together—if only for old times' sake."

"Is that so?"

He regarded her with suspicion, but she continued to pour on the charm. "We had some great times together, didn't we?"

"Yeah, I suppose so," he acknowledged.

"And now you've moved on. I get it," Amber told him believably. "We're all adults here, and you're entitled to pick and choose as you like. Consider this a going-away present. If you want to just have a drink with me and go no further, I'm okay with that. On the other hand, if you're up for recreating the magic we shared in bed one last time, that's cool too. I won't tell if you don't."

She watched while his deep blue eyes mulled this over—caught between suspicion and temptation—before the latter and perhaps his own libido won out, and Elliot relented, telling her with a lascivious grin playing on his lips, "Come in…"

Amber stepped through the double doors and was once again awed by the layout and furnishings. But any thoughts of sidestepping her purpose for being there by giving in to past feelings for him ran into a mental brick wall. She was not about to let him off the hook.

She put a fake smile on her face and said, while moving toward the gourmet kitchen, "I'll pour us some drinks, and we can have them wherever you like—"

If she thought it would be that easy, Amber was sorely mistaken. Elliot never took his eyes off her as he said, "I'll do the honors." He yanked the bottle out of her hands. "Why don't you make yourself at home. We can have that final drink in my room. I'm sure you remember the way—"

"Of course." She showed her teeth again, almost admiring his take-charge attitude, though suspecting it was more to err on the side of caution than anything. Apparently, he didn't trust her—and with good reason. That worked both ways, as he had already broken her trust irreparably. And would now have to pay the ultimate price. "I'll wait for you there," she told him and headed up the curved staircase.

She stepped inside the primary suite, put down the hobo bag, and kicked off her shoes before glancing about as Amber waited patiently for Elliot to show up. *Let's just get this over with*, she thought eagerly.

When he came into the room with the bottle in one hand and two wine glasses in the other, she was sitting on his big bed, her shapely legs crossed invitingly. She watched as he grinned lustfully and then poured wine into the glasses.

"Here you are," Elliot said, handing her one of them.

She smiled. "Thank you."

He grinned and sipped his own wine. "So, you're going back to Miami, huh?"

"Yeah. I have a few gigs coming up there, and it just seemed like a good time to make a clean break and start over."

"Cool." Elliot stared at her while drinking more wine. "Look, I'm sorry about the way things ended between us."

"It's all right," Amber lied, glancing at the wine in her hand. "Not all relationships are supposed to work out. It hurt for a while, but I'm over it now and just want to get on with my life. Just as you've done."

"Okay." He nodded and eyed her, emptying his glass. "You going to drink any of that wine, or what? I mean, that is why you're here—one drink for the road or whatever, right?"

"Right." She flashed her teeth, but didn't dare drink even a sip of the wine. Setting the glass on the floor, Amber opened her legs a bit and uttered, "On the other hand, I think I'd rather be sober for one last time in bed before we say our final goodbyes. You up for that?"

"Yeah, I'm up for it," Elliot was quick to agree. Even then, he was starting to wobble.

"Hey, are you okay?" Her expression was one of faux concern as Amber got to her feet.

"I'm fine." He sucked in a deep breath, and the glass fell from his hand and shattered on the hardwood. "Actually, I'm not."

"Let me help you to the bed," she told him. "Maybe if you lie down for a bit and shake it off..."

"Yeah, good idea," Elliot said as she allowed him to lean on her shoulder while barely making it to the bed.

She pushed him hard onto it and said, "Sweet dreams, lover." Then she laughed sardonically. "On second thought, I seriously doubt that they will be very sweet, Elliot. In fact, your dreams are about to blow up in your face, literally—"

Only in that moment did he seem to realize that something unnatural was wrong with him. "What did you do to me?" he demanded.

"Not much," she said sarcastically. "I just put enough Rohypnol in the wine bottle to knock out an elephant. Meaning it will kick in much easier with a slimebag human being like yourself."

"You bitch!" Elliot spat and tried to get up, but she pushed him back down and watched as he was suddenly out like a light.

Finally! Amber thought. She sighed and put her shoes back on. Then she grabbed her hobo bag and removed the box of matches.

Wasting little time, she glanced once at her unconscious former lover and love of her life, before leaving the room.

In the hall, Amber lit a match and then went to other rooms, where she set fire to as many flammable things as she could. She hurried downstairs and did the same throughout the house.

Till much of it was on fire.

She made her escape out the back door and went to the other side of the pool, where Amber slipped out the back gate and worked her way through a wooded area and back toward the front of the house—just in time to join several others who had gathered to watch the house as it went up in flames.

As Amber observed Elliot's property burn to the ground, with him inside, she felt a mixture of sorrow, relief, regret, and satisfaction.

Maybe someday she would join Elliot in hell.

Until such time, if it came, Amber intended to get on with her life as he suggested she do. Which may or may not mean that the pyromaniac in her, that she once thought was dead and buried for good, just might have a new beginning in reigniting the embers burning inside her like an inferno of the soul.

Only time would tell, she believed, as Amber walked unnoticeably away from the scene.

The Convenience Store Robbers

"So, what do you think?" Robyn Santiago asked, ill at ease, as the twenty-seven-year-old flipped her long, layered ash blonde hair over her shoulder while turning bold brown eyes toward her boyfriend. Brian Keebler, who towered over his petite girlfriend at six-four and was three years older, scratched his pate inside dark spiky hair that matched the color of his peach fuzz beard, held her gaze with solid blue eyes, and said determinedly, "Let's do this—"

She watched as he stuck a hand inside the pocket of his gray fleece zip hoodie, where she knew he had a Taurus GX4 9mm pistol. Though she hated guns, Robyn knew that Brian loved them. Moreover, it was necessary for them to have for what came next.

They stood outside the convenience store and gas station on Taylor Street in Golfton Hills. No one was pumping gas. Or otherwise hanging around as a potential witness when they robbed the place. This was good. The fewer complications, she believed, the better.

"Okay," she told him, though still feeling a bit jittery as though they should rethink this. But they needed the money and a ride, so there could be no turning back. Right? "Let's make it quick," she warned him. "In and out."

He cracked a smile and joked, "Yes, ma'am." Brian got serious again. "I'm ready…"

They entered the store, and while Robyn's primary job was to be an extra pair of eyes and ears, she also planned to use the opportunity to stock up on needed food, drinks, and some personal items.

It appeared to be empty inside, though looks at first glance could always be deceiving. Or at least this had been Robyn's experience in her life. Such as what she once thought was a loving mom who turned out to be little more than a crack addict. And her father wasn't much better. Apart from being a deadbeat dad, he seemed to have no problem getting into the pants of as many women as he could, with her mother often too wrapped up in her own issues to notice much.

Robyn eyed the clerk behind the counter. He was of medium build and tall, but not as tall as Brian. She guessed the man was about forty. He had grayish-brown hair worn in a faux mohawk and was wearing rectangle glasses in front of dark blue eyes on an oblong face that was clean-shaven.

After she and Brian exchanged glances, she gave him the nod to proceed. Robyn watched while he walked up to the counter, and the clerk said nonchalantly, "What can I get for you?"

"Anything I want," Brian declared hotly before he yanked the firearm out, pointing it at the man.

The clerk looked startled. "What do you want?"

"Give me all the money in the register!" Brian demanded. "And don't try anything stupid—like reaching for a gun under the counter…" His brow was furrowed in matching his tone to let the man know that he meant business.

The clerk complied with this, grimaced, then said, "Can't you go rob someplace else? Honestly, I really need every bit of what I make here."

"No, I'm afraid I can't cut you any slack," Brian insisted. "It doesn't work that way, dude. Now put the money in a bag—and hurry it up. Don't make me have to shoot you, 'cause I will," he assured him with pursed lips.

"If I were you, I wouldn't put that to the test," Robyn pitched in, glaring at the clerk while secretly hoping he wouldn't give them any trouble and they could walk right out of there with no further problems for anyone.

"All right, all right," the clerk acquiesced as he opened the cash register and began stuffing bills into a brown bag. "Don't shoot. I have a wife and three kids," he claimed. "I want to see them again."

"Then I guess we understand each other, don't we?" Brian continued to point the gun at him while looking around nervously.

Robyn did the same and was thankful that no one else had come in the store. Yet. If this were to happen, she feared that Brian might want to rob them too. Only giving them more to worry about. She grabbed as many items as she could carry in her hands.

"Here you go," the clerk said with a deep sigh, handing Brian the bag.

Brian glanced satisfyingly at the cash inside, then peered at him and said, "Oh, there's just one other thing... I need the keys to your car—"

"Really?" The clerk frowned frustratedly. "First, you rob me blind, and now you want to take away my only means of transportation, too? How is that fair?"

"It isn't," Brian conceded. "Nothing in my life has ever been fair. Get over it." He pointed the gun close to the clerk's face threateningly. "It's hard to drive around when you're dead," he snapped unfeelingly. "Now, hand over the damn keys. Or I swear I'll kill you right here and now and take them anyway—and more..."

Robyn wrinkled her nose at the clerk impatiently and nervously and cautioned him, "I'd listen to him if I were you. He's not playing games here. And neither am I," she added, trying to sound tougher than she truly was. "Move it!"

The clerk seemed to get the message loud and clear and begrudgingly took the key fob out of his pocket and handed it to Brian while stating accommodatingly, "It's the silver Subaru Outback."

Brian nodded and, gazing at Robyn, asked her, "You ready?"

"Yeah," she told him, having grabbed a basket to load up on what they needed while there.

"Good." He returned his attention to the clerk. "Show me your driver's license."

The man knitted his thick brows suspiciously and asked, "Why?"

"Do it!" Brian snapped, again aiming the weapon at him.

The clerk took out his wallet, removed the driver's license, and held it up so Brian could see.

"Guy Greenwood," Brian said musingly. He jutted his chin. "We need to keep your car for a few days, Guy, without needing to constantly look over our shoulders. That means you need to keep your mouth shut. Or what, you're probably wondering?" Brian narrowed his eyes. "I know where you live, Guy Greenwood. If there's even a hint of the cops on our case, we'll evade them and come after you to finish the job. Are you hearing me, Guy?"

"Yeah," the clerk said meekly. "I hear you. I won't call the police. I swear it."

"Okay, I'll take your word on that, Guy," Brian said, making good use of the clerk's name as part of the intimidation tactics he had mastered over a string of successful armed robberies. "Let's get out of here," he told Robyn.

She nodded and ran out first, with Brian right on her heels. They found Guy Greenwood's Subaru Outback, climbed in, and, with Brian behind the wheel, drove out of the gas station and onto Taylor Street.

"Think he'll call the cops?" Robyn gazed at her boyfriend, ill at ease.

"Nah," Brian voiced confidently. "The dude was practically sweating fear. The threat to come after him—and his family, in so many words—was more than enough to keep him from doing anything stupid. At least not before we can use his car long enough as transportation till we have to ditch it for another ride. Let's go home and see what goodies you brought with us."

"Cool." She grinned at him affectionately, even as she had an uneasy feeling that what they were doing in robbing stores—though they had yet to physically harm anyone, apart from the financial hurt—would eventually catch up to them.

* * *

Guy Greenwood waited a suitable amount of time before the armed robbers took off with his cash and car. He wasn't sure which theft miffed him most. Probably, they were equal in his rancor, in the sense of feeling victimized, violated, and powerless at the same time. Not to mention being caught off guard by the pair of desperate thieves.

But that was on him. He should have anticipated the possibility of this, having heard about the other local stores that had been hit by robbers lately. And little had been done by the authorities to prevent or capture the thieves.

The truth of the matter was that he had been too preoccupied with other things to be on guard against being targeted the way he was.

Guy rubbed his nose and reached beneath the counter, where he kept a loaded Korth Mongoose 2.75" Carry Special .357 Magnum revolver. As a U.S. Army veteran with two combat missions in Afghanistan, he knew his way around weapons. Or, to put it another way, he probably could have dropped the man who put a gun to his face at any time. And then killed his pretty female girlfriend—all in the blink of an eye—and been left unharmed himself.

But there was still no guarantee that it would have worked out that way. And he wasn't one who liked to play the odds with his own life on the line.

So, he allowed the robbers to have their way and gave them everything they wanted. That included standing by his promise not to involve the police in this brazen and foolish robbery.

But now the thieves would have to be taught a very costly lesson.

And he would get something extra out of it for the bargain.

Guy went to the front window, put the closed sign up, and then locked the door. He hated having to shut things down this early in the evening, but it had been a mostly slow day anyhow.

He thought about asking his employee for the night shift to come in early, but decided against it. With any luck, he would be back in no time flat without missing a beat.

But first, he needed to do a couple of things.

Guy walked to the back room and took a look at the surveillance camera footage. He saw the robbers enter the store and occupy it—getting a clear look at both of them. He homed in on the female robber for a long moment, finding himself smitten with her in ways she couldn't imagine—before erasing the video entirely.

As far as anyone knew, the two had never been there. And never robbed him.

Once he was able to retrieve his car, Guy would further remove any connection between him and the robbers.

Only then could he get back to his normal life and operate his place of business without it being intruded upon by people who were up to no good.

Guy grabbed his tablet off a metal table and accessed the app for his car GPS tracker. *There you are,* he told himself, as Guy spotted the vehicle making its way across the city. *Let's just see where you end up and then let the fun begin,* Guy thought, feeling giddy at the prospect.

* * *

Robyn and Brian made it home, safe and sound. No cops on their tails.

To Robyn, this was a good sign that their latest store robbery was going according to plan. They had obtained enough supplies and money to keep them going for a while, with neither being employed at the moment and living day to day on whatever they needed to survive.

They lived in a rented bungalow with an attached garage on Lester Lane. The stolen Subaru was parked inside and away from any potential prying eyes.

The modest-sized place was only sparsely furnished with mostly hand-me-down rustic furniture. This was fine by Robyn, as they didn't need much beyond each other.

They opened a bottle of white wine she had taken from the convenience store and drank about half while also getting high on marijuana.

"We did real good today, baby," Brian said sweetly.

"We did, didn't we?" Robyn agreed as they sat on a well-worn leather sofa. Her bare legs and feet were lying across his lap as he caressed her toes. It felt good. But she still needed to keep him grounded as much as possible. "I think we should lay low for a while so we don't press our luck."

She fully expected him to push back on slowing down on what had been a good way of financing their lives between jobs. But Brian looked her in the eye and said, "You're right. With the cops looking for us and who knows when we'll get greater resistance from store clerks or customers—we do need to take a step back."

"You're serious?" Robyn met his gaze doubtfully.

"Yeah, dead serious." He kissed the top of her foot while tickling the heel and making her laugh. "We'll play it cool and enjoy each other's company till things settle down."

"What about the car?" She still worried that Guy Greenwood might call the cops after all, and the police could end up at their front door to arrest them.

"We'll ditch it tomorrow," Brian promised.

They drank more wine and smoked more weed before heading to the bedroom to have sex.

* * *

Robyn heard a noise that, at first, she thought was only a dream. Till she felt something tickle her nose. When her eyes opened and adjusted to the darkness, she heard a somewhat familiar voice say tonelessly, "I believe you have something that belongs to me, and I intend to collect."

Only as she realized that the voice was that of Guy Greenwood, did Brian begin to stir, still under the influence of the wine and marijuana.

But before he could awaken fully, Robyn felt herself zapped with a stun gun, rendering her totally disoriented and all but helpless for what was to follow.

She saw Guy Greenwood yank the plump pillow from beneath Brian's head and put it over his face. Then, out of nowhere, he put the barrel of a gun right up to the pillow and fired twice into Brian's head, the cotton pillow muffling the sounds.

"I took the liberty of borrowing your boyfriend's own gun," the home invader mockingly told a shocked Robyn. "I'd thank him for leaving it out in the open on the kitchen table, but I'm guessing that he's already dead—and, thus, can't hear me."

Robyn was unable to react as Guy Greenwood grinned maniacally above her and, after tossing the gun to the brown carpeted floor, said, "With your boyfriend out of the way, it's just you and me now. Robyn, right? I caught the name, along with Brian's, on some mail, as we were never properly introduced when you decided to rob me and steal my car. Unfortunately, you chose the wrong convenience store to hold up. I think you're probably starting to realize that now, aren't you?"

Robyn saw him laugh as tears built up in her eyes and began to stream down her cheeks. How had he found them? Why did he need to come there? Was it revenge? Did he need to kill them for what was essentially a nonviolent crime they committed against him?

Did he even report the crime to 911?

As though he were reading her thoughts, Guy Greenwood said, "If you're wondering how I found you, I had a GPS tracker on my car, and it led me right to your door. So, I'll be taking back my car and the cash you took from me, if it's all the same to you, Robyn..." He laughed sarcastically. "Yep, I can see that you're good with that. I'm afraid, though, that isn't all I want from you. I usually like to wait a bit between kills, if only to keep the authorities off guard. But you've forced me to make an exception to the rule..."

Robyn saw him remove a long-blade folding knife from his pocket. Only then did it occur to her that a serial killer was on the prowl in Golfton Hills and elsewhere in the Panhandle. He had killed at least eight young women over the past two years, using a knife as his weapon of choice.

Was he the so-called Panhandle Killer, as the press had dubbed him?

She cringed at the thought of being stabbed to death, and tried her best to make her body cooperate with the will to live, but could not do so. Leaving Robyn only to pray that her death was quick, if not merciful.

As the blade was lifted above her face, she heard Guy Greenwood say pleasingly, "Thank you for allowing me the opportunity, by chance, to pick up with you where I left off with my last victim. If you run into her wherever you're headed—or your boyfriend—say hello for me, Robyn—"

With that and a derisive cackle, he sliced her throat with the knife, cutting deeply enough that Robyn had no time to think about wishing she could go back in time and do things over again, starting with the decision to rob Guy Greenwood, of all people—a serial killer. Or maybe go back even earlier than that, when after a miserable childhood and not much better as a young adult, she chose Brian to make a life with and struggled to make it work, leading them both down a path of no return.

Now, all Robyn was left with was hoping she would find peace in death, if not life, as everything quickly turned black.

* * *

Florida Department of Law Enforcement Special Agent Rita Hyland, working out of the Pensacola Regional Operations Center, pulled her blue Ford Mustang GT Fastback up behind a Golfton Hills Police Department squad car on Lester Lane. It wasn't exactly the way she hoped to begin her day. But, as duty called, it was her job to work with the locals in trying to get a handle on the double homicide that apparently occurred here last night.

Rita, who was African American, tall and slender, and had just turned thirty-one, exited the vehicle. She patted thick black hair that was in a braid-out style as her brown eyes gazed at the bungalow before she headed toward it.

After showing her identification to an officer, Rita went inside and made her way to the crime scene—the primary bedroom—where she met up with Golfton Hills PD homicide detective Antonio Fernández.

In his mid-thirties, taller than her and in good shape, with dark brown hair in a buzz fade cut, he turned to her with brown eyes and said somberly, "Hey."

"Fernández," Rita acknowledged him and then regarded the bed, where the two bodies, scantily clad, lay on a blood-soaked sheet.

"Looks like whoever did this caught them sleeping," he told her. "I'm guessing the male—tentatively identified as Brian Keebler—was shot first, with the Taurus GX4 9mm pistol lying on the floor."

"Who's the female?" Rita asked, noting that she was wearing only a blue thong teddy and didn't appear to have been sexually assaulted. Her throat had been slashed.

"According to her identification, her name's Robyn Santiago." Fernández furrowed his brow. "The pair matches the description of a male and female team believed to have been responsible for a number of local armed robberies."

"Hmm..." Rita scratched her cheek contemplatively. "Think there's a connection?"

"Possibly," Fernández said. "Could also be a home invasion that got totally out of hand. But my gut instincts are telling me something entirely different," he said, a catch to his voice.

"Mine too." Rita studied the female decedent. Before Fernández could get it out, she quickly told him, "Her manner of death has all the signs of fitting the modus operandi of the Panhandle Killer."

"Yeah, I was thinking the same thing," Fernández muttered matter-of-factly. "Keebler may have simply been in the way."

Rita considered that, if true, this would make the ninth female to have been killed this way over the last two years by the elusive serial killer whose case she was investigating. The last known victim, Sonia Naeole, had her throat cut just over a week ago. This murder seemed to go against the grain of the spacing of the unsub's killings.

I wonder what could have triggered him to go after her now? Rita could only wonder. Could their paths have crossed by happenstance? Or had Robyn Santiago been targeted from the start by a bloodthirsty killer who had become fixated on her and couldn't wait to make her another victim?

Her Secret Past Life

She ran for her life and freedom, naked and dead tired, wet from a downpour that seemed to come out of nowhere, and only vaguely familiar with her surroundings. But none of that mattered. Only survival. She knew that if he caught her, he would beat her badly, though not her face. He needed to protect her face so customers would still want to pay to have sex with her and not be totally turned off by her being bruised and swollen. Instead of pretty and desirable.

Then, he would drug her to make sure she didn't try to escape again. Or otherwise, would remain disoriented and docile for men to do with as they pleased. So long as they paid him the cash he demanded from each john.

She stopped just a moment to catch her breath before she once again resumed running barefoot through the woods that seemed to go on forever, ignoring the pain in her feet from blisters that had formed on her heels.

She would rather be dead than go through the worst experience of her life again as a sex slave. Like the other girls he still had under his thumb. They, too, had come from the foster care system in Florida, just wanting something better in life from someone who actually cared.

Instead, they ended up with far worse.

A pimp whose only interest in them was to sexually exploit them for his own profit and the sexual pleasures of other creeps who had no problem being with teenage girls with nowhere else to go.

But she decided there had to be somewhere where she could be free from him and make a life for herself. Maybe even find love with someone who could respect her and allow her to be the person she was meant to be. Instead of a sex object that had no say in what happened to her and when.

She saw what seemed to be a clearing up ahead through the old elm and dogwood trees and prayed that there might actually be a way out of this nightmare.

Maybe there was a house where she could go for help. Or a road in which she could flag down a car that could take her to safety.

Surely, someone will recognize that she was in danger and be willing to come to her rescue.

One could only hope.

She could hear footsteps behind her. He was gaining on her, though she was running as fast as she could.

She didn't dare look back, afraid of what she might see. Or who.

Stepping out in the opening, she saw that there were people moving about. Oblivious to her ordeal. Or the man who would gladly make her pay dearly for her disobedience.

But only if he could recapture her.

She would do everything within her power to make sure that didn't happen.

* * *

Special Victims Unit Investigator Nicolette Estefan, working for the St. Petersburg Police Department, was a member of the Tampa Bay Human Trafficking Task Force. They were in the process of a three-day sex trafficking sting in St. Petersburg, Florida. Nicolette hoped that they would be able to successfully rescue the underage girls who were being sexually exploited by their pimp and the johns he provided services for in a commercial sex trade operation throughout the city.

To Nicolette, this was much more than just a job to her. It was personal. At twenty-nine and Cuban American, she was still reeling from the loss five years earlier of her teenage sister, Hallie, who had been forced into prostitution by a sex trafficker named Aurelio Velasquez. Hallie had become a drug addict and stole money for Velasquez before she OD'd on cocaine laced with fentanyl, and that sick bastard was able to avoid apprehension.

Nicolette was determined to someday put him behind bars or see Aurelio Velasquez dead. But for now, she only wanted to do her part to stop the local sexual exploitation and violent victimization of children and arrest those responsible, whatever it took.

Armed with a SIG Sauer P320 semi-automatic handgun, she had her long blonde hair in a high ponytail as Nicolette trained her brown eyes on the duplex on Paris Avenue South on the other side of the street. She wondered how many girls they would find there. And what condition they would be in.

Only one way to know for sure.

She made eye contact with other heavily armed members of the task force, and the rescue operation at this location went into motion. Wearing a ballistic vest, Nicolette moved her tall and slender frame toward the house and past a cluster of saw palmetto palms and dark SUVs before they burst into the duplex, rescued the teenage victims, and made arrests.

* * *

Willow Sterling drove her white Toyota Camry down Trester Lane toward Kiki Elementary School as she responded to a call from her husband, Cliff, on speakerphone. "Hey," she spoke cheerfully.

"What are you up to?" he asked absentmindedly.

"I'm on my way to pick up Sissy from school," Willow told him regarding their five-year-old daughter.

"Right. My mistake," Cliff said apologetically. "I lost track of time."

"You're forgiven." Her aquamarine eyes lit up behind square glasses, not blaming him one bit for any excuse to talk to her. "And what are you doing?"

"I'm waiting for a meeting to start in a few minutes." He was an executive with a publishing company.

"Sounds like fun," she kidded, slowing down with traffic.

"Yeah, loads of it," he quipped. "Anyway, do you want me to bring home anything special for dinner?"

"Just yourself," Willow told him sincerely.

"That, I can do." Cliff chuckled. "But while bringing myself, maybe I'll pick up a pizza with everything on it that Sissy loves—and give you a break from cooking dinner."

"Sounds good to me...and thank you."

"Anything to make your life easier, honey."

"Ditto," she promised.

"Gotta go." Cliff spoke to someone else and then told Willow, "See you soon."

"All right. Love you."

"Love you more," he said in a syrupy voice.

I seriously doubt that, Willow thought, as she ended the call. She ran thin fingers through her shoulder-length raven hair with curled bangs.

They had been married for eight years now. Sissy had come three years into the marriage and was their pride and sheer joy.

Willow's pulse skipped a beat as she found herself slipping back even further in time when her life was so much different. Fifteen years, to be exact, when she was only sixteen. That was when she fled for her life from the sadistic and brutal pimp she was forced into working for as a prostitute in and around St. Petersburg.

When she'd finally gotten up the courage to break free of the sex trafficking world he operated, Willow had feared more than once that Aurelio Velasquez would track her down. Force her back into being a part of his stable. Or worse, kill her to send a clear message to any others who dared try to escape his clutches what the end result would be.

But he had never found her, thank goodness.

Willow had made her way to the Panhandle, settling into Golfton Hills, seemingly the perfect place to lay low and make a life for herself. It was there that she met Cliff Sterling, who won her over with his handsome looks, boyish charms, romance, and protective proclivity—making her fall in love with him and have a family as an extension of their marriage.

She had never told Cliff about her past life, fearful that he wouldn't understand. Or worse, would blame her somehow for getting caught up in the commercial sex trade. Or world of human trafficking.

Whatever the case, Willow didn't want to lose the best thing that had ever happened to her. Till Sissy came along.

In time, she fully intended to come clean with Cliff and hoped he was mature enough to forgive her. And not hold it against her.

She pulled up to the school and saw Sissy standing out front. Her daughter was talking to a man, his back turned to Willow. She assumed it was a parent of one of the other students, if not a teacher.

Willow got out of the car and approached them. Sissy, who reminded her of herself at that age, was small-boned with bold aquamarine eyes and mounds of dark hair with baby bangs.

"Sissy..." Willow got her attention.

Her daughter flashed a toothy smile and said, "Hi, Mommy. This is Mr. Velasquez—"

Willow was given a start as the man turned around, and she instantly recognized him as Aurelio Velasquez, her former pimp and abuser. It left her speechless.

"Hello, Willow." About six inches taller than her five-seven height, he lowered coffee-colored eyes with gold flecks, regarding her with a lascivious and self-satisfying crooked grin, "Long time, no see..."

Willow did not respond from the shock. He was fifteen years older now in his late forties, but hadn't changed much, save for adding a few pounds to his midsection. And a touch of gray blended in with dark hair in an angular fringe cut. New was the gunslinger beard and mustache. She couldn't help but wonder if this was meant to help alter his appearance, as if in trouble with the law.

I can't believe he found me, Willow told herself, feeling her knees shake and threaten to buckle under the weight of apprehension. She gazed at her innocent daughter and said, "Sissy, go wait in the car."

She frowned. "Why?"

"Just do it," Willow told her, trying to appear as calm as possible. "I just need to speak with Mr. Velasquez. I promise I won't be long."

Aurelio grinned at Sissy and said disgustingly, "Hope to see you again, Sissy."

Her daughter giggled, seemingly flattered by the attention. "Bye, Mr. Velasquez."

Willow waited till Sissy was in the back seat before facing her worst nightmare that had frighteningly reentered her onetime safe world. "How did you—?" The words stuck in her throat.

"Find you?" Aurelio laughed. "I never stopped trying to locate the best girl I ever had in my stable," he claimed. "No matter how long it took."

Willow cringed at the thought of being sex trafficked by him as a teenager and hated having to relive it. She glared at him. "I'm not going back with you, Aurelio, if that's what this is all about." Was he that arrogant to believe that would be the case?

"It isn't," he said matter-of-factly. He knitted his bushy brows. "I have to admit that I'm still pissed at you, Willow, for running away like you did. You had nerve, I'll give you that. If I had found you then...well, there's no telling how I would have responded. But that was then, and this is now..."

Willow still found herself intimated by the pimp and actually considered making a run for it—again. Or screaming at the top of her lungs to alert other parents or teachers that she was in trouble. But then, she glanced at Sissy in the car and realized that Aurelio knew where her daughter attended school—meaning she wasn't safe from him. Willow would kill the bastard before she ever allowed him to lay a finger on her daughter.

Peering at Aurelio, Willow asked point-blank, "What do you want?"

He gazed at her with a crooked grin and said smugly, "Now we're getting somewhere." He paused thoughtfully. "It's been fifteen years since you left me. The way I figure it, you owe me for each and every one of those years for what I would've made off of you. But because I'm not totally unreasonable, I'd say that half a mill should do nicely."

"Are you crazy?" Her eyes widened disbelievingly. "I don't have that type of money." Even if she did, she sure as hell wouldn't simply hand it over to him.

"I've seen your house." Aurelio jutted his chin. "You've obviously done damn well for yourself over the years, Willow. Half a million dollars should be just a drop in the bucket for you—"

He knows where I live? Willow thought, nearly at the point of panicking. Had he been stalking her and her family? Maybe even broken into the house, in spite of their advanced security system?

"You're wrong about that," she insisted brusquely.

"Am I?" he asked dubiously.

She looked him straight in the eye and said honestly, "The house was a wedding gift from my husband's parents. That's all. We're not rich." Would that be enough to get him to go away? Willow doubted that, making the situation all the more difficult.

"Maybe so and maybe no," Aurelio spoke tonelessly. "Frankly, I could care less. Other than the fact that you owe me—and I intend to collect—one way or another... I'm betting that you're resourceful enough, which you proved in having the wherewithal to escape from me, to find a way to get me what I want. You do so, and we'll call it even. Meaning, I won't come after you, your husband—or that cute little daughter of yours..."

Willow wanted to claw his eyes out in that moment of fury. Glancing at Sissy, who seemed intrigued as to why she was still talking with him, leaving her to have to try and explain later, Willow knew it was not a good idea to make a scene.

"If I get you the money, how do I know you'll keep your word and leave me alone for good?" she questioned, locking eyes with the sex trafficker.

"You'll just have to take my word for it," Aurelio said arrogantly. "The way I see it, you don't have much of a choice here, baby doll."

"Don't call me that!" Willow snapped, remembering it was one of the names he'd given her when she was part of his stable.

"Whatever you say." He chuckled. "So, do we have a deal?"

She sucked in a deep breath, knowing she was caught between a rock and a hard place, before answering, "Yes, we have a deal."

"Good." Aurelio smiled salaciously at her. "I'll give you a day or so to get the money. Meet me at eight tomorrow night at Golfton Hills Park by the playground. And come alone."

"All right," she snorted, wishing there was another way to deal with him.

"Oh, and I wouldn't call the cops, Willow," he warned. "Otherwise, it could end very badly for you and your daughter. But I would start off with the husband. Instead of killing him, I'd fill him in on all the lurid details of your former life in the sex-for-sale business. I'm guessing you've never told him about who you really are…?"

Willow bristled. "You bastard!"

"I've been called worse." He laughed. "See you tomorrow night, baby doll."

She watched as Aurelio walked away, still snickering like he was in full control of things as before, further infuriating Willow.

She took a chill pill and headed to her car, where Willow safely secured Sissy in her car seat before getting into the driver's seat.

"What were you and Mr. Velasquez talking about?" her daughter asked curiously.

"Just school stuff," Willow said coolly, hoping to leave it at that as she started the car.

"Does he teach at the school?"

"No," she told Sissy. "He was just passing through. I'm sure we won't ever see him again."

Or at least I'll make sure he never crosses paths with you ever again, Willow told herself with determination as they drove home.

* * *

At the dining table of their century old, but refurbished waterfront home, surrounded by longleaf pine trees that had everything Willow could ever have imagined in a house—spacious with an open concept, high ceilings, vintage furniture and a warm ambience—she found herself more than a little restless as they ate dinner. Aurelio Velasquez had put her in an impossible position by demanding money that she didn't have. Or was even capable of gathering in one day.

Moreover, she could never tell her husband about her past life. Could she? Would he ever be able to look at her the same way? Especially when they were in bed, being intimate.

When she looked up from her plate at him, Cliff's deep blue-gray eyes were already tuned in on her.

"Is everything all right?" he asked, concern in his voice.

She stared at his handsome face that came with a head of dark hair in an Ivy League cut, to go with a tall and solid frame. Forcing a smile, she responded believably, "I'm fine. Just a bit tired after a long day."

"Yeah, I hear that." He seemed to accept this while grabbing another slice of pizza and then asked, "So, who's this Mr. Velasquez that Sissy mentioned?"

Their daughter, who was making a nice mess of herself with her pizza, giggled and said nonchalantly, "I told you, he's just someone who knows Mommy and was just passing by at school."

When Cliff met her eyes for confirmation, Willow kept her cool and, with a soft smile, backed this up. "We don't really know one another," she stressed. "I think he has a son attending Kiki Elementary School and was just saying hello as I picked up Sissy."

Cliff nodded and tasted his red wine. Willow did the same, while paranoid that he could see right through her and somehow learn that Aurelio was her ex-pimp. And had shown up in town to bully and blackmail her into giving him half a million dollars.

But her husband moved on to talking about his workday, and she felt a reprieve for now as Willow tried to figure out what to do about this real threat to everything and everyone in her life that Aurelio presented.

* * *

I have to kill that son of a bitch, Willow told herself the following evening, knowing Aurelio had backed her into a corner with no wiggle room. It was the only way he would ever let her go, she decided. She needed to protect her family as best she could. Before her ex-pimp ruined her life more than he already had.

Though she didn't know what would happen to her thereafter, it was a bridge that Willow felt she would cross when she got to it. If that meant spending the rest of her life in prison, so be it. She only hoped that in time both Cliff and Sissy would understand that what she did was all out of love for them.

And pure hatred for the man who left too many scars for her to walk away from so long as he remained a threat.

While Cliff was taking a shower and Sissy was playing in her room, Willow opened the locked box they kept in the closet of the primary suite and removed the Beretta 92X Compact with Rail 9mm semi-automatic pistol, loaded it, and placed it in her shoulder bag.

When Cliff got out of the shower, she used the excuse of needing to run to the store to pick up a prescription and would be back shortly, which he seemed to accept readily.

Willow kissed her daughter and husband goodbye while praying it wasn't for the last time.

She arrived at Golfton Hills Park and parked her car near the playground on Ginger Road. There were a couple of other vehicles there, and Willow wondered if one of them belonged to Aurelio. Did he plan to kill her whether she gave him the money or not? Something told her, based on their past association, that he would not likely be willing to simply walk away—feeling that he was somehow justified in punishing her in any way he saw fit for daring to leave his stable against his wishes.

I'll have to take my chances, she told herself bravely, as Willow exited her vehicle while wearing dark clothing and her hair in a short ponytail. She had the dark leather bag strapped across her shoulder.

Approaching the lighted playground, she watched as Aurelio Velasquez emerged from the shadows. She stopped in her tracks as he asked unkindly, "Did you bring the money?"

"Yes," she lied. "It's all in here."

When she started to reach inside the bag for the gun, Aurelio said sharply, "Don't..."

"Do you want the money or not?" Willow asked nervously, fearful that he was onto her.

"I do," he admitted. "I'm just not sure I can trust you, that's all..." She watched as he pulled a handgun out of his pocket, pointing it at her. "Now, why don't you pass me the handbag, and I'll take the cash out, and then we can go our separate ways—"

If he finds the gun in the bag, I'm screwed, Willow told herself. Should she go for it and try to catch him off guard by removing the pistol and shooting him? Or would this fail miserably, giving him an excuse to shoot her to death, assuming this wasn't his plan all along?

As she contemplated the dire circumstances, with her life literally hanging in the balance with no money inside the handbag to give him, Willow watched as a tall and blonde-haired woman, holding a gun of her own, came up behind Aurelio and said authoritatively, "Aurelio Velasquez, drop the weapon and turn around slowly—"

Willow swallowed thickly as her ex-pimp, clearly caught off guard, swiveled quickly and tried to shoot the woman, who was quicker to the draw, and downed him with one shot to the head before Aurelio could ever get a shot off.

The woman moved over to him, checked his pulse, and only then, when she couldn't get one, did she place her firearm into a waist holster while declaring, "Velasquez is dead." She moved up to Willow and asked equably, "Are you all right?"

Willow nodded while trying to figure out who the woman was. Another former—or current prostitute—that was once under Aurelio's thumb?

The woman flashed her identification and said, "Nicolette Estefan, Special Victims Unit detective with the St. Petersburg Police Department. And you are…?"

"Willow Sterling."

"Ms. Sterling, we've been looking for Velasquez for some time now. Five years ago, he caused the death of my kid sister," Nicolette told her maudlinly. "More recently, he murdered one of the teenage girls he was trafficking and has been on the run ever since. I got a tip that he was spotted in Golfton Hills. Had to see for myself."

"Thank goodness for that," Willow stated gratefully. "Aurelio showed up here yesterday. Fifteen years ago, I was part of his stable of prostitutes when I was a sixteen-year-old named Willow Robinson and straight out of foster care. I managed to run away from that life and start a new one here. But he found me and demanded that I pay him half a million dollars for the time and money he lost in not being able to use me for his sex trafficking all those years."

"I see." Nicolette regarded her sympathetically. "That's quite a large sum of money. Were you prepared to fork it over to Velasquez?"

"No." Willow couldn't admit to a police detective that she had fully intended to kill Aurelio. Or die trying. "I was hoping to somehow reason with him," she asserted. "But I'm not sure it would have worked." Her voice choked. "Had you not shown up in the nick of time, I'm sure he would've killed me. You saved my life, Detective Estefan."

"It was either him or you, right?" she said in justifying her actions.

"Right." Willow was fully prepared to back her up on this. "I need to get home," she said, knowing she was late in returning, causing Cliff to worry. "I have a husband and daughter…" She sighed, meeting the detective's gaze. "They know nothing about my past life—"

Nicolette nodded with understanding. "Your secret is safe with me," she told her. "Go home to your family." She looked at Aurelio's body and said, "I'll phone this in and wait for the authorities to arrive. You'll never have to be a part of it."

"Thank you," Willow said tearfully and felt compelled to give the detective a hug.

Nicolette hugged her back briefly and said sensitively, "Now get out of here and live your life, Willow."

"You too," Willow told her with a nod and headed for her car.

When she returned home after having dropped by the drugstore to pick up an allergy prescription, Cliff was waiting for her at the door.

"You okay?" he asked, gazing at her.

"Yes, I got caught up in traffic after someone was in an accident," she said casually. Then Willow wrapped her arms around him and, while fighting the urge to cry, uttered, "Have I told you lately just how much I love you and Sissy?"

He laughed. "We can never hear it enough."

Willow chuckled, feeling as though an enormous weight had been lifted from her shoulders with Aurelio Velasquez now out of her life forever.

"Neither can I," she promised Cliff affectionately.

Her Abducted Son

S ingle mother Kimberly McGuire couldn't believe just how exhausting it was caring for a two-month-old infant. Seemed as though there was no rest for the weary, save for when her own mother gratefully volunteered to watch her son Johnny Franco Calderón while Kimberly took courses at Indian River State College in her hometown of Port St. Lucie, Florida.

But no such luck this day, as Kimberly had Johnny Franco in the infant car seat in the back of her red Kia Soul en route to the supermarket on Pedderton Street to pick up some baby formula and a few other groceries. At twenty-one years of age, Kimberly wished her son's father had still been in the picture to contribute to his health and well-being. Not to mention any type of child support. But Luke Calderón was behind bars and had been since before Johnny Franco was born, after being caught dealing drugs—illegally made fentanyl and crystal methamphetamine.

That left Kimberly to raise their son alone, more or less. But it was something she fully embraced. She loved Johnny Franco more than life itself and found that motherhood suited her in ways that Kimberly could never have imagined before this role was thrust upon her once she became pregnant. Now, she only wanted to do right by her son and give him the best life possible. And at the same time, complete her own education in making both their lives easier.

Kimberly pulled into the Pedderton Supermarket parking lot and found an empty spot near the front of the store.

"We're here," she told her son as Kimberly shifted her blue eyes at him.

Johnny Franco's wide eyes were the same color, and his dark curly hair was also a reflection of her own long sable locks in multi-layers with fringe bangs.

Johnny Franco, who had been unusually quiet during the drive from their apartment, giggled as if eager to get out of the car and breathe in some fresh air.

Kimberly laughed. "I hear you and feel the same way."

Moments later, at five-six and slim, while wearing a blue knit tank top, denim shorts, and flat loafers, she had exited the vehicle, placed him in the travel systems stroller, and rolled it across the lot and into the store. She grabbed a basket and navigated the two while picking up the things she came there for.

While in one aisle, Kimberly left the stroller in the middle momentarily unattended while she went to the end to grab some crackers off the shelf. She planned to have them with some day-old spaghetti and meatballs for supper. She collected the crackers and headed back to Johnny Franco, wondering if he had fallen asleep.

Only when she came up to the stroller, Kimberly was shocked to see that it was empty. As panic engulfed her, she looked frantically for her son—going from one aisle to the next while calling out his name in desperation. But he was nowhere to be found.

She ran outside, hoping to spot whoever had taken him from the stroller. Again, she saw no one.

Johnny Franco Calderón had simply vanished. Though Kimberly knew that her son had only done so with the help of a child kidnapper who had targeted him for abduction.

* * *

Ten years later, Kimberly McGuire drove her white Nissan Sentra down Wrendon Boulevard in Golfton Hills, where she was employed as an information technology specialist after getting her Associate's and Bachelor's Degrees in Digital Media Technology. As she moved down the palm tree-laden street and saw children at play, she imagined that her son, Johnny Franco, could be right before her eyes, and she wouldn't even know it. Necessarily. Or would she, on some level, be able to tell it was him?

It broke Kimberly's heart in a thousand places to think that her son had been gone from her life for a decade now, having been cruelly snatched away from her right under her nose. Since then, not a day had gone by when she hadn't thought about Johnny Franco and that fateful day at the Port St. Lucie supermarket that would change her life forever.

According to the Port St. Lucie Police Department, Johnny Franco had been abducted in broad daylight by an unidentified man and woman, who had fled the scene and somehow managed to disappear, as if by magic. Or black magic. In spite of the best efforts by the police and FBI to locate the missing child, their efforts had fallen short. Johnny Franco's kidnapping had turned into a cold case and remained an unsolved child abduction.

Kimberly was left to wonder if her son was still alive or dead. In her heart of hearts, she believed he was still alive somewhere. After all, wouldn't a mother somehow be able to sense it if her child was no longer among the living? Or was that more wishful thinking?

She felt her eyes begin to water at the unsettling thoughts and sought to brush them aside while returning to the here and now, where Kimberly had tried her best to move on with her life. Though still single at thirty-one years of age, she had managed to carve out an existence that gave her professional and social satisfaction, in spite of the void that would forever be there without her son to share her triumphs in life.

As Kimberly pulled up to the craftsman cottage-style waterfront house, where she had lived for three years now, she couldn't help but notice the new neighbors moving in across the street. The house had been vacant for three months since the previous owners relocated to California after a job transfer.

A couple of burly movers were taking the heavy stuff from a moving truck and into the house, which was also a craftsman cottage. In the driveway was a blue Hyundai Santa Fe.

Kimberly parked in her own driveway and wondered if the new neighbors would be as friendly as the ones who left. She hadn't exactly been very close to any of her neighbors, but she was not hostile to them either, mainly keeping to herself.

After exiting the car, she ran a hand through her shoulder-length brunette hair, styled in a comb-over lob, and glanced across the street, where she saw a tall and handsome fit man around her age with medium-length jet black wavy hair. He seemed oblivious to her as he grabbed some items from the car and headed up toward the house.

Just as Kimberly was about to turn away, she watched a dark-haired boy run out of the cottage, seemingly full of energy. She guessed him to be around ten and was height-appropriate and slender. Strangely, it was how she imagined Johnny Franco would look at that age today, giving Kimberly a chill.

The boy looked at her with curiosity, then smiled and waved. She waved back and watched him run inside the house. When the man, presumably the boy's father, came back out, he grinned and waved too.

Kimberly smiled and gave a little nod while wondering if he had a wife. Or lived with the mother of the boy.

* * *

Jesse Sloan caught the new neighbor checking him out. Or was it more the other way around? She was certainly a looker, as near as he could determine from across the street. He wondered if she was married. Or had children around the age of his son, Caleb, that he could become friends with?

After the movers finished unloading the truck, Jesse handed them a tip, and he and Caleb were left alone to begin the arduous but necessary task of unpacking and figuring out what should go where in their new home.

Though Jesse had been relatively happy living in a mid-century modern home on the other side of town, that all changed when his wife, Fiona, died a year and a half ago of bladder cancer. It left him and their son devastated while trying to cope with the loss.

To Jesse, moving seemed like a no-brainer. Besides wanting to give them a fresh start, he also wanted to live close to the water so Caleb could better enjoy the numerous activities it afforded them, such as beach walking, swimming, and boating—things Jesse loved when growing up before focusing more on his job as a civil engineer.

The one thing still missing was companionship. And maybe a mother figure in Caleb's life. Jesse didn't know if either were in the cards anytime soon. But the one thing he was certain of was that Fiona, courageous to the very end, wanted them to move on with their lives when she was gone. Including finding someone to love and be loved by.

In Jesse's mind, this was something he was open to, if it worked within his role as a father.

* * *

Kimberly peeked through the open faux wood blinds of the casement windows in the living room as the boy played in front of the house across the street. She lifted her tablet and zoomed in on him, snapping a close-up picture. She padded across the cork flooring and flopped onto a red velvet accent chair that was part of her traditional furnishings in the open-concept interior, then studied the boy's image for a long moment of contemplation.

She then brought up an age progression photograph that had been provided to her by a missing children's organization of what Johnny Franco might look like at age ten. In fact, Kimberly had been sent such pics every year for the last decade—to give her both a visual to keep her son alive in her head, as well as hope that this might someday lead to his being found alive and well.

Putting the two photos on a split screen, Kimberly gulped with a mixture of excitement and apprehension, as they were practically a dead ringer for one another. Was it even possible that the boy across the street was actually Johnny Franco? Or was she way off base and grasping at straws?

She allowed herself a long moment to let her imagination run wild with this possibility that she could be reunited with her son at long last. And that his abductor could be arrested and put behind bars—where, ironically,

Johnny Franco's birth father, Luke Calderón, remained, having been given a twenty-plus year sentence while making it clear that he wanted nothing to do with her or his son.

Kimberly broke from her reverie, but couldn't break away from the hope that Johnny Franco could be well within reach.

She pulled up on her tablet an article from ten years ago that gave a description of the child kidnappers, along with a vague image believed to be them at the supermarket.

Could the male abductor be the new neighbor? As much as she wanted to, Kimberly realized that she couldn't rule it out.

Not until she had more to go on.

* * *

That evening, Kimberly showed up at the new neighbors' home with a homemade apple pie and a bright smile across her face.

"Hi, I'm Kimberly McGuire," she introduced herself. "I live across the street."

The man she'd seen outside earlier, who was even better looking up close, grinned and held her gaze with deep gray eyes and said, "I kind of figured that out when I saw you drive up a few hours ago. I'm Jesse Sloan." He glanced at what she was holding. "What do you have there?"

"Apple pie." She lifted the covering. "Hope you have a sweet tooth?"

"I do," he confessed. "And so does my son. Thanks." He grabbed the pie from her and called out to the boy, who came running into the room. "This is Caleb."

Kimberly gave him a warm smile, trying hard to ignore the sense of familiarity in seeing the boy. "Hey," she told him.

"Hi." He looked bashful.

"I'm Kimberly, your neighbor."

"And look what she's brought us to feast on," Jesse told him excitedly.

Caleb's big blue eyes lit up. "Cool."

"You can set the table." Jesse handed it to him and, gazing at Kimberly, said, "If you're willing to excuse the mess inside, you're welcome to help us eat this if you like?"

"I think I can handle that." Kimberly smiled. "You're on," she readily agreed, knowing she needed access if she were to get proof that Caleb was really Johnny Franco.

And that his father just might be a child snatcher.

* * *

Kimberly was shocked to hear that his wife had passed away. But while saddened by his loss, this still didn't mean that the couple had not abducted her son ten years ago and passed him off as their own.

After finding herself surprisingly comfortable with Jesse Sloan, Kimberly was determined to keep her eye on the ball as she asked casually if she could use the bathroom.

She was directed toward one and waited till Jesse and Caleb were preoccupied with more unpacking, when Kimberly stepped inside Caleb's room that was a dead giveaway with the apropos furnishings and sports gear that she could imagine would be par for the course were this Johnny Franco's room.

Spotting a couple of hairs wedged inside a youth baseball glove, Kimberly confiscated them and slipped them inside a small plastic bag in the pocket of her jeans. She would have the hairs tested for DNA and compare them with her own in a maternity test—and go from there.

Though trying not to get her hopes up, Kimberly found them sky high as she rejoined Jesse and Caleb while eager to see what the results of the testing would be.

* * *

"You what?" Jesse narrowed his eyes at Kimberly as she just dropped on him out of the blue that she had gotten a sample of his son's DNA without his permission three weeks ago.

"I can explain," she told him, with a catch to her voice, as they sat on the modern farmhouse sofa in his living room beneath a ceiling fan spinning overhead. She sighed. "You know about my son being kidnapped ten years ago, right?"

"Yeah...?" He regarded her with curiosity as to how this could possibly relate to his son.

"Well, when I first laid eyes on Caleb, I thought it was possible that he was Johnny Franco."

"But how could you possibly think that?" Jesse demanded.

Kimberly lifted the tablet from her lap and showed him the age progression photograph in comparison with Caleb's picture. Jesse had to admit the resemblance was uncanny.

"I just felt I needed to see for sure, one way or the other," Kimberly said sorrily. "And as we'd just met, my suspicions weren't exactly something I could lay on you. So, I secretly took some hairs off Caleb's baseball glove and used them for a maternity test."

"And...?" Jesse knew what she'd discovered, but wanted to hear it from her mouth.

"The tests came back negative," she admitted. "Caleb wasn't Johnny Franco. I'm so sorry I took things to that level behind your back, as I really like you. It was just a spur-of-the-moment thing." She sucked in a deep breath. "I don't suppose you could ever forgive me?"

Even if he wanted to hold that against her, Jesse knew he couldn't. Apart from having fallen for the gorgeous neighbor, he could fully understand the love she had for her missing child and the lengths one would go to to find them. He would have done the same if anything like that had ever happened to Caleb.

But equally important to Jesse, in gazing again at the age progression photograph, it occurred to him that there was another local boy who just might be Kimberly's son.

Giving her the benefit of his attention, Jesse told Kimberly sincerely, "I forgive you." He paused. "Regarding your son, there is one more possibility here that might be worth checking out."

"Oh...?" She held his gaze interestedly. "I'm listening..."

* * *

Jesse tried to keep it as casual as possible as he went through the motions of his usual duties in coaching the youth league on the baseball field at Stabley Park on Zachare Avenue in Golfton Hills. He regarded Kimberly, seated in the stands, her eyes locked on the field; then Jesse spied Eddie and Valerie Packard as they sat two rows below her, cheering on their son, Ricky, who was the catcher while Caleb was pitching.

Eddie, who was in his late thirties, was of medium build and around Jesse's height, with dark hair in a middle fade and a short, boxed beard. He wore round eyeglasses over blue eyes. Valerie, also mid-thirtyish, was slender, hazel-eyed, and had brown hair with blonde highlights in a pixie cut. Jesse didn't know either very well, but they seemed to be nice people who loved their son.

But just how nice were they truly? And was Ricky really their son? Or was he actually Johnny Franco Calderón, missing now for the past decade?

Jesse felt compelled to find out. If only to give himself peace of mind—and ultimately the same with Kimberly—that her missing son wasn't actually living in the city, if not Caleb.

Studying Ricky Packard, Jesse could see the resemblance to Caleb, as he had come to mind when Kimberly confessed to suspecting that Caleb might be her kidnapped son. Ricky was a little taller and bigger than Caleb, and both had blue eyes and curly black hair, though Caleb's was in a fresh fade cut, compared to Ricky's in a mini quiff style.

I need to collect Ricky's DNA, Jesse told himself, while aware that the boy's overly protective parents were watching him like hawks, as though there was a reason to be beyond a loving mother and father.

When the game was over and Jesse went through his routine of giving every kid a high-five—or more like low-five—starting with his own son, Jesse noted when Ricky came up to him that the boy had some blood on one of his nostrils.

Must have been from that hard slide he took when racing to home plate earlier, Jesse mused. "You all right?" he asked the boy calmly.

"Yeah, just a nosebleed," Ricky voiced nonchalantly.

Jesse used the opportunity to remove the clean handkerchief from his pocket, hand it to Ricky, and said with no hint of ulterior motives, "Here, wipe it with this…"

"Okay." Ricky wiped his nose dry and seemed to wonder what to do with the handkerchief.

Jesse took it from him, as if not giving it a second thought, balled it up, stuffed it back in his pocket, and said, "Better not keep your folks waiting any longer to congratulate you for another good game, Ricky."

He flashed his teeth. "Thanks, Coach Sloan."

Jesse nodded and watched as Ricky met his parents halfway as Eddie and Valerie Packard gushed over the kid, oblivious to the stunt Jesse had just pulled in collecting his DNA for a maternity test.

Though feeling a bit guilty in so doing, if it turned out that the Packards were his real parents, Jesse justified this by going with the no harm, no foul adage. They need never know about the test if it proved negative. Whereas Kimberly could try and put this whole thing past her, to the extent possible, while waiting it out to see if the authorities should ever crack the case.

When he approached her after the coast was clear—with Ricky and his parents having gotten into their silver Jeep Grand Wagoneer and driven off—Jesse asked curiously, "So, what did you think?"

"I'm not sure." Kimberly hesitated. "After missing the boat with your son, I'm beginning to question my own judgment in wanting to believe that Johnny Franco is still alive. Or that he might actually be living in Golfton Hills ten years later like I am. I mean, what are the odds?"

"Not very good," Jesse had to admit. "But that's not the same thing as impossible odds either. Never reject a mother's instincts," he cautioned, as encouragement to her. "Till all options run out."

She favored him with a slight smile. "I'll try to remember that."

He removed the handkerchief from his pocket. "I got Ricky's DNA." He handed it to her. "There should be enough blood there to do the maternity

231

test."

Kimberly opened the hanky and gazed at what Jesse suspected was her lifeline to reconnect with her son ten years later. Or maybe needing to come to terms with his absence as something that was out of her hands, in spite of her best efforts to the contrary. "Thank you."

Jesse smiled thoughtfully. "Good luck."

Beyond that, he was left to wonder if she would be able to get past this either way so that maybe they could think about trying to build something special between them.

* * *

Kimberly was there when child kidnappers Eddie and Valerie Packard were taken into custody at their ranch house on Vale Drive, and their son, Ricky, was removed from the home by the Florida Department of Children and Families.

Initially, the Packards were in total denial, stubbornly insisting they were the boy's birth parents. Till a legal DNA maternity test proved conclusively that the home test Kimberly took was accurate in showing that Ricky Packard was, in fact, her son Johnny Franco. Eddie and Valerie Packard, unable to have children of their own, confessed to abducting the boy and were charged with kidnapping.

Now, Kimberly stood alongside Jesse and Caleb at the Golfton Hills Police Department, awaiting a reunion with her son. She was admittedly on pins and needles for a moment she once feared would never happen. On hand were missing persons' investigators from the Port St. Lucie Police Department and FBI, who had worked tirelessly to locate Johnny Franco through the years.

He emerged from a room with a tall and pretty, red-haired DCF social worker who had a big grin on her face as she eyed Kimberly and said, "This is your son—"

Kimberly glanced at Jesse, who showed his support, and then she approached the boy. He looked understandably confused and didn't move. She watched as, surprisingly, Caleb walked up to his friend, took his hand, and said supportively, "It's all right."

Seemingly encouraged by this, Johnny Franco walked up to her, and Kimberly said tentatively, "Hey."

"Hi," he spoke tonelessly.

Kimberly lifted her phone and showed him a picture of an infant. "This is you, Johnny Franco." He studied it with fascination. "I never gave up trying to find you."

That seemed to be all he needed to hear to wrap his arms around her waist. She took that as a strong indication that she had her son back and that they could be a family again.

Months later, Kimberly and Jesse walked barefoot on the beach, holding hands. Up ahead of them, frolicking in the sand, were Johnny Franco and Caleb, who had become even closer friends over the course of time.

"Seems like Johnny Franco's adjusting quite well," Jesse commented.

Kimberly agreed. "I think we all are." She noted that they had begun dating, with the approval of the boys, and seemed to have a bright future ahead of them. "And that's a good thing."

She smiled at him, and Jesse returned the favor as they caught up with Johnny Franco and Caleb and joined in on the fun.

A Note from the Author

Good day,

As a literary criminologist and crime novelist of long standing, I am thrilled in being able to bring to you my latest book, Mysteries of Golfton Hills, a collection of psychological suspense, crime, and thriller short stories. All take place in an interesting and idyllic beach town on the Florida Panhandle.

I hope you enjoy!

Also check out my Level Best Books crime novels, *Exposed Evidence:* A Jessica Frost Legal Thriller and *Till She Was Done:* A Psychological Thriller, equally riveting fiction.

Best,

R. Barri Flowers

Acknowledgements

I would like to thank the Dames of Detection at Level Best Books, and Lee Lofland of their imprint New Arc Books, for paving the way toward the publication of this riveting collection of crime driven short stories, *Mysteries of Golfton Hills.*

About the Author

R. Barri Flowers is an award-winning criminologist and bestselling author of psychological, legal, mystery, suspense, thriller, and crime fiction, along with criminology and true crime books. He has also edited several mystery and true crime anthologies. As an expert on criminal behavior, violent offenders, and serial killers, Flowers has appeared on the Biography Channel, Investigation Discovery, and Oxygen true crime documentary series. The author is a proud graduate of Michigan State University's renowned School of Criminal Justice and a recipient of its esteemed Wall of Fame Award. In his thriller novels, Flowers strives to bring verisimilitude to the characters and stories by using his expertise to go with creative juices and a vivid imagination to create gripping and realistic fiction.

SOCIAL MEDIA HANDLES:
   https://www.facebook.com/OfficialRBarriFlowers
   @RBarriFlowers (Twitter)
   RBarriFlowers (Instagram)

AUTHOR WEBSITE:

www.rbarriflowers.com

Also by R. Barri Flowers

Campus Killer (The Lynleys of Law Enforcement, Book 5)

Captured on Kauai (Hawaii CI, Book 1)

Chasing the Violet Killer

Christmas Lights Killer (The Lynleys of Law Enforcement, Book 2)

Cold Murder in Kolton Lake (The Lynleys of Law Enforcement, Book 4)

Danger on Maui (Hawaii CI, Book 4)

Deadly Defense (Grace Gaynor Christian Mysteries Book 1)

Exposed Evidence (A Jessica Frost Legal Thriller)

Fractured Trust (A Renee Steele Legal Mystery)

Honolulu Cold Homicide (Hawaii CI, Book 3)

Justice Served (A Barkley and Parker Thriller)

Kaanapali Beach Paradise (A Maui Contemporary Novel)

Mississippi Manhunt (The Lynleys of Law Enforcement, Book 6)

Murder in Honolulu (A Skye Delaney Mystery)

Murder in Maui (Leila Kahana Mysteries, Book 1)

Murder in the Blue Ridge Mountains (The Lynleys of Law Enforcement, Book 3)

Murder of the Hula Dancers (Leila Kahana Mysteries, Book 3)

Murder on Kaanapali Beach (Leila Kahana Mysteries, Book 2)

Murdered in the Gourmet Kitchen (Riley Reed Cozy Mysteries, Book 2)

Murdered in the Man Cave (Riley Reed Cozy Mysteries, Book 1)

Night Killers (A Crime Thriller Novel)

Persuasive Evidence (A Jordan La Fontaine Legal Thriller)

Special Agent Witness (The Lynleys of Law Enforcement, Book 1)

State's Evidence (A Beverly Mendoza Legal Thriller)

The Big Island Killer (Hawaii CI, Book 1)

Till She Was Done (A Psychological Thriller)